Verse and Vengeance

Also available by Amanda Flower

Verse and Vengeance

A MAGICAL BOOKSHOP MYSTERY

Amanda Flower

CROOKED LANE

NEW YORK

Copyright © 2019 by Amanda Flower

Published in the United States by Crooked Lane Books, an imprint of The Quick Brown Fox & Company LLC.

Crooked Lane Books and its logo are trademarks of The Quick Brown Fox & Company LLC.

Library of Congress Catalog-in-Publication data available upon request.

ISBN (hardcover): 978-1-64385-151-8
ISBN (ePub): 978-1-64385-152-5

Cover illustration by Stephen Gardner

Printed in the United States.

www.crookedlanebooks.com

Crooked Lane Books
34 West 27th St., 10th Floor
New York, NY 10001

First Edition: November 2019

10 9 8 7 6 5 4 3 2 1

For David Seymour
a Rainwater of my very own

Not a day passes—not a minute or second, without an accouchement!

Not a day passes—not a minute or second, without a corpse!

—*Leaves of Grass,* Walt Whitman

Acknowledgments

As always, thank you to my dear readers for loving the Magical Bookshop Mysteries, so much that the series has continued. Your support means the world to me.

Special thanks to my editors Matt Martz and Marla Daniels and everyone at Crooked Lane who worked on this novel.

Always thanks to my super-agent Nicole Resciniti, who makes me a better writer and encourages me to reach my full potential.

Thanks to Bobby Dimauro, who advised me on the bicycle accident in the story and lent me his name for one of the characters.

Thank you to my friend Mariellyn Grace for her encouragement while writing and editing this book and to David Seymour for his unfailing support. Also to my family for their support. I'm blessed to have all of you.

A very special thank you to Walt Whitman for writing Leaves of Grass. His poetry shares reality, vulnerability, love, and hope in brand-new way, and I am grateful for the impact his words have played in my own life and this novel.

Finally, to my Heavenly Father, thank you for poetry.

Chapter One

He was out there. I could feel him watching and waiting. He was searching for a mistake that would reveal the truth. I peeked around the curtain for a better look, but it was late, and all I could see was what was directly under the gas lamppost in front of my bookshop, Charming Books. He wasn't in the small pool of light it gave off. He would know to hide himself from my view.

I knew lawn chairs and ribbons already lined the street for tomorrow's bike race, a massive fund-raiser that was my grandmother's doing. When the village fell short of funding, Grandma Daisy—as the new mayor of Cascade Springs, our little village outside Niagara Falls, New York—went big. There was no simple bake sale for her. Nope, my grandmother had planned a regional bike race that had earned the village over twenty thousand dollars. Hundreds of riders had signed up.

"Violet?" a voice said behind me.

"Ahh!" I screamed and fell on the floor.

My grandmother stood above me in her usual jeans, Charming Books T-shirt, and gauzy scarf. Tonight's scarf was decorated with pineapples, a nod to the coming summer. Her cat-eye glasses slipped down her nose at she peered at me sprawled on the floor like a flattened spider. My grandmother's style hadn't changed a bit since she'd been elected mayor.

"Can I help you with something, Grandma?"

"Did you know they found a body at the bottom of Niagara Falls? According to reports, it's badly beat-up."

I scrambled to my feet. I could imagine that. The jagged rocks at the bottom of the American Falls would not be kind. "I had heard. It's all customers have been talking about today. Several customers mentioned it. What a tragedy. By everyone's guess, it was a suicide." I grimaced. Suicide by Niagara Falls was more common than anyone was comfortable admitting.

"I hope they can identify the body soon," she said. "Closure is essential for those left behind." She said this from experience that I knew came from having outlived her only child, my mother, Fern. I was raised right here in Charming Books by my single mother until she died when I was thirteen from cancer. After that, I lived with Grandma Daisy until I left Cascade Springs at seventeen. I came back only a little over a year ago to help my grandmother run the bookshop. My father was never in the picture. In fact, I hadn't known who he was until he'd shown up on our doorstep last Halloween. I still wasn't comfortable with the idea of having a father.

I went back to my window and peered outside.

"What has gotten into you, girl?" Grandma Daisy asked.

I glanced behind me.

My black-and-white tuxedo cat, Emerson, and the shop crow, Faulkner, seemed to wonder the same. Emerson walked over to me and put one white paw on my foot, and Faulkner flew down from the birch tree that grew in the middle of our shop, landing on his perch by the front window. The perch was a favorite spot for the large bird because he could glower at the tourists walking up and down River Road.

"It's Redding. He's driving me crazy. Every time I have left the shop in the last week, he has been there."

Joel Redding was a private investigator I'd met over the winter when my friend Lacey had been caught up in a murder investigation. He had been hired to solve the murder. From the get-go, Redding and I had been at odds. Mostly because he'd thought Lacey was guilty of the crime, and I'd known that was impossible. In the end, I was proven right, but there had been a cost. Redding had followed me often during that investigation, and because of his close observation, he'd started to take note of the odd things about Charming Books. The way the birch tree stayed green even in the winter, Faulkner and Emerson's curious behavior, and worst of all, my connection to the bookshop.

When the case was finally closed, I'd hoped that I would never see him again. He did leave, and it had looked like I would have my wish until he'd popped up again about a week ago in the village. Ever since then, I'd seen the man and his guitar case, which he supposedly used as a briefcase, everywhere I went. When I'd tried to confront him on several occasions, he'd run off. I didn't know what his game was or what had brought him back to the village. It was making my crazy.

My grandmother brushed dust off the back of my shirt. "We really need to sweep the floors more often, Violet. It looks like you rolled in dirt."

"I'd get a Roomba if I didn't think Emerson would attack it."

The little tuxie looked up at me and mewed. In his way, he was saying *Bring it on!*

I turned back to my grandmother. "I really do think Redding is up to something. Why else would he be watching the shop?"

"Have you said anything to David about it?"

I frowned. David was Chief David Rainwater of the Cascade Springs police department, who also happened to be my boyfriend. "It's not that simple. Our situation with the shop makes it complicated. We have Rosalee to thank for that."

When my ancestress Rosalee Waverly had moved to Cascade Springs after her husband was killed in the War of 1812, she'd built her home around the same birch tree that sat in the middle of the shop today. Knowing the mystical healing powers of the Niagara region and especially the natural springs here in the village, she'd begun watering the tree with the spring water, and that's where the magic began. She was the first Caretaker of the tree, and since then the job had passed down through the direct line of Waverly women until it had landed squarely on my shoulders on the cusp of my thirtieth when the responsibility was passed on to the next woman in line. My great-grandmother had turned the house into a bookshop, and today the shop's essence sent messages to the Caretaker, me, through the books themselves. It also had a knack for picking books for customers in the shop. It always knew what a reader wanted or needed. However, it never revealed itself to the customer. A book would fly across the shop when the customer wasn't looking, or he would reach for a volume on the shelf and come back with something completely different that he needed more. At times, I felt like the essence cut things a little too close. More than once a customer had almost seen a flying book, and that would have been the end of our secret. I know that's a lot to swallow, and at times I can't even believe it—and I have lived it close to a year now.

"Besides," Grandma Daisy said, interrupting my black thoughts. "Maybe Redding is just in Cascade Springs for a vacation. We do have an adorable little village."

"Right," I said. "Does his vacation have to include standing outside our shop watching us for hours? He never comes inside. Just watches. It's maddening." I stared out the window again. A shadow moved in on the lamppost. "I'm right! He's out there. I can see him." I marched to the front door and threw it open.

"What are you doing?" Grandma Daisy held on to the end of her scarf.

"I'm not going to sit in here and cower." I was down the steps and through the front gate before I thought about what I was going to say to Redding. It was just another example of me throwing myself into something without thinking it all the way through. I pulled up short a few feet from him.

He waited for me under that lamppost. "Hello, Violet."

I folded my arms. "What are you doing here?" The question came out harsher than I intended it to.

"That is not the small-town welcome I have come to expect in Cascade Springs."

I bit my lip. "I'm sorry for coming off rude, but what are you doing outside my shop in the middle of the night?"

He smiled. "I'm on an evening stroll. I thought that's what people in the village did."

"You've been out here every night for the last week."

"That's an exaggeration."

"Are you on a case?" I asked.

"I'm always on a case." He seemed nonplussed.

"What is your case, and what does it have to do with me?"

He cocked his head. "It's very strange for you to think that I would be investigating you, Violet. Should I have a reason to be curious about you?"

I didn't answer.

"You're a very interesting person, and your shop is fascinating. I find the tree particularly intriguing."

Despite myself, I shivered.

"Did you catch a chill?"

I folded my arms. "No, I'm fine."

His lips curled into another smile. "I should be on my way, then. Tomorrow is the big race. I'll probably see you around."

"Not if I can help it," I muttered.

He laughed, picked up his guitar case, and strolled down the street toward the Niagara River and the Riverwalk.

I went back inside Charming Books, where my grandmother was waiting for me. "What did he say?"

"Nothing. He said he was out for a walk."

"That could be true."

"Maybe. Maybe he's just visiting the village as you said and he goes for a walk every night outside my shop. It's not illegal, but it feels off."

"What do you mean?"

"I feel like I'm waiting for something to happen, but I don't know what it is." I rubbed my forehead. "Maybe I'm just tired. The last two months have been crazy, between finishing up teaching this semester at Springside and defending my dissertation and . . ." I almost added *juggling the shop alone since my grandmother became mayor of Cascade Springs.* I didn't have her to rely on as much to watch the shop when I needed to study or teach my courses. I would never say that to her, though.

My grandmother had run the shop and been the Caretaker for over forty years. She more than deserved a break to try something new. She would have given up her Caretaker duties much earlier had my mother still been alive.

"I just don't want to be the one who lets every Caretaker before me down by letting the truth of Charming Books get out."

She smoothed her perfectly straight silver bob that fell just below her ears. "My girl. The Waverly women have been able to keep the magical secret of this place for the last two hundred years. One small-time private investigator isn't going to topple that."

I hoped she was right.

"And, he won't have much luck gathering any information tomorrow. With the big race in the village, he will be lucky to get within twenty feet of the shop. The racers will ride right past Charming Books on the way to the finish line. Do you feel ready for tomorrow?"

My grandmother had organized the race with the hopes that she could continue to fund Cascade Spring's Underground Railroad Museum. The total cost of the museum was much more than the village budget could allow after a foundation problem was discovered during construction. To make up for the unexpected deficit, Grandma Daisy had been having a number of fund-raisers over the spring and summer, including the Tour de Cascade Springs tomorrow. Yes, my grandmother had come up with the name for the race. She claimed the name struck the right tone for the village. I suspected she just liked saying it.

The race was costing the village next to nothing to put on. All the swags, booths, publicity, and more were being donated by area businesses. The registration fees that the cyclists paid to enter the race were all being applied to the museum fund. Then there were the extensive private donations and racer sponsorships. It seemed people were inclined to donate toward this good cause, and the tax write-off helped too, of course. Grandma Daisy herself courted all those donors. She was a force to be reckoned with.

"I'm as ready as I ever will be. I've never ridden more than twenty miles at one time, so I'm more than a little apprehensive to do thirty miles tomorrow," I said, answering her question. "But I don't know why Rainwater got this idea in his head that we should ride together. He's going to be bored to tears if he's stuck in the back of the pack with me."

My grandmother smiled. "I think it's lovely he wants to ride in the fund-raiser beside you." She gave me a look. "And my dear, he wants to be beside you in all things. You need to be beside him, too."

I shifted uncomfortably and rubbed my back as if my fall had caused some sort of unseen injury. I knew what my grandmother was hinting at. David Rainwater was a very smart man. He knew I was hiding something. Just like I was keeping my connection to the shop from everyone else, I was keeping it from him. I thought he'd given me a pass all these months because I'd been so stressed over my teaching schedule and my dissertation, but now both of those "excuses" were off the table. If my relationship with the police chief was to go anywhere, I knew I had to take the risk and tell him. I just wasn't sure if I had the nerve to do it. It might ruin everything.

My grandmother studied me. "You don't know if it will ruin everything. Telling David might open everything up. You have to be brave, my girl."

I chewed on my lower lip. I would have to make the choice to tell him the truth or let him go.

She patted my cheek again. "David will understand. Trust in that, my dear." She took a breath. "Now, you need a good night's sleep, and stop worrying about Redding. The fates will take care of him. They always do."

Before I could ask her what she meant, she said, "I'm heading home, and you should go up to bed. I can see that Emerson is ready."

Just like every night when he thought it was time for me to go to sleep, Emerson sat on the bottom step of the spiral staircase that wound around the birch tree and led up to the children's loft and my one-bedroom apartment on the second floor of the house.

After Grandma Daisy left, Faulkner swooped down, dropping a book at my feet. I bent to pick it up. It was *Leaves of Grass* by Walt Whitman. After finishing my PhD on nineteenth-century New England writers, focusing primarily on transcendental writers like Ralph Waldo Emerson, the last thing I wanted to read was Whitman, a contemporary of Emerson. I picked up the book and held it out to the bird. "I'm taking a summer break from heavy reading. Why didn't you bring me something a bit lighter?"

Faulkner flew to the tree and landed on the second limb down from the top. He tucked his long black beak under his wing and pretended to be asleep. I wouldn't get any more information out of him that night.

"Okay, Emerson," I said to the cat. "Let's go to bed."

The tuxie mewed and then jumped to the next step. When he moved, I spotted the leather-bound book he had been sitting on. It was a second copy of *Leaves of Grass*. That's when I knew the crow hadn't picked the book to torment me at all. The shop itself had.

Chapter Two

There was barely enough room to get my mom's old cruiser bike through the crowd standing near the starting line of the Tour de Cascade Springs. There must have been five hundred riders in front of the imposing village hall that sat slightly elevated on a man-made hill overlooking the Riverwalk, the Niagara River, and Canada on the other side. My grandmother had told me that one of the things she loved most about being the mayor was having that view every day. It was the highest point in the village and had been intentionally built that way in the 1850s.

The village hall was what all of this was about. The building was decaying much worse than anyone in the village had known until my grandmother started construction on the museum. That was when the foundation issues were discovered and the ground underneath the village hall was ruled as potentially unstable. Although safe enough to hold the mayor's and a few other city offices, it wasn't deemed safe enough for tourists. Everything had to be fixed before the museum could be completed.

I recognized the slight form coming around the back of the museum. She was in her early twenties but looked much younger because of her diminutive size. Her dark curly hair was cropped close to her head. She made up for her small stature—and her childlike appearance, I thought—with a hoop pierced through her tiny nose. She wore leggings, a flannel shirt, and combat boots. A chain hung down just below the hem of her shirt.

I know teachers aren't supposed to have favorite students, but we would be lying if we said we didn't. Jodi "Jo" Fitzgerald was that student for me. She'd been in my composition class last semester, but even before that class, I'd gotten to know her because she worked in the English department office.

It was a tiny department that consisted of one full-time professor and a few other adjuncts like me. Up until this spring semester, Jo had worked for all of us. As I'd written my dissertation the last two semesters, I'd put in extra time at the office. Over that time, Jo and I had become more than student and professor—we'd become friends.

Jo was a talented writer, but when I'd had her in class, she was terribly late with her work. I gave her more extensions than I should have, but she had a gift. In my time as a teaching assistant and now as an English professor, I had read more than my fair share of terrible writing, which was why good writing like hers tended to stand out.

And she had always been polite when she asked for an extension by giving me free coffee from the campus coffee shop where she worked. Maybe I was taking bribes, but in the middle of the semester, free coffee was a lifesaver. I always ended up putting the money I owed her in the tip jar anyway. She was a hardworking student who went to school and worked two jobs to do it. She left working for the English department in December to take a job at the local bike shop, where she could get more consistent hours and higher pay. I didn't blame her for doing this, but I did miss seeing her around the office.

She was walking toward the street with a deep frown on her face. She looked over her shoulder a few times. I assumed it was because she didn't want to get run over by an overzealous rider, which was entirely possible. Jo was small. The rider might not see her.

I waved to her, and her face broke into a smile.

"Professor Waverly." She waved back.

I maneuvered my bike until I was at the edge of the sidewalk. It took some doing and a lot of apologizing. I got my share of dirty looks, but I thought most of those were from riders who thought I was trying to get ahead of them at the starting gate. That couldn't be further from the truth. I would very happily be at the back of the pack where I was in far less risk of getting run over by anything other than the police car that had the sad job of shepherding the slow riders to the end. Since I was dating the chief of police, I was guessing his officers would be very careful not to hit me.

"Jo," I said. "I told you, you aren't in my class any longer. You can call me Violet."

She grinned. "I think I'm actually supposed to call you Dr. Waverly since you received your PhD."

I laughed. "That's true, but Violet works just fine. Are you in the race?"

"Heck no," she said. "I'm not a crazy person."

I looked down at my bike.

"Dr. Waverly, you are a little crazy."

"Maybe a little. My boyfriend, David, really wanted to do this as a couple thing, so here I am."

"Where is he?" she asked, looking all around and going slightly pale at the mention of the police chief.

My brow wrinkled. "I'm guessing near the front. David hates to lose at anything. I'm definitely a back-of-the-pack rider."

"It's safer back there."

"Agreed."

"What were you doing behind the village hall?"

Her body jerked. "The village hall?"

"Yes," I said slowly. "That giant building behind you."

"Oh, right. I just was saying hello to my brother. He's working in there today."

"I didn't know you had a brother who worked for the village." My brow wrinkled even more. I would have thought Grandma Daisy would have mentioned to me that Jo had a brother who worked for the city. I had talked about the student enough because of the many times I had been worried about her throughout the semester. At one point, I'd thought I would have to fail Jo because she hadn't done enough of the assignments to pass, no matter how I reworked the math. In the end she came through and got a B-minus. Had she done the work in a more timely fashion, she would have had an A-plus based on her writing alone.

"He doesn't work for the village exactly. His company is working on the museum."

"He's the contractor?"

She nodded. "He lives in Niagara Falls, and I don't see him that often. It's been fun having him so close. Most of the time all he does is ask me about school, though." She rolled her eyes. "Like that's the only thing that matters."

"I'm sure he just wants you to succeed. Have you thought about transferring to a four-year college yet? There are several in Niagara Falls that would be a close driving distance for you, or you could take the bus. You wouldn't have to pay to live on campus. I would write a recommendation letter for you."

Her face closed off, and I knew I'd lost her. I had been pushing a bachelor's degree on Jo too hard. Springside was a community college, so the most we awarded was an associate's degree. Jo had the talent to go further than what we offered, but I was in real risk of alienating her completely if I brought it up again.

"Just keep that in mind," I said. "I won't mention it again."

"I know you're just trying to help, Violet." She said my name as if she was testing it out.

"There you go," I said. "That wasn't so hard, was it?"

"Jo!" a booming voice called from the Riverwalk.

"Yikes, that's Bobby. I had better get back. The bike shop booth has been nuts since six this morning. I think Bobby's in real risk of keeling over from the excitement."

I laughed. Bobby Holmes was the owner of Bobby's Bike Shop. He was a compact, bald, African-American man who talked fast and knew bikes like some people knew their shoe size or their phone numbers. My grandmother had recruited him to handle the registration for the race. In exchange for that volunteer work, he'd gotten a prime spot on the Riverwalk before, during, and after the race to sell his merchandise to the hundreds of riders.

"Violet!" Rainwater waved at me from near the starting line.

I chuckled. "Looks like I'm being summoned, too."

She nodded, and the worried expression she'd had earlier reappeared on her face. I didn't get a chance to ask her what was going on, because she waved at me. "I'll see you after the race. Professor—Doctor—Waverly. Ride hard!" With that, she ran across the street to where Bobby was waiting for her.

I watched her go with a furrowed brow.

Someone announced over the loudspeaker that the race would start in two minutes.

Rainwater appeared at my side and said, "Let's find a spot." He sounded more excited than I'd ever heard him. I followed him with my bike to a spot in the middle of the pack. "This is good." He squeezed my hand. "Are you ready to ride?"

I smiled back. "With you? Yes."

He grinned. "That's all I need to hear."

As the gunshot signaling the beginning of the race went off, my concern for Jo fell away as I concentrated on not getting run over by eager riders. Had I known what was to happen that day, the worry would never have left me.

Chapter Three

My thighs burned and my back ached. I leaned over the handlebars of my mother's bicycle as if my body weight would help propel me up the steep hill. I knew how ridiculous I looked huffing and puffing as I pedaled like the Wicked Witch of the West from *The Wizard of Oz*. Instead of a black cape, I wore a violet helmet askew on my head.

I shifted the bike into the lowest gear possible; my legs seemed to flail in space rather than propel the bicycle forward. I shifted back into third gear, and the chain ground as it moved, but finally caught on the gears. Other cyclists on bikes much better suited for racing flew by me. The wind cast off of them made my bike quiver.

I let out a sigh of relief as I crested the top of the hill and caught a glimpse of myself in the tiny side mirror attached to my handlebars. My eyes were bloodshot from the strain.

Rainwater stood next to his own bike at the top of the hill, waiting for me. "Vi, are you okay?" he asked as other riders zoomed by him. It took all my willpower not to growl at them as they waved and shouted, "Hello," "Hello," "Hello," one after the other. I was too tired for any form of social pleasantries.

I forced a smile, although I was afraid my expression looked much more like a grimace, but that couldn't be helped. "Doing great! Just catching my breath." I stared down the other side of the hill as riders whizzed by us. The incline was the steepest portion of the course and had been nicknamed Breakneck Hill by villagers. Not that anyone had ever broken her neck riding down it, but it was a good idea to test your brakes before you went. I gave my brakes a squeeze for good measure.

"It might have been easier to make it up the hill if you had stood up on the pedals." His voice was tentative, as if he knew he was taking a great risk. He was right about standing up on the pedals and about the risk.

I knew how to ride. I knew that standing and pedaling would have been more effective. It was exactly what I would have done if my legs hadn't been screaming at me to stop. We were twenty-five miles into the thirty-mile ride. My body could only do so much.

"I thought you liked to bike," Rainwater said. "You bike all over the village all day long."

"Riding between Charming Books and Le Crepe Jolie is not the same as a thirty-mile bike ride uphill both ways."

He laughed. "You sound like everyone's grandfather when you say that. It's not uphill both ways."

I adjusted the chin strap of my helmet. "Besides, when I leave the café, I usually am carrying a snack. Will there be snacks at the end of this?"

Rainwater smiled. "I'll make sure you get a snack at the end." His amber eyes twinkled. "And for what it's worth, you look adorable when you're hot and tired."

I could only guess how red my face was, perhaps as red as my strawberry-blonde hair. Super cute, I was sure.

"You better have some more water before we continue on," he said. "I can't have you dying from heatstroke on me."

I grunted and yanked my water bottle from the holder. After a long swig, I felt revived enough to know I was giving Rainwater a harder time than he deserved. "I'm sorry I keep slowing you up. I don't do much hill work in my rides around the village."

He smiled, and his white teeth shone against his damp, tawny-colored skin. Even when he was sweaty and tired, he was still the most handsome man I had ever seen. Sometimes I had to remind myself that he was my boyfriend.

Rainwater leaned forward and kissed me on the cheek. "You're doing great. I know you weren't keen on doing this charity ride, but I'm so proud that you did it."

I stepped back. "Ick. You don't want to kiss me. I'm sweaty and gross," I protested.

"So am I, and I don't care. You deserve a kiss for encouragement. You looked so determined coming up that hill. I don't think I have ever seen anything like it." There was a slight chuckle in his tone.

I narrowed my eyes. "Are you making fun of me?"

"No, I would never." His grin was full-on now. He leaned forward and kissed me again, this time on the mouth, as four more riders whizzed by.

"People are going to talk about us if you keep that up." I hoped that my blushing cheeks could be blamed on the ride.

He laughed. "I'm pretty sure that everyone in the village already knows about us. Daisy practically threw a parade when we got together."

I sighed. He was right. I opened my mouth to make another joke about it when a bike passed us but at a much slower pace than the others. The rider had blond hair and a mustache and held up a small digital camera as he flew by. The flash caught me directly in the eye, but not before I saw the man behind the camera. Redding.

I blinked away the dots as I stood there with my mouth hanging open. "Did you see that?" I asked Rainwater.

He got back on his bike. "Wasn't that Joel Redding? What is he doing back in Cascade Springs?"

I bit the inside of my lip. That was something I would like to know, too.

"Why was he taking photos of you?" Rainwater asked.

I licked my lips. "How do you know he was taking photos of me? He might have just been photographing what he could of the race. Maybe he's investigating someone in the race? Or maybe he cycles in his free time?"

Rainwater arched his brow. "He was wearing an oxford shirt at a bike race. He's not here for the Tour de Cascade Springs."

Yes, that blue-and-white button-down shirt wasn't your typical athletic clothing. Redding stood out like a nun at a circus.

As David's eyes narrowed further, I could all but see his police chief hat slipping on over his bike helmet. And the last thing I wanted was to be on the receiving end of one of his interrogations. While I'd never lie to him outright, I didn't want to unload all my worries and concerns, especially as they pertained to my Caretaker role, in the middle of the Tour de Cascade Springs bike race. As it was, our brief pause atop the hill had only barely allowed me to catch my breath.

He opened his mouth as if he was going to say something more, but I cut him off by jumping back on my bike. "Let's go. We have to have a respectable showing in this race. We don't want to embarrass the mayor, do we?"

I started down Breakneck Hill. Trees lined either side of the narrow two- lane road and felt like they were closing in on me just as they had when I was a child. I coasted down the hill and was breathing hard. It wasn't from the pedaling. I was out of breath because Redding was here. I had been right—he was watching me. I'd acted like Redding couldn't possibly be taking photographs of me, but I knew better than to think I'd fooled Rainwater. David was far too smart and observant. Thankfully, he was also a gentleman. And as a gentleman, he'd not called his girlfriend out on her bumbling attempt to deny the obvious.

As far as Redding was concerned, I knew he was taking photographs of me because he wanted to expose my secret. I supposed if he found out the truth behind Charming Books, he could make a lot of money, and from what I knew of Joel Redding, making money was his prime objective as a detective.

But I wasn't going to let that happen. I would do whatever it took to keep him from finding out the shop's secret.

Rainwater came up alongside me as we made it down the hill. "Violet," he began.

I pretended I didn't hear him and pedaled faster, like the tires of my bike were on fire. I knew I couldn't outrun Rainwater forever or even until the end of the race, but I wanted to get my story straight in my head first.

"Whoa!" Rainwater cried. "Violet! Slow down."

I looked over my shoulder.

"Don't look at me! Look ahead of you!"

I spun my head around and saw at least a dozen people standing in the middle of the road. Some of them were riders still on their bicycles and some were onlookers. Bikes that were still in the race careened around the spectators as they tore by. I squeezed my handle breaks with all my might, leaving a thick layer of rubber on the road. I careened off the course and into the grass, barely missing a tree as my bike bounced to a stop and I leaped off.

Rainwater came to a stop beside me. "Violet, are you all right?"

"I'm fine, I think. Why where all those people in the middle of the road like—"

"He's dead!" a voice in the crowd screamed.

Rainwater hopped off his bicycle, let it fall into the grass, and took off running even before I could process what I'd heard.

Chapter Four

My reaction time wasn't as quick as Rainwater's, but I took off after him, not even bothering to take off my violet helmet as I made my way through the crowd.

The bike race had come to a complete stop at this point as more and more riders and onlookers gathered on the road. I pushed my way through the throng. "Excuse me. Excuse me. I'm with the police."

Most of the people were tourists who didn't know me, so claiming I was with the police didn't seem like too much of a risk, especially since I was with Rainwater.

The spandex-clad crowd parted ways for me. I saw Rainwater and the EMTs who were there to treat injuries for the race, but I doubted they'd expected a death. I cringed to think what I would find and what it would mean for the village or my grandmother if a rider had died during the Tour de Cascade Springs. Like all races, this one had required each participant to sign a lengthy waiver acknowledging that if he or she was maimed or killed during the ride, it wasn't the village's fault and the village couldn't be sued, but the bad press was certainly unavoidable.

"Excuse me," I said to a large man in my path. His biker shorts were stretched to the limit.

He glared at me so hard that I stumbled back in surprise. He wasn't a person I knew, but that didn't mean much. In the late spring and summer, Cascade Springs was overrun with tourists from all over the world. It was a popular place on the bed-and-breakfast circuit for those visiting the majestic Niagara Falls.

I edged around the man.

"Looks like a bad accident," someone said.

"I think I've seen him in the village before. Wasn't he here in the winter when all that went down with the Morton family?"

I shivered as I started to realize who must be lying on the ground. Maybe I was wrong—I was still holding out hope that it wasn't who I thought it was. It couldn't possibly be.

"Looks to me like he lost control while coming down the hill."

"What an awful thing to happen at a wonderful charity event," another bystander mused.

I pushed through the crowd and made my way to the front. Finally, I spotted Rainwater leaning over a man lying on the ground. A few feet away, the man's red-and-silver bike lay crumpled on the road. The front wheel was bent; the spokes had broken loose from the rim. It was clear that whatever caused the accident had thrown him over the handlebars.

I edged around the scene, taking care to keep my distance. Rainwater wouldn't want me to be there, but he wouldn't be surprised I was here either.

I saw a foot sticking out next to Rainwater. What caught my attention most about it was that it was a loafer, which wasn't exactly a regulation cycling shoe. I inched a little to the left and looked at the face of the person on the ground, but I already knew who it would be. Joel Redding. This was definitely a time that I didn't want to be right.

I hadn't cared for the man in life, but in death, I had sympathy for him. What a terrible way to die. I swallowed hard. Had the shop revealed Walt Whitman to me after I saw Redding the night before so I would know to warn him? Had I failed somehow and contributed to his death by not understanding what the essence wanted me to do? I knew from past experience that when the shop's essence put a book in my path repeatedly, there was a reason. It was its way of giving me clues of what was to come, to help me understand what had happened, and at times to warn me. Honestly, it would have been a whole lot easier if it would just come right out and say what the heck was going on, but according to my grandmother, it had never worked that way.

"This was on him, Chief," Officer Clipton said. She was a curvy female officer and wore a reflective yellow smock over her uniform. All the police on the sidelines of the race were wearing them so that visitors and villagers alike could find the police quickly during the race if the need should arise. And boy, had it ever.

Rainwater looked up, and by the flicker in his amber eyes, I knew he took notice of me standing there with my mouth hanging open. "What is it?" Rainwater asked.

"A book. It was in the pack on the back of his bike." Clipton shook her head. "Who rides in a bike race with a book?"

"Maybe he wasn't a part of the race," Wheaton, a male officer with a buzz-cut and a massive chip on his shoulder, suggested. "He's not dressed for it. What book?"

"He was on a bike. Poetry. *Leaves of Grass*," Clipton said. "I'm sure you've never read it."

The other officer scowled back at her.

I felt woozy at hearing the title.

"We have to secure the scene," Rainwater said. His voice was sharp.

"I just got radioed that there is another pack of riders coming this way."

"We need to divert them," Rainwater said. "Clipton, take a couple of officers and make the pack of riders turn around. They can come down Chickadee Street since it runs parallel to this road. We can add them back into the course. The riders might have to wait for a moment to get everything settled, but it won't cause too much trouble."

"Got it, Chief." Clipton was all business as she ran up the hill we had all just come down. I doubted she would even been winded at the top.

Rainwater made no comment about me being there. Another of his officers was diverting the riders back on course.

"I have to get back in the race!" one man in bright orange biker shorts yelled.

"I'm sorry, sir," the officer said. "But there has been an accident. If you want to get back on the course, you will have to go back up the road and follow the detour."

The orange-shorts guy's face turned bright red, which didn't go with his ensemble at all. "This is completely messing with my time. I was making good time until you stopped me."

"Sir, I understand you're upset, but this is a police order."

"I don't care what it is. I'm in a race."

Rainwater's brow furrowed. "Take the detour, or one of my officers will detain you until the end of the race."

Riders who were determined to return to the race walked their bikes back up the steep hill so they could rejoin the newly diverted course. I wasn't among them. I was less than five miles from the end of the race, which was a great physical accomplishment for me but didn't seem to matter now. A man was dead. A man I knew. A man who had possibly been following my every move for that last week.

A high, clear voice broke through the crowd. "Out of my way. Village mayor coming through. Step aside!"

I grimaced. I loved Grandma Daisy with my whole heart. She was my favorite person when it came right down to it, but this was the last place I wanted her to be right now. I knew her well enough to know that the moment she saw Redding, she was going to make a scene, which would only draw attention to the fact that Redding and I had had a dispute in the past. I would much rather everyone in the village forgot my connection to the private eye.

I pushed through the crowd to reach her and spotted my grandmother a few feet away, standing in front of Officer Wheaton and shaking the end of her silk bike-printed scarf at him. Wheaton glowered at her, but then again, Wheaton glowered at everyone, so that really didn't mean anything at all.

"What on earth is going on here?" Grandma Daisy asked Wheaton. "I was cheering at the finish line, and then suddenly the stream of riders coming through slowed to a trickle, and one of the final riders said there had been an accident. I'm the mayor of this village, and I have a right to know what is going on!"

"Ms. Mayor," Wheaton said as coldly as possible, "there has been an accident, but I'm not at liberty to say more at the moment. I will tell you that the course has been diverted to the next street over and the race has resumed. You should see riders coming in to the finish line at any moment now. I would advise you to return to your post at the end of the race."

"Who do you think you are talking to, Wheaton?" my grandmother asked.

"Grandma!" I hurried over to her and grabbed her arm.

She blinked at me. "Violet, what are you doing here? I thought you would be on the course. Aren't you going to finish the race?"

I squeezed her arm. "I'm not going to finish it now. Something has happened."

"I know. I have been trying to find out what it was from Wheaton, but the officer isn't saying a word. Where's David? I know the police chief will tell me." She narrowed her eyes at the young officer.

"Let's talk privately. I can bring you up to speed, at least with what I know."

She glared at Wheaton one last time and then let me guide her to the patch of grass where I had abandoned my bike.

"Violet, what on earth is going on? We can't let anything ruin the Tour de Cascade Springs. We have a lot of money for the museum riding on this event. What is this about an accident? Was anyone hurt?"

I bit my lower lip. "It's much more than an accident. A man is dead."

Chapter Five

I told her about the accident at the bottom of Breakneck Hill but didn't have a chance to tell her who that man was before she burst out, "What? This is a disaster!"

Most of the riders had gotten back on the revised course by this point, but there were still a good number of onlookers standing around. One of Rainwater's officers went from spectator to spectator, asking them what they had seen at the time of Redding's accident.

I turned my grandmother away from the crowd and whispered, "It gets worse, but you have to keep your cool. People are watching."

Grandma Daisy looked over her shoulder at all the staring faces. "What could be worse than having a rider die at our first annual Tour de Cascade Springs, a race that one day will be the high point of the cyclist season in New York State?"

I shook my head. Leave it to my grandmother to set her aspirations higher than anyone else would dare. I leaned close to her and whispered, "It's Joel Redding."

Grandma Daisy removed her cat-eye glasses and rubbed her eyes. "I can't even process that. We saw him just outside Charming Books yesterday. He's been following you around the village for near a week. *That* Joel Redding?"

I nodded. "The very one."

She put her glasses back on and resumed holding her scarf like it was some kind of security blanket. "I'm sorry to hear he's dead. The poor man."

I felt a *but* coming on and waited.

"But," she began.

There it was.

"But at least he won't find out about you-know-what at you-know-where."

"Grandma, a man is dead. We shouldn't be thinking about the shop right now."

She blushed. "You're right. You're right. And Redding told you he was just out for a walk. That doesn't mean he was following you."

I frowned, thinking of the photos Redding had taken of me standing at the top of Breakneck Hill. They would be the last photos he ever took. I shivered.

Grandma Daisy twisted the end of her scarf around her hand. "Are you sure it's Redding? Maybe it's just someone who looks like him," she said, with a little too much hope in her voice. "With all the spandex and biker shorts going on in the village, everyone is looking the same at the moment. I hardly recognized you in that getup." She looked me up and down. "You have a beautiful figure, my dear, but not many people can pull off this look."

I crossed my arms around my chest. "Grandma, this is not the time for jokes."

"I'm not joking."

I scowled. "I knew it was Redding before I saw his dead body with my own eyes. It's him."

Grandma Daisy straightened her shoulders. "I had better take a look for myself. It might be gruesome, but I'm the mayor and it's my job to look at the underbelly of life in Cascade Springs." Without so much as a backward glance at me, she marched over to the crime scene.

Until that moment, I hadn't even known that Cascade Springs had an underbelly.

With a sigh, I followed her. At least most of the spectators had been interviewed by this point, or perhaps the police had just taken their names and their race numbers and then asked them to leave the area. Only law enforcement, Grandma Daisy, and I were left behind at the bottom on the hill.

"Mayor coming through," Grandma Daisy announced again. Although she was hard to miss. My grandmother's sleek silver bob was perfectly in place, her signature eyeglasses were back on her face, and she was wearing her favorite uniform: jeans and T-shirt. Instead of the Charming Books tee she usually sported, she wore a T-shirt advertising the Tour de Cascade Springs. Grandma Daisy was a big proponent of wearing what you support on a T-shirt.

"David, tell me what's going on," Grandma Daisy said the moment she reached Rainwater.

Rainwater was crouched next to the body, having a whispered conversation with a crime scene tech who must have arrived when I had been trying unsuccessfully to calm my grandmother down. The police chief stood up. Even out of uniform and in biking shorts like the rest of the riders, he had a commanding presence. "Daisy, I don't think you should be here. I'll be sure to inform you of everything that is going on when I know more."

Grandma Daisy put her hands on her narrow hips. "I don't have to remind you that I am the mayor of this village and have a right to this information the moment something goes down. It's my job to keep everything on an even keel, and how am I supposed to do that when I don't know what's going on in my little village?"

Rainwater's cheek twitched. I didn't know if he was fighting a laugh or a groan in exasperation.

Grandma Daisy leaned forward to take a better look at the deceased. Leave it to my grandmother not to be afraid of a dead body. I averted my eyes.

"It's Redding, all right," my grandmother said, as if her announcement made a difference in some way. "I never forget a face. Names are a different story. I can barely remember my own name on some days."

Rainwater looked at my grandmother curiously. "When was the last time that you saw him?"

I inwardly groaned, but Grandma Daisy kept her cool. "I remember him from being in the village this winter. He hung around the bookshop back then because he wanted to know what Violet knew about the murder."

He nodded as if he wasn't completely convinced and then said, "We will have to get to the bottom, then, as to why he is back in the village."

I felt like I might be sick.

"My officers have gotten the names and numbers of the people who may have witnessed the accident to follow up," Rainwater said.

My grandmother cocked her head. "You think it was just an accident, then?"

His cheek twitched. "We aren't making any assumptions at this point, but this is a steep hill." He glanced at me. "He may have just lost control of the bike. I'm more curious about why a copy of Whitman's *Leaves of Grass* was on his person." In his gloved hand, he held up the book.

I felt the color drain from my face as he said that.

"And why Violet went so pale when she saw it."

Rainwater noticed everything.

"Chief," the crime scene tech called. "We found something!"

Rainwater turned back to the scene. I peeked around him and saw the tech leaning over the handlebars of Redding's bike.

"Violet," Grandma Daisy whispered in my ear. "What is this about a book? Do you have something against reading the first great American poet?"

"Not all scholars agree he was the first great American poet. I mean, most do, but there is still some debate on the topic."

"Violet . . ."

"Sorry, I'm still trying to defend my dissertation. I'm experiencing post-traumatic oral exam."

"Violet." She yanked on her scarf for emphasis.

"It's the same book that the essence revealed to me last night," I said, barely above a whisper.

She sucked in a breath. "Then how did it get out here? The shop has never been able to send books outside Charming Books before."

"That's something I would like to know," I said out the side of my mouth. "Could it be it's just coincidence that the shop wants me to read *Leaves of Grass* and Redding just happens also to be a big Whitman fan?"

"I don't believe in coincidences when it comes to the shop's essence."

"Me either," I said, and scooted closer to the scene so I could overheard Rainwater's conversation with the crime scene tech.

"What is it?" Rainwater asked.

"The brake line, Chief. It's been cut."

"What?" Rainwater asked.

I swallowed and shared a glance with my grandmother.

Grandma Daisy ducked under the crime scene tape. "The brakes are cut how?"

I didn't follow my grandmother but stopped at the edge of the scene.

The tech looked at Rainwater as if to ask if he could speak about it in front of Grandma Daisy and me. Rainwater gave a slight nod.

"Well," the tech said, "I noticed the tube around the brake line was a little loose, so I pulled it back and could see both the front brake and back brake had been cut about three-quarters through. The last quarter on both was frayed, so my assumption is someone moved the tubing over the brake wire back, cut the wires most of the way, replaced the tubing, and then waited. Something like this couldn't have happened on accident. When the victim had to hit the brakes on this big hill, the brake lines snapped, which made him lose control and crash." The tech looked up at Rainwater. "I'd say you have you more than just an accident on your hands, Chief."

Rainwater didn't say a word. Instead, he looked back at me. There were so many questions in his amber eyes.

"There's something else," the tech said.

Rainwater turned back to his tech with a sigh. "What is it?"

The tech adjusted the department ball cap perched on his head. "I know where he got the bike."

"How?"

The tech pointed under the crossbar. "It's a rental from Bobby's Bike Shop. There is a sticker under here."

I had a sinking feeling in my stomach as I thought back to when I'd seen Jo making her way to Bobby's booth. Could she be involved? She couldn't possibly know Redding, could she? Or could Bobby be involved? At the very least, one of them would have to know how Redding had gotten one of their bikes.

It looked like I needed to have a conversation with Jo and Bobby.

Chapter Six

Rainwater turned back to Grandma Daisy. "I promise to tell you more when I can, but now that we are dealing with a possible murder, I need to ask you to leave, even if you are the mayor."

Grandma Daisy ducked back under the crime scene tape to come to my side. "I understand, David. You have a job to do. Besides, I need to get back to the finish line to greet and congratulate the winners. Violet, you're out of the race now; would you mind going back with me to the finish line?" She gave me a meaningful look and did everything but wiggle her eyebrows Groucho Marx style.

Rainwater rolled his eyes at me to let me know he didn't miss Grandma Daisy's expression.

"Sure, Grandma Daisy," I said, glancing back at Rainwater. "Do you need me here? Do I need to give a statement or something?"

The police chief shook his head. "I'll stop by the shop later. I'm going to be here for a while."

I nodded, knowing Rainwater was going to feel the weight of Redding's death heavily on his shoulders.

Grandma Daisy and I walked back to where I had left my bike, I picked it up, and we walked back to the top of Breakneck Hill. I never would have believed it would one day live up to its name.

When we reached the top of the hill, I said, "I know you don't have your car here. I can walk my bike with you to the finish line."

"Who says I'm walking?" my grandmother asked. "I've got wheels, too!" She pointed at a nearby golf cart. Ms. MAYOR was painted on the hood in neon-blue paint.

I closed my eyes for a long moment and let out a breath. "Where on earth did that come from?"

My grandmother blushed. "Charles Hancock made a donation to the village. He thought it would be easier for me to fulfill my mayoral duties if I could travel around the village more quickly. As you know, having a car in the village is too cumbersome. I'm not much of a bike rider, so a golf cart is just right."

I suppressed a smile. Charles Hancock was a determined eighty-something man who happened to have a very public crush on my grandmother. He made no secret of his affection for her, having gone so far as writing a sonnet about her that he recited the day she was sworn into office, and now apparently giving her a golf cart.

Charles had pined for my grandmother for years, and just in the last few months she had started to soften toward his advances. However, I took care to make no mention of her change of heart when it came to him. Grandma Daisy could be very prickly on the topic. I think she had been resisting Charles for so long, she might have felt like she was conceding something by giving in to him now.

I must not have hidden my amusement very well, because my grandmother narrowed her bright-blue eyes—the same color as mine—at me. "Are you laughing at me, Violet Waverly?"

I couldn't hold back the chuckle bubbling in the back of my throat. "Laugh? I would never laugh at my grandmother."

She snorted. "I don't believe you for a minute. You've laughed at me plenty of times."

"Because you're so funny." I smiled sweetly.

She grunted and climbed into her royal golf cart. "You're just jealous of my new wheels. You wipe that smug expression off your face or I won't let you take it for a spin of your own."

"Was the title painted on the hood Charles's idea or yours?"

"It doesn't matter whose idea that was." She tossed the end of her scarf over her shoulder.

Her response was all the answer I needed.

"The golf cart needs to be quickly recognizable to anyone in the village as an official vehicle. You know golf carts aren't generally allowed on our streets."

"But mayors can have them?" I asked.

She grinned. "There is privilege at the top."

I didn't doubt that in the least.

I rolled my bike alongside her and straddled it. "Grandma, does your golf cart have a leather interior?"

She grinned. "And Bluetooth!" With that, she gunned the engine and took off. I had to pedal double time to catch up with her.

Fifteen minutes later, I rode off the course through the residential streets of the village in what felt like a parade in my grandmother's honor, as I was one bike length behind her new wheels. It was clear Grandma Daisy felt the same, because she returned the royal wave to all her subjects. I wasn't enthused when she took her hand off the wheel. However, much to my surprise, my grandmother seemed to have a better handle on maneuvering the golf cart than I'd expected she would.

Thankfully, it was a quick trip, as we took a shortcut through back roads to the finish line. My legs were little better than Jell-O after riding twenty-five miles.

The finish line sat in front of the village hall. I could hear the roar of the spectators as we merged onto River Road and rejoined the pack of riders. With my bike, I blended in well. Grandma Daisy was another story. She continued her mayoral wave as she turned on the street, not taking care to watch out for the dozens of riders that she almost sideswiped with the cart.

Grandma Daisy parked the golf cart on the sidewalk in front of the village hall, and Cameron Connell was waiting for her. Cameron was a member-at-large of the village council and the most outspoken member in the group of seven. He was a realtor and investment banker in his forties who dreamed that Cascade Springs was a quiet, boring town. That dream would never do as long as Grandma Daisy was mayor. Quiet and boring weren't her style. Not surprisingly, Cameron was adamantly against the new museum, so he and my grandmother were at odds much of the time.

I hopped off my bike and walked it over to where the pair stood, just in case my grandmother needed backup.

"Daisy!" Cameron cried. "We have to have an emergency council meeting. I have taken the liberty to gather what members I could. I couldn't find Logan Duffy. He appears to be shirking his duties again. We might have to think about ways to get him off the council. A resignation would be the least messy option."

My grandmother turned to me. "Violet, you will have to excuse me, my dear. Duty calls." She straightened her shoulders and walked up the steps to the formidable building with its two- feet-thick stone walls, clock tower, and domed roof. The hall was beautiful but far too large to govern a village as tiny as Cascade Springs. My grandmother was right. It would have made a wonderful museum if this latest turn of events hadn't ruined its chances.

Riders fresh from the race and visitors walked around me on the sidewalk as I stared after my grandmother. I wondered how there could possibly be another murder in our quaint little village. In a place like this, the worst I would have expected would be a rash of jaywalking, not a rash of murder.

"Violet, Violet!" My friend Lacey Dupont waved from the café, Le Crepe Jolie, that she and her husband, Adrien, ran. Lacey, Adrien, and their waitress, Danielle Cloud, stood outside the café handing out free crepes and other French goodies to the riders as they came in.

I walked my bike over to her and parked it on the side of the café.

She beamed at me. "You made it!" She put a fresh cheese crepe in my hand, and Adrien was soon at her side and put a bottle of water in my other hand. They really were the best people to meet at the end of a bike race.

I drank the entire bottle of water and wiped my mouth before speaking. "Not quite. I only rode twenty-five miles."

"What happened?" Lacey looked around. "Where's David? Is he okay? I expected the two of you to come in together."

"He's fine, but he's not going to be coming to the finish line anytime soon." I leaned in close and whispered to Adrien and Lacey what had happened at the bottom of Breakneck Hill.

Lacey gasped. "That's the same terrible investigator who thought I killed my sister earlier this year!"

Danielle's head snapped in our direction.

"Shh!" I scanned the area around us and saw a piece of crepe fall from a nearby rider's mouth at Lacey's outburst.

I smiled at me. "She's joking."

"He got what he deserved," Adrien said in a dark voice.

"He's joking too. Aren't they hilarious?" I asked the man with the crepe, who edged away from us.

Lacey's eyes went wide at her husband. "How can you even say such a thing? True, he wasn't a nice man, but I could never wish any ill on him or anyone."

Adrien touched her cheek with his large, callused hand. "And this is why I love you, *ma chère*. You are pure of heart. I will do the hating for the both of us. What are you going to do, Violet?"

"What do you mean?" I asked.

"Well." Lacey lowered her voice. "Are you going to find out what happened to Redding?"

"Rainwater won't like it."

"That doesn't mean you won't do it," Lacey said in a knowing voice.

"Why was he in the race?" Adrien asked.

41

"That's probably the biggest question. He rode and had a racing bike, but he wasn't dressed to ride. He was wearing casual business attire, not spandex," I said.

Lacey's mouth fell open. "You saw the body?"

I nodded.

Adrien tilted his head. "That doesn't sound to me like he planned to be in the race."

"That was my thought," I said, and not for the first time, I wondered why Redding had even been in the race. Did it have to do with me? As Rainwater noted, the private eye had been taking photos of me, and I couldn't forget the copy of *Leaves of Grass* with the body. The book the shop's essence had revealed to me the night before the race.

"And you will want to talk to Bobby," Lacey said. "If Redding registered, he will be on Bobby's list."

I nodded. "The bike he was riding was from Bobby's shop."

"That makes sense," Adrien said. "There's nowhere else to rent a bike at the last minute in the village. He should be at the registration table. You can't miss him."

I knew that was true. Very few people missed Bobby.

Chapter Seven

A cross from the village hall and the café was the Riverwalk; it was a three-mile-long path that followed the Niagara River in and out of Cascade Springs. It was the largest piece of green space in the downtown area and the location for all the festivals, celebrations, and events.

At the moment, the long stretch of green was dotted with race spectators, tired riders, and dozens of booths that catered to both groups. Even so, Bobby Holmes of Bobby's Bike Shop wasn't hard to find. He wore his ever-present Atlanta Braves ball cap. Bobby, an Atlanta transplant, frequently wore the colors of his favorite team proudly, and he spoke so fondly of his old life in the warm South that it made me wonder how he had ended up in Cascade Springs, which was under snow a minimum of four months of the year. That was a low estimate.

Not to say that the village wasn't a good locale for a bike shop. Bicycles were a popular form of transportation in Cascade Springs, which was a small village with only a few thousand year-round residents. In the summer months and then again in January, during ice wine season, our tiny village was inundated with people from all over the globe. Bikes were the best and quickest way to travel through the narrow nineteenth-century streets congested with white carriages, cars, and pedestrians. On two wheels, a rider could swerve in and around the bewildered tourists or avoid them altogether by taking the many bike paths that cut through the village park that stood behind Charming Books and led to the famous springs.

Bobby tipped his Braves hat at me. "Violet, good to see you. How did that old cruiser bike work for you on the race? Usually those types of wheels aren't built for these sorts of things. I can show you a sleeker and faster model that would serve you better in your next race."

I laughed. "This was my one and only race, and I did it more for Rainwater than myself. I much prefer tooling around the village at my own pace. My old bike is perfect for that."

He nodded. "You can't fault a man for trying. You may change your mind someday. I'm always there when you want to upgrade."

I laughed, not surprised that Bobby's shop did so well. He was the affable salesman.

"If you're not here for a new bike, is there something else I can do for you?" he asked.

"Actually there is. Could I take a peek at the race registration list?"

He arched his brow. "I'm not sure I can do that. You're not on the committee. You're a competitor."

In my case, *competitor* was used loosely. Even if I had finished the entire race, I hadn't been a threat to take home any medals. "It's for my grandmother, actually. She got caught up in a village council meeting and would like me to check the registration list."

Bobby got an odd look on his face. "If Daisy can't trust me to manage the race . . ."

"Oh, it's nothing like that." I waved my hands. "Grandma Daisy was so very happy when you volunteered to manage the race. It was quite an undertaking on very short notice. You've done a wonderful job."

His chest puffed out just a little at my compliment. "Thank you. That's very nice to hear."

He walked over to the race check-in table, which was no longer manned by volunteers, since the race was all but over. The leaders had rolled across the finish line well over two hours ago, and the stragglers were coming in now. Flyers and pamphlets were strewn across the table, and a laptop computer sat in the middle of the mess.

He opened his laptop and tapped on the keys. "Let me see. We have over six hundred people riding today. Your grandmother did an excellent job of getting the word out."

I smiled. Grandma Daisy was a good salesperson too.

"Do you really want to look at all these names?"

I wrinkled my nose. I didn't. "Not really."

"Is there anyone in particular your grandmother wants you to find? I can do a quick search of the spreadsheet to find a particular name." He said *grandmother* like that detail of my story was suspect. I would have to tell Grandma Daisy the fib I made up so she would go along with it should Bobby ask. I knew she would. She loved a good "undercover op," as she called them.

"Joel Redding," I said.

"Redding, Redding, Redding," Bobby muttered to himself.

I peered over his shoulder for a peek at the spreadsheet listing all the riders' names in alphabetical order. Bobby went through the *R*s twice, and neither of us spotted Redding. Just to be safe, I suggested he use the find feature on the spreadsheet for Redding and then for Joel. Neither came up. It was surprising that of all those racers, there was not a single Joel in the bunch.

I stepped back from the screen, deep in thought. Redding could have registered under another name. After all, he was a private detective who would have experience going undercover. Perhaps he hadn't used his real name for fear that Grandma Daisy, as the instigator of the race and the village mayor, would have spotted it and given him the boot. That made sense, but it still didn't answer why he was dressed in street clothes for the race on such a warm day. I was wearing a biker shirt and shorts—definitely not the most flattering outfit on the planet—and I had been terribly hot during the race.

Someone cleared her throat behind me. "Violet, should I even ask what you're doing over here?"

I jumped back from the computer as if I'd been caught with my hand in the cookie jar. "Hey, Clipton." I knew my voice was much higher than it normally would be.

Bobby's thick eyebrows disappeared under the brim of his hat. "Violet just asked to see the registration list. She said Daisy was asking about a certain rider."

Clipton smiled. "I'm sure she did. I'm going to need a printout of that list, Bobby, with names, addresses, and phone numbers. The works."

The bike shop owner bristled and looked from Clipton to me and back again. "Why? I don't see any reason why you would need that. Unless something has happened. I heard that one of the riders crashed near the end of the race. Is that what this is all about?" He looked to me for the answer.

Clipton cocked her head and reminded me of a curious cocker spaniel. "I'm surprised that Miss Waverly didn't tell you about the accident. A man by the name of Joel Redding was killed on the course."

Bobby's head whipped around in my direction. "That's why you asked me if Joel Redding was registered?"

Busted.

"Grandma Daisy did want to know for the reason you said." I shot Clipton a look. "I didn't tell you about his death because I didn't know if the police wanted to make it public yet."

"Nice save," Clipton muttered.

I scowled at her.

She folded his arms. "So what was the verdict? Was he registered?"

"We couldn't find his name," Bobby said.

"That doesn't mean he wasn't riding under an alias," Clipton said.

I wasn't the least bit surprised that Clipton came to the same conclusion I had.

The police officer studied Bobby for a long moment. Clipton could have a penetrating stare when she wanted to. "At least twenty riders and just as many spectators saw the accident and heard that a man had died. How did you not know about the death?"

"I guess I wasn't at the Riverwalk when that group came in." His eyes flicked back and forth as if he were looking for someone to save him.

Bobby was everyone's good-time guy. I couldn't remember ever seeing him so jittery. Was he hiding something?

"Where were you?" Clipton tried to sound casual.

He wouldn't meet her eyes. "I had to run back to the shop for some parts to repair some of the bikes. That took about an hour. Maybe my assistant heard something. I haven't been able to speak to her since I got back."

"Who's your assistant?" Clipton asked.

"Jo Fitzgerald."

I scanned the area, but I didn't see Jo. I was about to ask where she was when Clipton beat me to it.

"Where's Jo now?" Clipton asked.

"I don't know." Bobby licked his lips. "It seems she's wandered off. She does that at times."

"She doesn't sound like she's a great employee." Clipton cocked her head in the other direction. "I want to talk to Jo," Clipton said, and then she turned to me. "If you see her first, tell her that. I assume you will be looking for her now."

I held up my hands in innocence. "Why do you assume that?"

She had the humor enough to laugh. "Before I go, Bobby, I need a list of all the registered riders."

He licked his lips. "Don't you need a warrant to take that?"

"This is a public village event. You don't have any property rights to that information, now, do you?"

His forehead broke out in a sweat. "You can have it. I don't want anything to do with this mess. I'm sorry that a man is dead, but keep me out of it. I don't know anything about it."

"Really?" Clipton almost cooed. "Then why was he riding a bike from your shop?"

The color drained from Bobby's face.

Chapter Eight

Bobby opened and closed his mouth for a moment like he was deciding what to say, but no words came out. He swallowed. "I don't know what you are talking about."

She glanced at me. "There's a sticker on the undercarriage of Redding's bicycle stamped with the bike shop's name, phone number, and address. I'd say that's a pretty good calling card."

Bobby removed his hat, scratched his head, and replaced it. "I don't know how he got it."

"Are any of your bikes missing?"

"I—I don't know. I haven't started inventory yet. The race is just ending, and sales of accessories have been busy. I'm the only one here."

"Because Jo wandered off," Clipton said.

Bobby's Adam's apple bobbed up and down.

She leaned closer to Bobby. "If you don't know how Redding got your bike, maybe Jo does. I think you will want me to have a chat with her, don't you?"

Bobby shook his head. "She doesn't have anything to do with this. She's a good kid."

"Violet!" A voice called me from the other side of the street. I turned to see Sadie Cunningham waving at me. She was dressed for summer in a lemon-printed bubble dress and peep-toe sandals the same color as her lemons. Her silky black hair was secured in a bun on the very top of her head, and she wore red lipstick.

Sadie had her arm linked through the arm of her boyfriend, Simon Chase, a tall, bookish, African-American man who was an insurance adjuster and wrote poetry by night. He adored Sadie and her sunny personality. He couldn't have been more different from her ex, who was gruff and critical. I was thrilled that my best friend had finally fallen for the right guy.

Clipton smiled at me. "Go on, Violet, visit with your friend. You don't need to be here for my conversation with Bobby."

I knew I didn't need to be there, but I wanted to be there. I wanted to know what had Bobby so worried. I wanted to know what he knew.

Clipton waited. When it was clear she wasn't going to go any further with the interview while I was standing there, I shrugged as if I didn't care. "I'll see you later, Bobby."

He didn't reply as I turned and walked to the street.

Crossing the finish line at the end of a thirty-mile bike race was as hard as it sounded. As the riders came in, they were so tired and yet exhilarated to be done that many of them didn't watch their steering. I almost got hit twice running across the street to meet Sadie and Simon.

"Violet, OMG! You almost got hit by that bike," Sadie cried.

"By two bikes actually, but who's counting?" I smiled at Simon. "Hey, Simon."

He gave me a small smile in return. Simon was as quiet as Sadie was bubbly.

"I'm so glad I caught you. I have something for you." She pulled up short and wrinkled her nose as she was about to hug me. "What on earth are you wearing?"

I looked down at my biker shorts and brightly colored spandex shirt. It was good for the ride to keep cool, but it wasn't really walking-around-town clothing. It showed everything. I folded my arms awkwardly about my waist, and my paper bib crinkled. "I was in the bike race."

"Still . . ." She trailed off. "I could have found you something better. This can't have been your best option."

"You had something to show me?" I asked, changing the subject. My clothing choices were something Sadie and I would never agree upon.

"Yes." She thrust the book out to me. "It's here, and I wanted you to have one of the very first copies. My author copies just came in the mail today, and I wanted you to have one right away."

I took the paperback book from her. On the cover, a woman's feet were dangling off what looked like a dock with a sunset reflected in the lake, which I knew from the story was Lake Ontario, where Sadie's debut romance novel was set. The cover read SUMMER MELODY / SADIE CUNNINGHAM.

Sadie wrapped herself around Simon's arm as if she needed something to hold on to. "Have you ever seen anything so beautiful?"

I smiled at her glowing face. "Never," I said, meaning it. The book represented years of hard work on Sadie's part and a lifelong dream fulfilled. She had owned and operated her vintage clothing shop, Midcentury Vintage, across the street from Charming Books for years, but being an author had been her true dream since she was a child.

She beamed at me. "I'm going to show it to everyone at the Red Inkers meeting tomorrow night."

The Red Inkers was a writing critique group that met twice weekly at Charming Books. Sadie was the first member to have a novel published and the youngest of the group, too. You would have thought there would be jealousy among the writers, but everyone was honestly thrilled for Sadie and her success. She had worked hard for this moment, and I was so happy that no one appeared to want to take that away from her.

"Of course, you and Simon have already seen it." Sadie looked up at her boyfriend. "I wouldn't have gotten published without Simon. If he hadn't written that referral to his agent, this never would have happened for me."

Simon shook his head. "You would have gotten there, Sadie. Don't be silly. You have the talent and drive. That's what it takes."

"He's right, Sadie," I said. "And I know all of the Red Inkers are so proud of you. I will be at the meeting tonight, but I'm not sure Rainwater will be able to make it." I quickly told her about Redding's death.

"Murdered? How terrible? Is David sure?" Sadie asked.

"He didn't say, but if the brake line really was cut, it is a malicious act, if not murder in the first degree," I said.

"Manslaughter, then?" Simon asked.

"That would be my guess," I said.

Sadie hugged herself. "What has our little village come to that this is normal conversation in Cascade Springs? And did you hear a man died by going over Niagara Falls last night too?"

I nodded. In all the upset from Redding's death, I had forgotten.

Tears came to her eyes. "It's just all too horrible. I just can't stop think about that man going over the Falls. What a terrible way to die. And now this!"

Simon wrapped his arm around her. "Sweetheart, you are too tenderhearted for your own good sometimes."

She looked up at Simon as if hurt.

"But that's what makes you such a wonderful writer and person."

Her face broke into a beautiful smile.

I rubbed her arm. Sadie was the sweetest and most compassionate person I knew. If anyone was going to cry over Redding's death and the death of the nameless man at the Falls, it would be her.

"I wonder," Sadie mused with clear eyes, "if Redding isn't done with Lacey yet and that's why he came back. Is that why he came back?"

I bit the inside of my lip, remembering Adrien's comment that Redding had gotten what he deserved. I shivered. Had Adrien seen Redding around the village the last several days and come to the same conclusion Sadie just had? Did he think killing Redding would remove the problem? The café was right across the street from where Bobby's Bike Shop was temporarily set up for the race. I shook the black thoughts away. Murder didn't fit Adrien at all, but then again, did it fit anyone?

I held up the book for Sadie to see. "I'll display it in the front window of the bookshop with pride. It will be great to show this off, for your launch party at Charming Books in two weeks. Everything will be perfect. I promise."

Her cheeks turned a lovely shade of pink. "Oh, I have another copy for the bookshop. I already dropped it off at Charming Books. Richard said he'd put it in the window."

Richard Bunting was my English department chair. With the spring term concluded, he'd wanted to make a little extra money and had asked if he could fill in some hours in the shop. Now that Grandma Daisy was the mayor of our little village and not at the shop nearly as often, I'd jumped at the chance. However, it felt a little strange telling my austere department head what to do.

Thankfully, not much instruction was required. Richard had been coming to Charming Books between browsing and Red Inkers for years, and he was almost a daily fixture in the shop. In some ways, he knew the store as well as Grandma Daisy and I did, and he certainly could answer any questions about literature that came up. But he knew nothing about the tree, the water, or the shop's essence. At first, I'd been nervous about leaving him in the shop alone, but Grandma Daisy insisted that the essence revealed itself only to the Caretaker or past Caretakers. That's how it'd been for the last two hundred years and that is how it would remain, or so she told me.

"How's Richard coping with Emerson and Faulkner?" I asked.

A little smile played on Sadie's lips. She was far too sweet to laugh outright at the English professor's troubles. "Faulkner seemed to be behaving himself. He was on his perch the whole time I was there. Richard said he and Faulkner were giving each other some distance."

I pressed my lips together, wondering what that meant.

"I didn't see Emerson, though," Sadie added.

I wasn't surprised. My cat hated being penned up, and he would think staying behind while Grandma Daisy and I were at the bike race was sheer torture. He was also known to stow away in my bicycle basket. I had checked it at least half a dozen times before I started the race to make sure he wasn't there. He was an expert hider as well as an escape artist.

"I just hope he's staying out of trouble," I said.

"Not likely," Simon said.

He was probably right.

"I can't believe what's happened at the race. I'm so glad you're okay. Rainwater is okay too? Daisy?" Sadie's face creased with concern.

I nodded. "We're all fine."

"It could have been an accident. That hill is steep," she argued.

"Maybe," I said, but doubt was obvious in my voice.

"I just don't want another murder to hang a black cloud over our little village," she said sadly.

"Neither do I, and I know Rainwater doesn't want that either."

"I need to get back to my shop." Sadie pulled on Simon's hand. "It's a busy day with so many people in town, and sales have been strong. I think people wish for some other kinds of clothes when seeing so many people in spandex." She shivered.

I laughed. "It does make you pine for another look."

She smiled. "See you tonight!"

"I'll be there," I said.

Sadie hopped in place. "Perfect." She grabbed Simon's hand. "Now, we really must get back to my shop. Bye!" She spun on her heel and pulled Simon after her down the Riverwalk. The tall man stumbled for a moment but was able to right himself before falling to the ground.

Simon put his arm around her as they made their way through the crowd that was finally starting to thin out as riders and spectators began to leave. The concession booths were packing up too, and the band that had been playing throughout the race was finishing their last set. I found myself smiling at them, but the smile faded when my gaze locked with that of another man's.

He was tall, with long gray hair tied back into a ponytail with a piece of leather. He had a guitar strapped around his body, and his guitar case sat open at his feet, ready to collect tips and donations. I recognized the song he played as an old folk tune, but I couldn't name it. Every time someone dropped a bill or coin into his case, he nodded his thanks and kept on playing and singing.

I couldn't move. I couldn't breathe. It was the first time I had seen my father in six months.

Chapter Nine

My father, Fenimore James, had come back to the village last Halloween with the purpose of finding me. I'd never gone looking for him. I hadn't known his name. My mother had never told Grandma Daisy and me and the father line on my birth certificate had been left blank. My mother had had her reasons for this. She'd believed, as the next Caretaker of Charming Books, that she was destined to be alone, just like all the women before her.

For a large portion of my life, my father hadn't even known I existed. He didn't find out until my mother sent him a letter telling him about me while she was dying from cancer. Of course, I'd had no idea she'd done this. Fenimore had told me and given me the letter, which now was hidden at the bottom of my sock drawer.

He'd known for over seventeen years who I was to him but had never come looking for me even though he knew where to find me, or at least knew where to find Charming Books. After he'd left last Halloween, I hadn't heard from him again.

Perhaps it was my turn to go looking for him. But life got busy, and I made excuses. I couldn't bring myself to do it.

"Move out of the way!" an angry voice shouted at me.

I jumped and stumbled off the sidewalk into the grass. I hadn't realized I had stopped in the middle of the street. I had been caught completely off guard by seeing my father.

"I can't believe you brought me here, Edith, on such a wretched weekend," the red-faced man said as he brushed past me. "You know I have no interest in athletics, and this entire village is overrun by cyclists."

The woman didn't seem the least bit put off by her husband's outburst. "You know, dear, this is our thirtieth wedding anniversary this weekend. I wanted to come back to the place where you proposed all those years ago. It may be crowded today, but one of the vendors assured me that it's only for today and we will have all of Sunday to bask in our love."

"I'm not basking in anything in this terrible place. I think I threw my back out when that biker cut me off," he grumbled. "I've never understood why anyone wanted to ride a bike anywhere anymore. That's why cars were invented. If you wanted to come here for our anniversary, we should have come another weekend, a weekend when no one was here."

"It wasn't like I could move the date of our anniversary, dear," she said, nonplussed by his harsh tone.

She was a stronger woman than me. I would give her that.

They moved down the sidewalk and finally were far enough away that I couldn't hear the man complain any longer. His grumbles were swallowed up by the chatter of the crowd.

When I turned back to Fenimore, I saw that he had stopped playing the guitar and singing. Instead he was staring at me.

He made a move like he was going to approach me, but he looked back like he thought better of leaving his guitar case full of money unattended. Which was a good call in such a large crowd, but it also gave me just enough time to get away.

I weaved through the bikes and riders who had just crossed the finish line. Tired squealed, but I didn't care.

"Violet! Where are you going?" Lacey called after me. "What about your bike?"

I ignored her. I knew my bike was in safe hands with Lacey and Adrien, and I doubted anyone would want to steal my painted violet helmet.

The street, just like the grumpy man had said, was choked with riders and tourists who were now trying to make their way out of the Riverwalk area.

Was I being a coward for running away from my father? Yes, I was. Was I proud of it? Not really, but I had to process the fact that he was back in the village before talking to him. In a way, I hadn't expected him to return to Cascade Springs. Before he revealed his identity to me, he had been in the village often doing his traveling troubadour thing, but since then he hadn't shown his face. Which had been fine by me; I had been far too busy to deal with the baggage of learning I had a father after thirty years of having none.

I told myself I just needed a moment to compose myself and I could deal with it. I had just seen a dead body not that long ago, too, so didn't that give me a pass to some extent to deal with my daddy issues?

It would be far too difficult with the riders coming down River Road to make it back to the shop in any short order. Instead of going home to my shop, where Fenimore could easily find me, I ran up the twenty-some stone stairs to the front door of the village hall. I stepped into the hall and took a breath. The large wooden door closed with a thud behind me and the sound reverberated throughout the cavernous space.

I knew the building well because I grew up here, and because more recently I had seen every nook and cranny of it while my grandmother was deciding the best location for the museum.

The main entrance featured a grand rotunda with an antique wooden staircase that led up to the second floor, where the village offices were located. I knew that my grandmother was in one of those rooms now, meeting with the village council. The main floor of the hall was rarely used for anything other than a special event. My grandmother's idea was to use this great room for the museum, and construction had already begun before the money ran out.

At my feet, a large section of the marble had been ripped up out of the floor. Orange cones and hazard tape circled it. The hole was deep and went under the building into the man-made hill. The construction crew was in the process of bracing up the foundation. I stared down into the hole. It looked like an endless pit and smelled faintly of wet earth and old paper, and it was what had stopped construction on the museum. The foundation issue had been discovered when trenching began in the marble for electrical and Internet.

When the village hall was built in the 1850s, it was built over an aquifer, the same groundwater that fed the river and natural springs. All the water in this village is interconnected. When the hall was built, the aquifer was better contained and deeper under the surface, but as time passed and erosion occurred, it became much closer to the surface and made the ground unstable beneath the building.

The village had enough money to cover the foundation repair, but not enough to finish the museum or even repair the hole in the marble floor.

Where the museum would stand was to my left. A section of the rotunda had been portioned off and framed out. The wood framing was up, but that's where construction stopped.

I started through the doorway.

"What are you doing here?" A sharp, high-pitched voice echoed off the rounded walls, so I didn't know where it was coming from.

"Look up!"

I did, and I saw Bertie Rhodes, my grandmother's secretary, a woman who'd been in the position for the last forty years through five different mayors. Not one of them, my grandmother included, had had the nerve to get rid of this particular irritable public employee.

She ran the mayor's office with an iron fist. In the past, she had been able to boss the other mayors around. She hadn't had much luck in that regard with Grandma Daisy. It seemed that Bertie had finally met her match. My grandmother and Bertie didn't agree on anything when it came to managing the city or even what brand of paper clips to buy for the office. Every decision put the two strong women at odds. For one, Bertie thought the Underground Railroad Museum was a complete waste of money even though the museum was being paid for through private donations and fund-raisers, not by the taxpayers.

I suspected Bertie didn't like the idea of the general public entering her sanctuary. She was the only person who had been a constant fixture in the village hall for the last forty years, and she felt more than a little ownership over it.

My grandmother said she kept Bertie around because the secretary was just six months shy of retirement. It seemed cruel to oust her this close to the end of her career. However, Grandma Daisy was counting the hours until Bertie's last day.

Bertie came down the stairs. "You shouldn't be in here."

"Did my grandmother call you in to take minutes for the impromptu council meeting?" I retorted.

"I don't need anyone to call me in," she said bitterly. "Some of us have to work even if the village has completely lost its mind over this cycle race. It's a good thing that I happened to be here when everything happened."

"Is my grandmother still in the meeting? Can I see her?"

"No one can interrupt a private session of the council. I know that Mayor Daisy has been lax with this rule, but I will uphold it."

Oh-kay, so chatting with my grandmother for the time being was out of the question. That was probably for the best. Grandma Daisy would take one look at me and know something was wrong and that it was something more than a murder in the village.

"Did you see part of the race?" I asked, doing my best to make small talk with the prickly woman.

She sniffed. "I have no interest in this event or anything that has to do with the fiasco created in the village hall. It's downright shameful. This was a beautiful place until Mayor Daisy got ahold of it. Look at it now." She pointed at the hole in the marble floor. "I hope she's happy. We're the laughingstock of the state."

I doubted that any of the other cities or villages in the state cared that there was a giant hole in the marble floor in the

Cascade Springs village hall. If they didn't read the village paper, it was unlikely they even knew about it.

I looked down at the hole and felt a twinge of sympathy for her. "If the construction hadn't started, the foundation problem could have gone on to the point that it was irreversible, so in the long run it was a good thing this was discovered now."

Bertie stared at me like I was speaking another language. "People who go and look for problems are the ones who find them. That's always been my experience. If you don't look for trouble, trouble won't find you."

I felt my brow wing up. Was Bertie's comment pointed? Did she think I went and looked for trouble and that was the reason I kept getting caught up in murder investigations? I shook my head. She could be talking about something else entirely.

"I won't keep you," I said. "I know you need to be getting back to the council meeting."

She scowled at me. "You shouldn't be in here alone. You don't work for the city."

I frowned. "I'm going to do a walk-around of the exhibit to make sure everything is all right for Grandma Daisy. She's been too busy to check on things herself. Would you like to visit the exhibit with me?"

"No, I have no interest in that." She waited.

I waited too.

She crossed her arms.

I crossed my arms too. "If you want, you can stay here while I check the exhibit. It might take a little while."

She sniffed. "I don't have time for that. I have somewhere that I have to be." Without another word, she marched across the rotunda floor.

The hall's door closed with a thud after her, and I walked over to one of the windows that looked down on the street. I couldn't see Fenimore any longer, but that didn't mean he wasn't there, watching and waiting for me to reappear. The previous October, he'd told me he was my father, proving it with a letter in my mother's hand. Since that time, I hadn't heard a peep from him. He'd made his announcement and then disappeared. Why would he come back now? And maybe I was being too self-centered to think he had come back to Cascade Springs to see me. Maybe he was just here to make tips off the thousands of bike riders and spectators on hand for the bike race. Maybe, like all those riders and spectators, he would be gone from the village tomorrow.

I frowned. It had been a trying day, and I wasn't ready to decide whether or not I wanted to find Fenimore and confront him or pretend I never saw him. I should return to Charming Books and check on Richard and Faulkner and find Emerson. And I had a murder to solve, if the copy of *Leaves of Grass* with Redding's body was any indication.

I would be returning to the shop a bit earlier than I'd planned, since I'd told Richard I wouldn't be back until later this afternoon, but I was certain the English department chair wouldn't mind the help. He was a great teacher; he wasn't as great at running a credit card machine.

I had turned to open the front door of the hall when movement caught the corner of my eye. A flash of black and white that I recognized all too well darted into the museum construction site. I'd told Bertie I wanted to check on the site for my grandmother, and it looked like I was going there after all because of my wandering cat.

Chapter Ten

I pushed back the plastic sheeting that was protecting most of the construction site from view. "Emerson?" I asked. "Are you in here? You're in so much trouble and are so grounded."

I didn't get so much as a meow in response. Maybe starting off telling the cat he was grounded wasn't the best way to entice him to come out.

Emerson was a master at getting into odd and impossibly small spots, causing me to find him in all sorts of complicated predicaments. To date, the most confusing had been when he hid behind a secret wall in a mansion. To this day, I don't know how he got there or how he planned to get out if I didn't come along.

I adopted Emerson—or more accurately, the cat adopted me—after his previous owner, Benedict Raisin, who also happened to my grandmother's last love, died. Benedict had been a Cascade Springs carriage driver, and he'd let Emerson tag along on all his rides, which was a charming addition for Emerson and riders alike. The only downside that came out of it was that Emerson was accustomed to traipsing around the village. While other cats wanted to lounge in a sunny spot or on a favorite pillow, he had a need to explore. It was almost impossible to keep him in Charming Books, and the times that I had been able to keep him in the shop, he had made his disgust more than apparent, usually by shredding a pillow. Or if he was really mad, he might go after my jeans that I had carelessly left lying across the chair in my bedroom. Bottom line, Emerson didn't like being told what to do. He was a true Waverly that way.

I looked around the space that was half drywall, half studs and plastic sheeting. The ceiling was as high as it had been in the rotunda, so I guessed twenty feet up. My grandmother had wanted to keep that height because she thought it would be a good place to suspend signs and perhaps a hanging timeline of Cascade Springs during the nineteenth century.

However, this part of the museum was much further along than the entrance. There were even a few artifacts sitting in a corner as if waiting to be displayed. An old yoke, a wagon wheel. There was a set of chains that made me shiver. I didn't know if they were actual chains slave catchers had used to drag people back into slavery or replicas. Either way, they were chilling. I was ready to leave.

"Emerson," I hissed.

Still nothing.

I shivered again, this time not from the artifacts but from the cold. I was wearing only biking shorts and a race shirt, and it was at least thirty degrees cooler in here than it had been outside. The building was well insulated with stone.

"Emerson!"

This time there was a faint mew in response, but it came from above me.

I looked up. Emerson was crouched above my head on top of the scaffolding that went all the way to the ceiling twenty-some feet up. The scaffolding was under some water damage in the ceiling, another expense for the museum.

I put my hands on my hips. "Emerson, get down here this instant."

He flattened himself on the wooden plank above my head.

"I'm not coming up there after you," I said like I meant it.

He meowed.

"I'm serious."

He meowed again.

We were getting nowhere with this fast. I could always leave the cat in the museum. Goodness knew he'd gotten himself into and out of scrapes of all sorts in the past.

Emerson yowled again.

My shoulders slumped. Who was I kidding? I wouldn't be able to walk away from him. I stood below the scaffolding and studied it. It appeared to be easy to climb, and I knew some of the men that were working on the project. Several of them outweighed me by at least one hundred pounds. If the scaffolding could hold them, it could hold me. Even so, the last time I'd climbed something like this, I had fallen a story to the ground, hurting my shoulder and my pride in the process. The pride had required the longer recovery time.

Emerson yowled again.

"I'm coming," I muttered, and put my hand on a rung.

Emerson peered over the edge at me.

"You're really going to make me climb up there? The woman who loves you and cares for you and gives you plenty of food to eat?"

He meowed and shuffled back on the landing. I guessed that was cat for *yes*.

I started to climb and the rungs held my weight, which made me bolder, and I climbed faster. The sooner I got Emerson down, the sooner I could go home and take off this spandex.

I was halfway up when Emerson jumped onto my head and then my shoulder, then used my shoulder as a springboard to the marble floor below.

I rubbed the top of my head, looking down at him. "You used me as a trampoline!"

The cat didn't say anything back. A year ago, if a cat had spoken to me, I would have fallen to the floor. If it happened to me now, I would wonder why he hadn't spoken sooner. I suppose that's what happens when you find out you are a magical Caretaker of a birch tree and bookshop. Reality is skewed.

I was about to make my way down when something caught my eye. A piece of metal glinted on the landing. I hesitated for a moment, then climbed all the way up. On the edge of the scaffolding was a delicate garnet necklace on a broken golden chain. It was clearly a woman's necklace. I couldn't see it being worn by any of the men working on the project. I tried to remember if I had seen any women on the work crew. I couldn't remember any, but that didn't mean there wasn't a female carpenter among them.

The necklace didn't look old enough to date back to the Civil War like the other artifacts in the display. Also, jewelry and small trinkets hadn't been brought into the museum yet.

I debated for half a second if I should leave the necklace where I found it, but I didn't know how whoever lost it would find it on the scaffolding twenty feet in the air.

I picked up the necklace and tucked it in the minuscule key pocket at the waistband of my shorts. I would show it to my grandmother and see if she might know who it belonged to. My only guess was a member of the village council. If that was the case, my grandmother would be able to return it to its rightful owner immediately.

I started down the ladder again. It was time to go home and put on clothes I was much more comfortable wearing. At least Emerson was the only one seeing this unflattering view of me in biking shorts. I shivered to think of anyone else seeing me climbing around in that outfit.

The rungs creaked. Emerson watched me from the floor below, and his narrow black tail swished back and forth across the cool tile.

"Don't you look at me like I should hurry up," I scolded the tuxie. "It's your fault that I'm here in the first place."

"Excuse me?" a deep male voice asked, causing me to misstep and miss a rung. My foot dangled out in space, and I lost my balance. Strong hands caught me around the waist, plucked me off the scaffolding, and lowered me to the floor. "Easy there."

He let go of my waist, and I turned around to see a man with light-brown hair and hazel eyes giving me the once-over. "Judging from your dress, you were in today's race. Did you get lost on the way to the finish? You shouldn't be in the museum. This is a construction site."

I dusted myself off and sidestepped to put some space between us. "I was looking for my cat."

"I don't see a cat."

I glanced around. Sure enough, Emerson was gone. I inwardly groaned. "He was here a moment ago. I'll let my grandmother know so she can be on the lookout for him. I'm Violet Waverly."

Recognition lit his eyes. "I work for Museum Fabricators. I'm Vaughn Fitzgerald."

I nodded. "You're Jo's brother. She told me you were working on the museum."

"You know my sister?"

"I teach English at Springside Community College. She's a good kid and a great writer."

A strange expression crossed Vaughn's face when I said his younger sister was a good kid. It was almost as if he didn't believe me. "Have you seen my sister recently?"

"Not since before the race."

"You really shouldn't be in here, and climbing on the scaffolding is absolutely off-limits."

I crossed my arms. "And I was in here looking for my cat," I repeated. "He was up there." I pointed to the top. "He's a black-and-white tuxedo cat. You might have seen him around. His name is Emerson."

His face cleared as if the expression had never been there. "Now that you mention it, the mayor told my team to be on the lookout for a black-and-white cat. That's yours?"

I nodded. "He kind of considers himself the deputy mayor of Cascade Springs and goes wherever he pleases in the village."

"Why were you up the scaffolding, though?"

"That's where Emerson was hiding. I climbed up after him, and he used the top of my shoulders as a trampoline. Now I can only guess where he might be hiding in the hall." I sighed. "Daisy is my grandmother, so I think that's why Emerson believes he should have run of the village hall."

"Makes sense," Vaughn said with a smile.

"What are you doing here? I thought work stopped on the site when the money ran out?"

"Oh, well." He looked surprised. "I just like to come to the site every so often to make sure everything is where we left it. It's a great project, and it was very hard to leave when we ran into those issues. However, I know that if your grandmother has anything to do with it, we will be back at work in no time."

"How many people are on the team building the museum?" I asked, trying to sound casual.

"There are six members of my crew, but we have any number of contract workers going in and out all the time, or at least we did."

"Any women?"

He frowned. "No. You want to sign up? I saw you scale that ladder, so you might be good at it."

I shook my head. "I already have more work than I know what to do with." And it was true. Between being an adjunct professor at Springside Community College, running Charming Books, and being the Caretaker of the birch tree and the shop's essence, I was fully booked, literally.

I started to put my hand to my pocket and ask him about the necklace, but something stopped me. I would ask my grandmother about it first.

"I was hoping to run into Jo again. Have you seen her? I thought she was working for Bobby's Bike Shop during the race, but she wasn't there. Bobby didn't seem to know where she'd gone."

"Jo's got a bit of growing up to do." He stopped just short of rolling his eyes. "She needs to settle on something." He said this in such a way that I guessed it was something he'd repeated to Jo many times before.

He arched his brow. "I can tell from your face that you think I might be too harsh on her. I just want her to pick something to do. She's twenty-two years old and should have some sort of path by now. Instead she flits from part-time job to part-time job, half-heartedly taking classes at the community college. I would like her to settle on something." He sounded much more like a parent than an older brother, but I guessed that Vaughn was eight to ten years older than Jo. Perhaps because of the age difference, he had always treated her that way.

Vaughn clapped his hands, and the sound of the smack echoed throughout the hall. "The site looks fine. I'll be glad when we have the green light to get back in here to work."

"I know Grandma Daisy is looking forward to it too. The museum is a special project to her, and it will add to the culture of the village. Cascade Springs is much more than ice wine."

"Yes, it is much more. It's a special project to me, too." His voice softened. "Some of my ancestors came up through Cascade Springs as runaway slaves. I feel honored to work on this project and preserve their history. I probably wouldn't be standing in front of you today if not for them."

My eyes fell on those horrible chains again, and I shivered.

Chapter Eleven

As Vaughn and I left the hall, we found Emerson sitting in front of the main door with his black tail wrapped around his white paws, as if he were a perfectly behaved feline that would never run away.

"This must be the mysterious cat," Vaughn said with a laugh.

"That's one name for him." I quietly approached Emerson and gave a sigh of relief when he allowed me to pick him up. He placed his forepaw on my shoulder as if he wanted to give me a hug.

"He seems to really like you. I can't imagine this little cat using you as a trampoline."

I smiled. "Appearances can be deceiving."

"I know all about that," Vaughn said in a much darker voice than I would have expected. He shook his head. "I should get back to the office. Even though I can't work here at the museum today, there are other projects that could use my attention. It was nice to meet you, Violet." He paused. "And if you see my sister, can you tell her I'm looking for her?" He didn't wait for an answer and went out the door.

Emerson and I shared a look.

After I left the village hall, taking Emerson with me, I made my way up River Road toward Charming Books and away from the finish line. The further I moved from the Riverwalk, the quieter it became. I blew out a breath, hoping some of the stress I felt would leave with the exhale of air.

That didn't seem to work. As I walked, my eyes darted in every direction, searching for any sign of Fenimore. I wasn't sure what I would do if I saw him again. Would I be a coward for a second time and run away? I couldn't say I was proud of ducking into the village hall. A more adult thing to do would have been to face my father head on. I promised myself I would work up the nerve in case I got another chance, which I might not. Last time I'd seen Fenimore had been six months ago; he could be gone for another six months or more before I saw him again. I didn't know if that made me relieved or disappointed. Maybe both.

Charming Books came into view as soon as I turned the corner south. The periwinkle-blue Queen Anne Victorian with its wide wraparound porch, tower, and gingerbread was the showpiece of the street.

I opened the gate in the white picket fence that wound around the yard. Emerson jumped from my arms when I stepped on the porch and ran through the open door and into the shop. He ran straight to the base of the stairs that went around the birch tree. The little tuxie licked his right paw like he didn't have a care in the world and he'd been there all day.

Richard Bunting was in the middle of the room sitting on the floor, surrounded by books. The English professor wore brown dress pants and a white button-down shirt. His glasses were perched precariously on the tip of his nose, and his goatee was perfectly groomed. His only concession to the fact that it was summer vacation and he wasn't teaching was the fact that he wasn't wearing a tie. Even so, finding him on the floor with all those books was unexpected.

I blinked at him. "Richard, are you okay?"

He wiped his brow. "I think so. It's just that everywhere I look, I see a new book I want or need. You have an amazingly versatile collection. Some of the volumes about British literature are out of print. How is it that you are able to have them, and how are you able to fit them all in this shop? It's not a huge space. Some of these books I have been looking for all my life."

I glanced at the tree. The shop's motto is "Where the perfect book picks you." That couldn't be any more true. The shop knows exactly which books someone needs or wants to read and by magic puts them in the person's path while they're in Charming Books. Sometimes books fly across the room when customers aren't looking, and sometimes they just appear on a shelf right out of thin air. The shop's essence was working overtime with Richard, and if it had any say in it, the poor man would spend the entirety of his salary in the shop.

I picked up one of the arcane volumes. "You don't have to buy all these books. As much as I would love it if you did, I know you can't afford it. All these together would cost more than you will earn here all summer."

"What good is money if you can't buy books?" he asked, lovingly brushing his hand over the cover of a leather-bound tome. "Besides, some of these I think Renee would like too." His face reddened. "In my experience books make the very best gifts."

I did my best to hide a smile but don't think I did the best job. Renee Reed was the outspoken librarian at Springside Community College, and Richard was more than a little in love with her. The hardest part about it was everyone knew it. I think even Renee suspected, but Richard, as of yet, hadn't gotten up the nerve to ask her on a date. Part of me wanted to shake him to wake him up. Women, at least most women I knew, didn't want someone to pine for them from afar. They wanted to know they were desired; they wanted to know they were loved.

"I'm sure she would," I said diplomatically. "It's fair to say that Renee loves books just as much as we all do in the Red Inkers."

He nodded, stood, and blinked, as if he saw the massive circle of books around himself for the very first time. "My goodness, I can't possibly take all these home."

I smiled. "Why don't you narrow it down to two or three? I'm certain the others will be here when you need them. Maybe it will be best to buy them or read them in spurts."

He smoothed his goatee. "That's probably wise. I'll take the three I picked out for Renee. This small token will make the long summer days at the library go much more quickly."

"I'm sure they will." I didn't even bother to hide my smile this time.

Maybe it was time to give Richard more than a little hint as to what he should do next when it came to Renee. "If you leave now, you can make it to the library before it closes. It's only open until two on Saturdays in the summer. I bet Renee would like to go out for a coffee to talk over those books, or maybe a stroll around campus?"

He wrung his hands. "No, now isn't a good time. She'll be wanting to return home. I think it will be best if I just talk to her about it at the Red Inkers meeting tomorrow night. You do remember that we have a Red Inkers meeting."

"Sadie reminded me," I said. "But I still think you should take those books to Renee this afternoon. Maybe you could talk about them at the meeting?"

He shook his head. "I don't want to be a bother to her."

"It's not a bother. You're her friend. It is not strange for friends to hang out outside of a larger group."

"Friend?" He said the word like it was somehow foreign to him. "Renee is my colleague. I wouldn't presume anything more than that." He bent and picked up one of the books.

I rolled my eyes. It seemed I wouldn't be able to convince Richard to make the first move when it came to these two. Maybe I should start working on Renee.

He gathered up the three books he'd selected. "I'll take these and put the others away." He frowned. "Except I can't quite understand your shelving system. They seem to be all over the store. I found books on the same topic in four different places. One of my literature books was in the area labeled travel."

I forced a laugh. "You know Grandma Daisy. She has her own way of doing things, including shelving books. She must have put that book in travel because of armchair traveling."

"Oh," he said dubiously. "That seems like an odd way to shelve books, even for your grandmother."

I shrugged and helped him stack the remaining books on the sales counter. "Anything else happen while I was out? Did you have many customers?"

"Several came in near the middle of the race. Sales were good. I was amazed how everyone could find what they needed with very little help from me."

The shop's essence had been at work again. I knew it. "I'm glad to hear that. I think I will—"

Richard snapped his fingers. "I almost forgot something."

"What's that?" I asked.

"There was a man here very early this morning looking for you." He added the last book to the stack on the counter.

"Who was it? Did he give a name?"

He shook his head. "No, but he said you knew each other."

I froze as I picked up a book. "Did he have a guitar and a ponytail?"

He shook his head. "No ponytail, but he did have a guitar case with him. I assume there was a guitar with it, but I never saw it."

I frowned. When I'd seen Fenimore earlier, he'd definitely still had his guitar with him. Then I remembered that Private Investigator Redding also carried a guitar case. He used it as his briefcase. He said it put people at ease. He had never opened the case in my presence, so I didn't exactly know what was in it. I bit the inside of my lip. If the guitar case was his briefcase of sorts, I wondered if he had information about me and Charming Books inside it. I very much wanted to know what was in that guitar case.

"Did the man have a light-blond beard and glasses?"

He nodded. "Yes, he did. You do recognize him, then?" He nodded approvingly. "He said you would."

My stomach ached. "When did he stop by?"

"It was right after I opened the shop for the day. I opened it at nine sharp like you asked. An hour earlier than usual so we could take advantage of the early spectators. That was an excellent idea."

"What was he wearing?" I asked.

"Who?"

"The man with the guitar case."

Richard's brow went up when I asked the question. "I don't remember really. Normal clothes. Pants and a shirt. I don't pay much attention to fashion. I'm not like Sadie in that regard."

"So he wasn't wearing clothes for the bike race."

"I should say not. He was wearing just everyday clothes. Perhaps a button-down shirt, but not a racing outfit. I know that much. He did ask if people could the join the race that was starting just about then. I said I didn't know and he would have to ask Bobby who was in charge of registration."

His comment made me think of something else. If Redding had come to Charming Books looking for me and found out I was in the race, then decided to join the race wearing his street clothes so that he could catch up with me, that still didn't answer how he had gotten one of Bobby's bicycles.

"So it would have been just before the race began," I mused. "Did he tell you what he wanted?"

Richard shook his head. "But then, I didn't ask. I didn't want to intrude on any business you might have had with the man."

"Why do you think it was business related?"

His face reddened. "Well, I know that you and David Rainwater are"—he searched for the right word—"a close pair, so I knew it must not have been a gentleman caller."

Gentleman caller. Sometimes I thought Richard actually believed he lived in the seventeenth-century literature he taught at the college.

"That was the correct assumption. Did he say he planned to join the race?"

Richard pressed his lips together like he was thinking hard. "He did mention that he wanted to. He asked where he could find a bike on short notice, and I told him to talk to Bobby about that too."

Things were starting to become clear as to how Redding had acquired the bike and joined the race, but I still didn't know why he'd bothered. If he'd wanted to pester me, he could have just waited outside Charming Books like he had been for days on end. There had to be a big reason why he wanted to join the race so badly. What did he think he was going to see?

"If he comes back when I'm here, I will take care to question him more thoroughly."

I didn't tell Richard that wouldn't be necessary because the man he described was dead. He would learn that soon enough.

"Did he do anything while he was in the shop?"

He rubbed the bottom of his goatee. "He seemed to have a great interest in the birch tree. He asked me many questions about how old it was and how it was able to grow inside the shop. I told him it had always been a part of the shop as long as I've lived in the village and I didn't know anything more than that. I said that it was just something the people of the village had accepted as part of the Waverlys' business."

I felt cold. "And did he ask anything else?"

"No, but he told me to tell you something."

I grew very still. "What was that?"

"I can read it to you. He had me write it down."

I knew Redding's message from beyond the grave was something I needed to hear.

Chapter Twelve

"Oh," Richard fussed, rubbing his brow. "Where did I put that scrap of paper with the message on it? I was so distracted when he told me because of all the books I was finding." He snapped his fingers. "I know. I was using the note as a bookmark inside those books." He paused. "Or was it another book?"

I grimaced. There had to have been thirty books on the floor around where Richard had been sitting. One of the books on the counter fell with a thud to the floor.

I bent down and reached for the book on the floor, and its pages fluttered. A scrap of paper flew out. I grabbed it out of the air before it could fly away. "I think I found your note," I said to Richard.

"That's extraordinary." Richard removed his glasses and polished the lenses on the hem of his shirt. "Extraordinary. By some bit of dumb luck, the book that fell from the counter was the one with the note in it. What are the odds of that happening?"

The odds were pretty high if you lived and worked in a magical bookshop like I did. I unfolded the note. ALL TRUTHS

WAIT IN ALL THINGS. THEY NEITHER HASTEN THEIR OWN
DELIVERY NOR RESIST IT.

Truths. I glanced at the tree. Was Redding trying to tell me
he would get to the bottom of what was going on at Charming
Books?

I recognized it as a quote of poetry. I picked up the book
the note had fallen from, flipped it over, and smoothed the
cover. It was a paperback edition of *Leaves of Grass*.

"Yes," Richard said. "Now I remember. I thought it was
quite strange that he was quoting Whitman, but then again,
nineteenth-century American is your specialty. I thought perhaps he was also an American literature scholar. When I asked
him this, he seemed not to have any interest in talking about
it." He frowned. "I have found that most scholars love nothing
more than to speak about their field of study. He was quite an
odd fellow."

"Did he buy a book?" I asked.

"Now that you mention it, he did. He bought a copy of
Leaves of Grass. I told him it was a very wise selection and challenging too. Scholars have been debating Whitman for over
a hundred years. I agree with many that he was the father of
strictly American poetry, but I, of course, am more partial
to the British greats, such as Keats. The way he was able to
write beautiful poems and break all the rules including iam-
bic pentameter is a mystery to me. Whitman's free-verse style,
although very American, doesn't soothe my need for order in
the same way."

"Whitman wasn't trying to cause order," I said, thinking
of the poet and wondering why Redding had chosen this line
from his work.

I knew Walt Whitman just as I knew all of my dead nineteenth-century American authors. He was a contemporary of Ralph Waldo Emerson, whom I had spent the better part of my adult life studying. Because of that, I knew Whitman too. I knew all the writers who moved in and out of Ralph Waldo Emerson's life. Whitman was one of the more unique of the bunch. He wasn't a cultured man of substance. He'd left school when he was ten to work to help his family. Many of his siblings in the large family were troubled. He did many jobs over his life, but focus was hard on the day-to-day for him. He read that Emerson called for the first great American poet with a truly American voice. Whitman, who had no doubt in his own potential for greatness, thought he was that poet.

Emerson did too, to some extent, and complimented Whitman's first edition of *Leaves of Grass* that came out in 1855. Perhaps it was praise that Emerson later regretted, as Whitman used Emerson's letter as fuel to continue his career. He even published the complimentary letter in the newspapers of the time without Emerson's permission with the hope of increasing sales. In many ways, Whitman was one of the first self-promoting authors and saw his career as a business, which at the time was a new perspective on the art of writing.

Richard gathered up his books. "Was there anything else you needed, Violet? I've been thinking maybe you're right and I should take these to Renee now. It will save her time from carrying them home from the Red Inkers meeting tomorrow. It seems like the easiest solution. I hope she will enjoy them."

Despite my anxiety over *Leaves of Grass* and Redding, I smiled. "I know she will, but before you go, mind if I run upstairs for a few minutes and get cleaned up?"

He looked at me and blinked, as if he was noticing my disheveled appearance for the first time. "Yes, of course. The ride must have been challenging. You appear to be a bit . . . um . . ."

For the first time since I had known him, Richard was at a loss for words.

I didn't want to be there when he thought of the word, because chances were high I wouldn't like it. Taking the note and the volume of Whitman with me, I went up the winding staircase to my apartment on the second floor.

Inside the safety of my apartment and standing in front of my bathroom mirror, I grimaced, seeing why Richard had been taken aback by my appearance. My hair was a tangled mess and my face red and blotchy.

I turned away from the mirror, peeled off my clothes, jumped in the shower, and washed away the grime of the day. I wished that it was just as easy to wash away the events of the day, but it looked like they would be with me for some time to come.

In the shower and while I dressed and dried my hair, I kept thinking about the message Redding had made Richard record verbatim. Why had he chosen Whitman? Why had the shop chosen Whitman? Had Redding known what the shop could do? All I knew was that I had to find out Redding's connection to Whitman and what it all had to do with his murder and with me.

*   *   *

Feeling more like myself, I headed down the stairs. Faulkner fluffed his wings as I walked by. It was midday, and the crow was taking a siesta—or, I thought, he might just be pretending to be sleeping in the hopes that his ploy would make Emerson bored of watching him.

That wasn't likely. The little tuxie sat on the step just below Faulkner's favorite branch, watching the bird with the same intensity he had when he watched the laser beam Rainwater had gotten him for Christmas. Just like with the red dot, Emerson was determined to catch Falkner . . . someday. It was a day I hoped would never come.

"There she is," I heard Richard say as I reached the main floor. He was speaking to a young woman at the sales desk.

She turned around, and I gasped. Finding Jo Fitzgerald was to be my number-one mission when I started investigating Redding's death, and there she was standing in the middle of my bookshop.

Richard smiled at me. "Violet, I can't tell you how excited I am about the selection of books that you have. I'll be sure to tell everyone on campus that this is the place to come when they need research."

I smiled back. Something I appreciated about Richard the most was his cluelessness. It worked to my advantage at times. "Thanks, Richard. That means a lot."

My eyes flitted to Jo. It was clear that Richard had no idea how uncomfortable she was. The girl shifted her weight back and forth between her feet. Her eyes darted around the room as if she expected someone to jump out and scare her at any moment. Jo was many things, but most of all, she was scared.

The chain hanging from her pocket rattled when she pivoted away from me and faced the giant fireplace on the wall to the left of the sales counter. It was May, so there was no fire in the hearth.

"Thanks again for watching the store, Richard," I said. "Now, you had better hurry if you want to make it to campus before the library closes."

"Right," he said, and gathered up the books he had purchased for the librarian. "We will see you at the meeting tonight."

I followed him to the door. "See you then."

As soon as the front door closed, Jo turned around, and there were tears in her eyes. "Professor Waverly—Violet—I need your help."

Chapter Thirteen

"What—"

I didn't get to finish my question, because the front door opened and a family of four trooped in. I bit my lip.

She shook her head. "Go help your customers. I'll be fine."

"I—"

"Miss," the man in the group said.

I looked back to Jo and then to the man and felt my shoulders droop. I turned and walked over to the family. I put a smile on my face. "How can I help you?"

When I looked over my shoulder again, Jo was gone.

I had a rush of customers. Most of them bought multiple books, but I wished they would all leave so I could find Jo.

When the last customer left, I gave a sigh of relief and looked around in case Jo was still there. She was nowhere to be seen. Emerson sat on the steps that led up to the children's loft and meowed. He looked up.

Taking the hint, I climbed the steps. I found Jo sitting on one of the toadstools in the middle of the room. She stared at her hands, which were folded in her lap. The hand-painted woodland fairies that peeked out from around the bookshelves watched her.

Jo looked up. "Redding is dead, and everyone is going to think it's my fault."

I grabbed a second toadstool and put it in front of her. "Why do you need my help?" I tried to keep my question neutral, but inside I was shaking. Maybe I would be able to clear up Redding's murder before the day was even over. Not that I believed Jo could do this. She might be flighty, but she wasn't a killer.

She looked down at her hands again.

"Jo?" I prompted.

"I gave him the bike. The one he was in an accident with. I didn't know anything was wrong with it. Bobby said the police questioned him about it and said the brake line was cut. He said because I was the one who gave him the bike, I was responsible."

"Did you know that the brake line was cut?" I asked.

"Of course not! I would never give someone a bike if I knew it was broken or tampered with."

"Did you know Redding?"

She looked at her hands again. "No." Her answer was barely above a whisper.

She was lying.

"Jo." I leaned forward on my toadstool. "If you want me to help you, I have to know all the facts. If you know Redding, you have to tell me how you know him. Chief Rainwater will want to know."

"I'm not talking to the police." Her voice was bitter. "That's why I'm talking to you."

I frowned. That wasn't how it worked. Rainwater would want to talk to her himself if he knew she was somehow involved with Redding's death or a witness. I didn't say that to her, though. It was clear she was upset. Jo might be flighty and a little prone to giving away things that didn't belong to her, but she was a sweet girl. She was scared and needed my protection.

"Why did you give Redding the bike?"

"He asked for one. He said he was joining the race."

"But he wasn't registered?"

She shook her head.

"Did he say why he wanted to join the race at the last moment?" I asked. I watched her face carefully for a reaction again.

Again, she looked at her hands, which I was discovering was a type of tell for when she was lying. "No."

That was definitely a lie. I would have bet the whole of Charming Books that Redding had told her why he was joining the race.

I sighed. "Just tell me what happened this morning, from the beginning."

She seemed to deliberate over that request, her whole body motionless and her gaze far away for several seconds. Then she nodded. I was glad. If she'd continued to lie to me, I would've had to call her out on it, and I didn't want to put added strain on her.

"I was helping Bobby with registration," she began. "Just before the race, after I saw you, Bobby had to leave for a bit, so I was alone at the registration desk for a little while."

"Where did Bobby go?" I shifted my position on my toadstool.

"I don't know. I didn't ask."

"Okay." I nodded, encouraging her to continue.

She took a breath. "So the race was about to begin, and this man—Redding—came up to me, said that he wanted to register for the race and needed a bicycle to ride. I told him that it was too late to register. The race would start in five minutes, but he wouldn't take no as an answer."

"What do you mean when you say he wouldn't take no as an answer?"

She looked at her hands again. "He just wouldn't."

"When he didn't take no as an answer, what did you do?"

"The booth was so busy with the race about to begin, and there were some last-minute riders who needed to check in and get their bibs, and Bobby wasn't there. Everyone was angry with me, so I gave him the bike to make him go away. Before he left, I told him to take a helmet too. I made him promise that he would return the bike at the end of the race."

"Why did you give him that particular bike?"

She licked her lips. "It was the last bike we had. He was so insistent that I just gave it to him. I know that I shouldn't have. Bobby was furious with me when he got back that I let Redding take the bike."

So then Bobby knew about Redding and the bike. Interesting.

I hadn't thought Bobby was lying when I'd purposely questioned him about the registration, but then I didn't know his tells the way I knew Jo's.

Jo's story wasn't quite aligning, though, and I was inclined to ask, "How did you know what his name was when he took the bike if you didn't know who he was?"

Her face flushed red, and still she wouldn't look at me. "He must have told me."

Uh-huh. "Do you have the rental paperwork from the bike?"

"We didn't do any paperwork," she said regretfully. "There were so many people there needing so many things that I didn't have time. Bobby is going to kill me."

I grimaced. He might not literally killer her, but he was going to be mad, that was for certain. At least this all explained why Redding wasn't on the roster of riders Bobby had shown Officer Clipton and me.

"Where were you?" I asked.

"What do you mean?"

"Near the end of the race," I said. "After Redding's accident. Where did you go? I went to the Riverwalk to talk to Bobby, and he said you had wandered off."

"Oh." Her face flushed. "I had something to do."

"What?" I asked bluntly.

"It doesn't have anything to do with what happened."

"I need to know. The police are going to want to know."

She jumped off her toadstool. "I came here because you're my friend and I thought you would help me. Looks like I was wrong."

"Jo, I do want to help you." I stood up too. "I can't help you if you're not telling me the truth. I know you're holding something back."

She spun around and ran down the steps to the main floor. Faulkner cawed in the birch tree and flapped his wings. I was halfway down the steps when the door slammed closed after her.

I ran to the front door of Charming Books just in time to see her disappear across the street around the corner of Midcentury Vintage. My shoulders sagged. I felt like I had just failed that young woman as her teacher and as her friend.

Chapter Fourteen

After Jo left Charming Books, I tried to call Rainwater to tell him what had happened, but he didn't pick up. I wasn't surprised. He was in the middle of a murder investigation and the village was in the process of cleaning up after the race. I sent him a text to call me and left it at that. I knew he would when he could.

I didn't have time to think about Redding, Jo, or even Walt Whitman until around four when my grandmother waltzed into the shop. "Violet," she said. "There you are, my girl. I had wondered where you'd gone."

I raised my brow at her. "Where did you think I'd be?"

"My dear, there has been a death, so I expected you to be in the thick of it. Didn't we have Richard watching the store for us?"

"I let him go home," I said.

"Violet, you should have kept him on so you could do a little bit of sleuthing. You're so fond of it."

I sighed. "I was about to do a bit of sleuthing, but I don't know what good it would do." I gave her an abbreviated version of Jo's visit.

"That poor girl. She sounds scared. She knows more about Joel Redding's death than she let on. She trusts you. She'll come to you again for help when she's ready."

I nodded, wishing I had handled her with more care. Maybe she would still be in Charming Books now if I had. Although part of me felt that the secrets Jo was keeping might take more than a little while to come to the surface. Jo was an enigmatic girl, a private person, and while she trusted me, I couldn't help but think Jo didn't trust anyone wholeheartedly. I only hoped Grandma Daisy was right and I'd get another chance to help the young girl.

"Violet, I know that David will clear up this mess with Redding—with your help, of course."

I didn't think Rainwater wanted my help, but I didn't bother to say that. I think everyone in the village knew I was going to poke my nose in the case. I had to now, in any case. Jo had asked for my help. It didn't matter that she had been lying to me about how she knew Redding. She was a scared young woman, and as her professor, I had to help her.

Grandma Daisy beamed. "I do have a bit of good news. We raised over twenty thousand dollars just today. I believe between this event and the others we have planned throughout the summer, we will have no trouble of reaching our goal. The museum will happen! I have to call Vaughn to tell him to get back to work."

Her mention of Vaughn reminded me of the necklace I had found at the village hall. "Wait here for a moment. I have something I want to show you."

"Oh, part of the mystery, is it? I would love to see. I knew that you would be on the case, Violet. Is it something the books have revealed to you?"

I shook my head. "It doesn't have anything to do with Redding. Hang tight, and I'll go get it."

When I'd gone to my apartment to freshen up when Richard was still at the shop, I had completely forgotten about the necklace. I hoped that it was still in my pocket. I plucked my biking shorts from the hamper and checked the one tiny pocket. The necklace was gone.

I swallowed. That couldn't be right. The pocket was too small to let anything fall out of it. It was one of those slit pockets in the waistband of activewear that was just big enough to slip a key into. A penny wouldn't even have been able to escape it.

I shook the shorts out just to see if the necklace would fall to the floor. Then I pulled every bit of clothing from the hamper and poured over each piece of laundry. The necklace was gone.

I went into the bathroom and checked the counter, floor, and shower. I even looked behind the toilet, although heaven only knew how it could have gotten back there. Still nothing. The necklace was truly missing.

Where could I have lost it? I remembered thinking of showing it to Richard, but I had thought against it. Then I remembered when Vaughn had lifted me off the ladder. Had he pulled some kind of magician's trick and taken the necklace? But why? How would he have known I even had it? I hadn't told him.

"Violet," my grandmother's voice floated from my living room. "What on earth is going on up there? I can hear you running around all the way downstairs. And what was it that you wanted to show me?"

I came out of the bedroom and sat on the arm of my sofa. "It was a necklace, a garnet necklace, actually. There were three stones and they were shaped into three teardrops."

My grandmother nodded. "It sounds lovely. Did David give it to you as a gift? I do love that man. As your grandmother, I was more hopeful that it would be an engagement ring."

I rolled my eyes at the comment. I wasn't going to be pulled into a conversation about engagement rings with my grandmother—or anyone, for that matter.

I shook my head. "It's not mine. I found it at the museum."

"When were you in the museum?" she asked.

"I went there after the race," I said.

"Why?" She cocked her head.

I bit the inside of my lip, wondering if I should tell Grandma Daisy that Fenimore was back in the village. I assumed that if she'd known, she would have mentioned it to me. She was the only other person who knew who he was to me, who he was to both of us.

Then I remembered the cat.

"Emerson."

"Ahh." She smiled as if that made perfect sense.

As if on cue, the little tuxedo cat walked into the room from my bedroom with no explanation as to how he'd gotten there. I hadn't seen him in the bedroom when I had been looking for the necklace. I had long ago given up on asking Emerson how he moved about the world. It was far too confusing.

"So you took the necklace from the museum? Why?"

Yikes. When she put it like that, it certainly sounded suspicious . . .

I went on to tell her about Emerson, the scaffolding, and Vaughn's unexpected arrival. "I assumed it belonged to a woman on the village council, and I was going to give it to you to return to her. Now I wonder."

"What happened to it?" she asked.

"I don't know," I said. "I can only guess that Vaughn took it when he helped me down."

"Why would Vaughn take the necklace from you? I know him. He and his company have done an amazing job on the museum so far, and they have been so patient with the financial troubles we've had. I know other companies would have abandoned us at this point, or worse, sought to litigate, but Vaughn and his team hung in there."

"He said the museum was important to him, too," I said.

She nodded. "Then why do you suspect him?"

"I don't know what else could have happened to it. It was in the pocket of my bike shorts when I climbed down the ladder, and now it's gone."

"Well, could you just ask him?" she asked reasonably.

"I just realized that it was gone, but I will." I frowned. "I need to talk to him about Jo, too. I'm worried about her."

"It sounds like you have every reason to be."

"Yes." I paused. "But what am I supposed to say when I ask him about the necklace—'Hey, did you put your hand in my pocket and take a necklace that wasn't even mine?'"

"Good point, but you can mention that you saw it at the site and wondered if anyone picked it up. Watch him closely and see if he gives anything away. Truly, I can't believe Vaughn would do this. Of the two Fitzgerald siblings, he is the more responsible one."

Grandma Daisy must have seen the look on my face that showed I was about to protest. "Nothing against Jo, in the least. I like the girl very much, but you have told me of the many times she didn't turn in her classwork. I can't imagine

Vaughn doing that. He's always been punctual with everything at the museum."

I rubbed my forehead. "I wish I knew where Jo went. She needs help."

"I can tell that you won't be able to rest until you track this down," Grandma Daisy said. "And you have been stuck in the shop most of the day. Why don't you go into town and see if you can find out what's going on?"

It wasn't a bad idea.

"David was still at the Riverwalk when I left," she said.

I bit my lip. "Did he ask you anything more about Redding?"

She shook her head. "What is worrying you, my dear?"

"I'm afraid that Redding was here in the village to investigate us. All the signs point to that." I lowered my voice even though we were the only ones in the building. "He asked Richard questions about the tree."

She pursed her lips together. "That is worrisome. He might have asked others too."

"That's what I think, too." I paused. "It could be seen as motive . . ."

She snorted. "David would never believe that about us."

I didn't bother to say that Rainwater had thought it about us both before. She knew it as well as I did.

Chapter Fifteen

"What would we do if others found out about the shop's essence?" I asked my grandmother. "That's what we don't know. That's what you've never told me." I couldn't keep the accusation from my voice.

Her eyes went wide. "Violet?"

I bit my lip trying to hold back the words, but I couldn't keep the questions at bay any longer. "Grandma, you tricked me to come back to Cascade Springs almost a year ago to take my place as the Caretaker of the shop and the tree, but you have told me very little about them."

I supposed part of me was still a little miffed at my grandmother's methods to convince me to return to Cascade Springs last summer. I had been in Chicago, where I'd lived ever since I left the village at seventeen. The moment I'd graduated high school, I was out the door. Most of that had to do with being accused of killing my best friend, Colleen. She had died in a tragic drowning accident in the Niagara River. It was later proven that no foul play was involved, but I was a teenager and couldn't get over how most of the village had been convinced I was somehow behind it. I had to get out of there, and I planned to never come back. I had stuck to that plan for twelve years until one day Grandma Daisy called to tell me she was dying. I was terrified of losing her. She was all the family I had in the world. I was in the middle of my doctoral studies at the University of Chicago and dropped everything to come to Cascade Springs to be at her bedside. What I found when I arrived was a woman in perfect health. In fact, my grandmother had the physical fitness of a person half her age.

I was furious and was about to leave when she told me I was the next Caretaker. She told me the books weren't communicating with her like they once had. It was time to turn the job over to the next generation: me.

Now she started to speak, and I held up my hand. "Please let me finish. I know the story of Rosalee, and I know that the shop's essence communicates with the Caretaker. I have seen that with my own eyes. But why do we have to keep it a secret to the point that we drive away people that we love?" I said this thinking of my own mother and father and every Waverly woman who had ended up alone before me.

She sighed. "I think it's time."

I blinked at her. "Time? Time for what?"

She held up a finger. "Lock up the shop, and I will be back in a moment. We don't want anyone else here when we have this conversation."

She walked to the back of the shop and into the kitchen. Part of me wanted to follow her and demand what was going on, but I did as she told me and closed up the shop. Emerson walked behind me as I locked the front door and then checked the windows to make sure they were locked, too. Faulkner flew down from the tree and landed on the mantel. He sat on the corner of it looking more like a Halloween decoration than an actual living bird.

By the time my grandmother returned, the shop was closed and I had balanced the cash register for the night, locking the money and credit card receipts into the safe below the counter. I came around the side of the sales counter. "I was starting to think you might not come back."

She laughed. "I will always come back, my girl. You can count on that." As she said this, I noticed that she was carrying a leather-bound ledger in her hand that appeared to be very old. The leather on the spine was cracked and peeling.

"What's that?" I asked.

"Let's sit down." She walked over to one of the two sofas in front of the fireplace and sat.

Emerson leaped onto the seat beside her, and, frowning, I sat on her other side. Faulkner's talons clicked on the mantel as he moved down to the end closest to the rest of us, all the while keeping a close eye on Emerson.

"I haven't told you everything about the essence."

I waited, biting my tongue to hold back from shouting, *I knew it!*

She sighed. "Let me say first that I thought I was doing the right thing by not telling you. In hindsight, maybe I was wrong. I should have trusted you to come to your own conclusions. Perhaps I was no better than my own mother."

I wrinkled my brow. "What do you mean?"

"I'll start from the beginning. I have already told you about Rosalee Waverly, who moved here to Cascade Springs after her husband died in the Battle of Lake Erie during the War of 1812."

I nodded.

"She brought her baby daughter here and built her home around the birch tree. She was mystic and knew the power of the spring water here. She began watering the tree with the spring water, and the Caretakers have been doing that ever since. When Rosalee was alive, people in the village and the surrounding town knew she was someone who could help them. She was a healer, and using her special herbs and the water, she was able to care for many people. She was accepted. That wasn't the case for all the Caretakers.

"Over the next two centuries, the village started to turn against the family. There were those who said that what Rosalee and her descendants did was evil, although no one was ever hurt by a Caretaker's actions. People fear what they can't understand, and scientific advances over time couldn't explain our gift. This came to a head with my great-grandmother, Dahlia Waverly. She was born in 1878, and she was the one who made this house into the beautiful Victorian home we have today. She had the gift of visions. I have told you that all the Caretakers had a different gift. She was able to warn villagers when something was about to happen. Every prediction she made came true, including bad things like death. Some in the village thought she was the source of these bad events, and she was shunned. It got so bad that one night when she walked to the springs to collect the water, she never returned. Her body was found three days later in the woods."

I swallowed hard. "She was killed?"

She nodded.

I blinked. "You mean murdered?"

"We don't know for sure. She died in the middle of winter. She was found frozen to the ground."

I gasped. "How awful."

"My grandmother, her daughter, told me this story. She was just a teenager at the time. After that, my grandmother decided she would keep the essence a secret, and it has been so ever since. My own mother knew of her grandmother's death and rejected being the Caretaker of essence. She wanted nothing to do with it or the tree. I wouldn't have known about it myself if my grandmother hadn't told me when she was too old to water the tree any longer. I started to water it then, but I never told my mother, who threatened to cut the tree down so many times during her lifetime. I begged her not to, and she never did. I like to think she couldn't bring herself to do it.

"Instead of being the Caretaker, my mother made the old house into the bookshop it is today. I think she believed that by making the house into a bookstore, she would be able to ignore the tree. It would just become a curiosity in the shop to attract shoppers. What she never knew was that the essence started to communicate with me through the books. They led me to the people who needed my help like they have you. Although it never directed me to solve murders like it has you. I help people in other ways. The books would tell me when they were ill or needed a friend to visit them." She brushed the palm of her hand over the cracked leather cover of the ledger.

"What's that?" I pointed at the ledger.

"This is where our history is recorded. You can read about each Caretaker who came before you and her gift, from Rosalee's gift to heal to Dahlia's visions. The essence has been different for each one of us." She set the ledger on my lap. "Now, it's your turn to record the people you have helped."

My hands hovered above the leather-bound book. "I wish you had trusted me with this from the start."

She bowed her head, and her silver locks fell over her face. "I should have." Her voice dropped. "I was just so afraid that you would leave, and I couldn't bear you leaving again. I thought, after everything that happened with your mother's death and with Colleen's, that this would be too much and keep you away from the village forever."

I touched the book, and some of the leather flaked off the cover. I would have to be very careful with it not to damage it more. "So this is why we kept the secret, because of fear?"

Grandma Daisy nodded. "Yes." She paused. "And I don't know if that's fair to the Caretaker or the people she loves. It might be time to let others in."

I knew she was thinking of Rainwater. I bit the inside of my lip. What she had told me might change everything for me and for David.

"But we have to be careful who we tell," she warned. "Not everyone will be accepting if they know the truth about Charming Books, about us. Dahlia taught us that lesson."

"We don't have the essence; the shop does," I argued.

She frowned. "I don't think those who fear or mistrust such things would see it that way."

I knew she was right, and it was more than I was ready to think about just then. At the moment, my concern was Jo and how I could help her out of whatever mess she'd found herself in. I knew that's what the essence wanted me to do, even though it wasn't very clear how exactly I should do that.

I cleared my throat. "I saw Bobby at the finish line. I went down there to talk to Rainwater and Bobby again. Maybe I will be able to track Jo down too."

She nodded, as if she accepted that I was done talking about the essence for the time being. I would have more questions later. We both knew that.

"Bobby could have done it," she said. "I hate to think that, but the bike was from his shop. Jo told you she didn't know it was tampered with when she gave it to Redding," Grandma Daisy mused, and then she shivered.

"I hate to think that about him, but he and Jo had the most access to the bike. They are the most likely suspects. I can't believe Jo would do it. What would her motivation be?" As I asked this, I remembered how Jo had lied to me about knowing Redding. I knew she'd known him somehow. I didn't mention this to my grandmother. I wanted to talk it over with Rainwater, but then again, did I want the police chief to consider her a prime suspect in the case?

"It's hard to believe," Grandma Daisy said, shaking me from my black thoughts. "Bobby is such a nice man. Everyone in the village likes him. I can't think of anyone who would have a bad word to say against him."

Neither could I.

She nodded. "Find out if we are wrong about Bobby."

I swallowed. "Or wrong about Jo."

Chapter Sixteen

I left Grandma Daisy at Charming Books and headed back down to the Riverwalk. I was surprised when Emerson didn't follow me to the door. Typically, the tuxie was always ready for adventure, but he sat by the front door and watched me go with little more than a twitch of his whiskers. I found this suspicious. One never knew with Emerson. It was actually a blessing that the cat and the crow generally didn't get along—although they tolerated each other well enough. If they had combined their mischief, Grandma Daisy and I would never have had any peace.

I tried to shake off the eerie feeling Emerson's uncharacteristic behavior gave me as I made my way through the garden gate, around the shop's front yard, and onto the sidewalk and strolled toward the river. Even though the race was officially over, there were still a good number of people milling around the Riverwalk. I spotted Adrien and Lacey in front of Le Crepe Jolie, handing out leftover baguette sandwiches.

Aster, David's niece, was with them. In the summer, Lacey and Adrien let Danielle bring the little girl to work with her.

She did on most days. Rainwater thought it was great, because, he said, they needed a chef in the family.

Lacey waved at me. "Violet, you're back." She paused. "And I see that you are back in normal clothes."

I looked down at my T-shirt and jeans. "Yes, I feel much more human in this."

"How are you feeling?" Adrien asked. "You didn't do the whole race, but most of it."

"I feel okay," I said.

"The worst of the pain from the long ride will come in twenty-four hours," he said knowingly, and I knew that Adrien knew. If he wasn't at the café, he was working out to keep his body in top shape. "I suggest you take some aspirin tonight so you can sleep."

I grimaced. "Thanks for the tip."

Aster looked up from the book she was flipping through, dropped it on the sidewalk, and ran to me, hugging me around the legs. I swallowed hard. My exposure to children had been limited to those who came into Charming Books. I was finding I had missed a lot, spending my life exclusively with adults or with my nose buried in my studies.

She looked up at me. "Mommy and Uncle David went for a walk!"

I gave Lacey a questioning look.

She shook her head. "David came by a little while ago and said that he needed to talk to Danielle. He said it was important. We agreed to watch Aster." She smiled at the girl. "We're having fun. As soon as we're done passing out the last of the sandwiches, Adrien is going to teach her how to make crepes."

"I love crepes," Aster said.

"Me too," I said with forced brightness. Something felt wrong about David taking his sister from work and talking to her. I hoped they were both all right. By the concerned look on Lacey's face, I wasn't sure they were, and I didn't want to ask her for more details in front of Rainwater's niece.

"Have you seen Bobby or Jo?" I asked.

Lacey's face cleared, as if she was relieved I had changed the subject. I might have dropped it with her, but I was certainly going to ask Rainwater about it.

"Not for a little while. After the police left and the race ended, Bobby wasted no time closing up his registration booth and packing up his store. I think if he stayed on, he could have made a few more sales, but he seemed to be in a hurry."

"Violet, were you looking for the chief?" Adrien asked.

I looked up to see Rainwater and his sister walking down the street. Danielle had her head down, staring at her feet.

"Mommy!" Aster called and ran to her mother.

Danielle kneeled on the sidewalk and buried her face in her daughter's neck. After a moment she stood, and I saw the tears in her eyes. "Excuse me." Danielle ran into the café crying. Lacey went in after her.

Aster looked up at me. "Is Mommy okay?"

I swallowed. "I'm sure she's fine." I made eye contact with Rainwater. His amber eyes were like hard stones, giving nothing away.

"Well." Adrien cleared his throat. "Aster, why don't we start practicing those crepes?"

"Yeah!" Aster pumped her fist. Then she spun around and gave her uncle a hug. "Love you, Uncle David."

The hard mask he had been wearing started to crack.

Adrien led the little girl into the café.

Rainwater stood in the middle of the sidewalk and watched them go.

"David," I whispered. "What's going on?"

"I—"

His cell phone rang and cut off the conversation. He looked at the readout. "Violet, I have to take this. I'll stop by Charming Books later, and we can talk then."

I nodded, and he strode away.

After Rainwater left, I collected my bike from behind the café where Adrien had stored it. As soon as I started to pedal, my legs began to ache. I guessed Adrien was right and I would need to take some aspirin tonight if I was to have any hope of sleeping.

To save both my legs and myself some time, I decided to cut through the park to Bobby's Bike Shop, which was just outside Springside's campus. When I'd had classes and the weather was good, I'd always ridden my bike to the college, so I was familiar with the shortcut.

This late in the spring, the trees were filling out again after the long winter. The leaves were bright green and new. Late-afternoon sunlight shone through them, casting a neon-green glow on the path in front of me.

Just a quarter mile into the park, I stopped my bike beside the springs. The water bubbled and flowed over the large boulder and other rocks into a pond. This was the place that I gathered water for the birch tree.

I didn't have my watering can with me to gather more water, so I kicked off the path and continued on my way toward campus. Bobby's Bike Shop was directly across from Springside

Community College. It was a great location, as the students often rented bikes from Bobby throughout the semester. Also, it was on a major road that allowed for easy access from the highway coming into Niagara Falls for out-of-town customers.

It was a busy shop, but not today. The gravel parking lot of Bobby's crunched under the tires of my bike. I slowed the bike, and a few pebbles flew in front of me. There was a long bike rack in front of Bobby's shop with at least ten bikes in various stages of disrepair locked up. I parked my bike beside it and didn't even bother to put the chain on. I wouldn't be at the shop very long—I just wanted to ask Bobby about Jo.

I walked to the front door, but before I got there, I could tell no one was there. All the lights were off except security lights. There was a hand-written note on the door: Bobby's is closed today and tomorrow. Thank you for your patience.

I stepped back from the door. What had caused Bobby to close the shop for two whole days just at the beginning of the summer season? Now was the time people needed their bikes tuned up and were thinking of getting new ones. Had David or one of his deputies taken Bobby into custody? The thought chilled my blood. Bobby was a nice man, a part of the community for many years. In my heart, I couldn't believe he was the killer.

I rang the bell, knocked. I turned the doorknob. Nothing. The place was locked up tight. However, it was worth checking every possible way to get in. I walked around the back of the building. There was another door there, and it was also locked. Next to it was a large patio area with a green awning over the top of it. It was an outdoor bike repair space. Handlebars, spokes, chains, and other pieces of bicycles lay all over the patio. Some were organized in crates, while the rest were just on the concrete floor or table, as if Bobby had been in the middle of a project and had just walked away before he was done.

A sharp-looking knife and a pair of wire cutters lay on the worktable in the very middle of the space. I shivered. Either one of those tools could have been used to tamper with Redding's bike, but would Bobby do that? Just because he had the opportunity didn't mean he was the killer.

There was a book on the table with the tools. I took a step closer, peering at the cover. Part of me wasn't the least surprised that it was *Leaves of Grass*.

Was the shop now able to show me books outside the bookshop? I didn't know how I felt about that. In the past, when I'd left Charming Books, I'd been able to escape the essence. I didn't take its following me around the village—if that was what was happening—as a good sign.

Chapter Seventeen

I couldn't run around the village looking for Jo all day long. She was my student, but she was also an adult. If she wanted to stay hidden for a little while, that was her choice. However, I was still my nosy self, and I couldn't help wanting to check one more place for her before I gave up for the day.

Her apartment was close to campus, so I didn't think anyone would blame me for stopping by to see if she was there when it was just a few yards away. I hopped back on my bike and road through the campus to the cluster of apartments just to the south of college property. There was no on-campus housing at the community college, but a small developer had built three two-story buildings nearby to capitalize on the students and faculty in need of apartments. The buildings were well cared for and in keeping with Cascade Springs' high standards of architecture. Each building had a name—one of the Great Lakes. As one of my students had once said, there should have been five buildings, then. Huron was left out. If I remembered correctly, Jo lived in Ontario.

One day in February, I had given her a ride to her apartment from campus. Yes, it was only a short drive, not even a mile, but the wind had been howling and the wind chill thirty below. She'd only had a light jacket on.

Now I was grateful for that moment because I knew where she lived, sort of. I knew the building but no more than that.

I parked my bike in the rack in front of her building and walked up to the door. It was locked. I shook my head. Of course the building was locked. It had been a waste of time coming here.

I was just about to leave when a young man, who I assumed was a student, came through the door.

"Need to get in?" he asked.

"Yes." I hurried forward and grabbed the door. "Thanks so much." I paused. "Do you know if Jo Fitzgerald is here today?"

He stared at me blankly. "Who?"

"She is petite, just five feet, and has black hair and an eyebrow ring."

He shook his head. "She must be new. I've lived in the building for three years and have never seen anyone like that." He walked away.

I frowned. I knew for a fact that Jo wasn't new. She had lived in this building at least a year.

I stepped inside and found myself in a wide entryway. There were doors that I assumed led to five apartments on this level and stairs going up to the second floor that led to another five units. Of the ten apartments, how was I to know which one was Jo's when her neighbor didn't even know she had been living there? I had dropped Jo off at the building once but had never been inside. I didn't see a mailroom where I could look at the names, either.

I may have my braver moments, but I wasn't brave enough to knock on all ten doors in the building, asking where she lived. That was a good way to get attention from the police. Rainwater had enough to deal with without being called to the complex because of a prowler, especially if that prowler was me.

There was a bang on the floor above me, and then nothing. At this point, a wise person would have left the building, but I was close to campus and felt relatively safe. I also patted my pocket to make sure my phone was still there. I promised myself that at the first sign of trouble, I was out of there.

I crept up the stairs. My footsteps were noiseless on the carpet. I reached the second-floor landing, which looked almost identical to the first floor. All the doors were closed except one at the end of the hallway. This would have been one of those times I wouldn't have been the least bit surprised if my cat Emerson just popped out of the open door. The cat had a penchant for being in places he wasn't supposed to be. I was grateful when he didn't appear.

I removed my phone from my pocket and made my way down the hallway. Light came out of the doorway, and I could hear someone moving around inside. Was Jo's apartment being tossed? Was I even right to think this was Jo's apartment? I stepped in front of the open doorway. I peered into the room. There was a tiny kitchenette and a living space. The area was neat and tidy. I just wanted to peek in a bit more to confirm that this was Jo's apartment; then I was out of there.

Whoever was in the apartment was in a back room. I didn't step inside the apartment, but the refrigerator was right beside the door. On it was an elaborate calendar for the month of May. Each day listed all the places Jo had to be between school and her three jobs. Most of the listings were back-to-back.

It made me realize how hard Jo tried to make her life work. I wanted her to go to a four-year college, since she had so much potential, but seeing that calendar, I realized she was just trying to keep her head above water most of the time to pay her bills and go to school. Most of my students were juggling a lot. College students today were expected to handle more than ever before, but Jo's was the worst case I had seen. I wished there was a way I could help her.

"What are you doing?" a male voice asked me.

I jumped. I hadn't realized I had stepped all the way into the kitchen to take a better look at Jo's calendar.

Vaughn glared at me. "Do you know where my sister is?"

I blinked at him and then sidestepped until I was in the hallway so that I would a have means of escape should I need it. He didn't stop me. "No, that's why I'm here. I wanted to check on her to see if she was all right."

"Have the police been here?"

I shook my head. "I don't know. I just came because Jo's my friend and student. Like I said, I wanted to make sure she was all right."

He seemed to relax after that. "Oh. Because the police asked me to meet them here."

"They did?" I asked. "In your sister's apartment?"

"I have a key, and they wanted to take a look around."

I swallowed. Neither of us said it, but we both knew the police wanted to take a look around because of the murder.

"There's no sign that my sister has been here since she left this morning. Everything is in its place, like it always is with her."

Now that he mentioned it, I noted that the apartment was impossibly clean. There wasn't a stray spoon on the counter or a piece of junk mail. The furnishings were sparse but well cared for. The neatness of the space and her crazy calendar gave me a new perspective on my student. It seemed to me that she was doing her best to control her life, and in her apartment at least, she had mastered that.

I backed out into the hallway a little more. "Well, I should be going before the police get here. I know you will want to talk to them alone." I said it like I was doing him a huge favor, even though I was desperate to get out of there before Rainwater or one of his officers arrived. I knew if I was still there, I would get an earful from them.

He nodded. "Thanks for looking in on my sister." He swallowed. "If you see her, can you tell her to call me? I know that we haven't always been the closest, but I'm worried about her and about . . ." He trailed off.

I was about to ask Vaughn what else he was worried about when I felt someone behind me. I turned to see Officer Wheaton walking down the hallway. It had to be Wheaton, didn't it?

"Violet, well, goodness, it is such a surprise to see you here," Officer Wheaton said sarcastically.

Vaughn stepped out into the hallway. "Finally, you're here. You took your time getting here. I'm a busy man and have more important things to do than stand around here waiting for you to show up."

"Sorry, sir," Wheaton said with a scowl. "But a man is dead. That takes a little more time to deal with than a jaywalking violation."

Vaughn's cheeks flushed. "I know. I'm sorry. I didn't mean any disrespect. As you can imagine, I'm worried about my sister."

"So finding your sister isn't as important as those other things you have to do?" Wheaton cocked his head.

"I didn't say that, but I know Jo. She can take care of herself. She's been taking care of herself for most of her life. If she decided to leave for a little bit, I don't know where she would have gone."

"It is a concern when a man that she spoke to just a few hours ago is dead. She has a part in the case, and we would like to talk to her."

"My sister didn't kill anyone," Vaughn said.

"I just said that we would like to talk to her. Why would you jump to killing?" Wheaton asked.

I frowned. It seemed to me that Wheaton was having far too much fun tormenting Vaughn by drawing out this conversation. "Just look at the apartment, Wheaton," I said. "Jo isn't there. It's a tiny apartment. It shouldn't take you long to verify that we are right."

The officer scowled at me. "What makes you think you can tell me what to do, Violet? Is it because you are dating the police chief?"

Vaughn's mouth fell open, and he looked at me as if I had betrayed him somehow. I had a feeling I wouldn't have any more luck getting information from him about his sister.

I glared at Wheaton. "I have to go." I turned to Vaughn. "I care about your sister and will keep a lookout for her. If I find her, I will tell you."

He nodded, but he looked at me with suspicion now. I had Wheaton to thank for that.

As Vaughn went back into the apartment, I started down the hallway, but I had made it only two steps before the young officer grabbed my arm. His grip was loose, but it was enough to stop me. Wheaton worked out obsessively and was fully aware of his strength. "I want to know the real reason why you're here," he said.

"I don't know what you're talking about."

"Everyone else might have forgotten, but I remember that you and Redding didn't get along too well last winter. I know that you disliked him. It was clear on your face whenever his name came up."

I cursed my expressive face. I wished I was better at hiding my feelings. "I didn't like him because of what he put Lacey through when her sister died. I had no other reason."

He narrowed his eyes. "I don't believe you."

I wrenched my arm from his grasp. "No one is asking you to. I'm just asking you to leave me alone, Wheaton. That's all I've ever wanted from you."

"I wish I could, Violet," he said.

As I wondered what that might mean, he said, "If you run into your friend Jo, tell her the police want to talk to her."

I scowled. He would be the last person I would tell.

Chapter Eighteen

At the Red Inkers meeting that evening, Richard shifted in his seat as he read an essay he'd written. I glanced at the other members of the group. Everyone was paying attention. It seemed to me that I was the only one with a wandering mind. It was little wonder. I still hadn't heard from Rainwater, and it had been hours since I'd last seen him outside Le Crepe Jolie. I had texted him several times with no answer. I'd finally broken down and called Officer Clipton to see if she could tell me where he was. She wasn't any help. She said, "The chief asked not to be disturbed. I guess, since you don't know where he is, that means you too."

Richard closed his notebook at the end of his essay and cleared his throat. "That's all I have so far. I'm still thinking of an ending."

"That was lovely, Richard." Sadie, who never struggled to come up with a compliment, said. "I like the way you compared the earth to your mother's mac and cheese. I don't think I have ever looked at our planet in such a way."

Nor has anyone else, I thought.

Simon and Renee gave Richard praise for his essay as well. The only member of the group not present was Rainwater, and he was the one I most wanted to see. I bit the inside of my lip. I couldn't get the look on his face outside the café out of my head.

"Violet," Renee asked. "Do you have any comments to add to Richard's piece?"

I blinked. "I liked it," I said quickly. "Richard, you should have enough essays now to publish a collection if you want."

He shook his head. "I don't think my work is ready to submit yet. I have much to do."

"You need to work up some nerve, Richard," Renee said. "Time isn't going to stand still for you, and opportunities will pass you by."

Simon and I raised our eyebrows at each other, and Sadie placed a hand over her month to hide a smile. Everyone in the room knew Renee was talking about something much more than Richard's essay collection.

"Besides, we know that it can happen." Renee held up her copy of Sadie's book. "Sadie is proof of that. I predict we will all be published one day and look back at this time fondly. We'll laugh over what caused us to wait so long in the first place."

Richard didn't look nearly as certain. "In any case, it will be Sadie's turn to read at our next meeting, which is fitting with her release of her book in a few weeks. Will you be reading from the book, Sadie?"

She shook her head. "No, the sequel. I hope you'll all like it. I have a bit of fear over the sophomore slump."

"I'm sure we will." Richard stood. "Another great meeting. I only wish that David could have been here with us."

Sadie looked to me. "Have you heard from him, Violet?"

I stood up and folded my chair and then Richard's chair next. "I haven't heard from him since this afternoon."

"It's such a strange thing that a man would die in the bike race. Does Rainwater know what happened?" Richard asked.

I shrugged. "I don't know what he knows. He's on the case, and I'm sure that everything will be clear soon."

I hoped what I said was true.

"Will you help him, Violet?" Renee said.

I didn't say anything.

She laughed. "We know that you will. You can't resist poking your nose in a case."

"Well," I said, thinking of Jo and how much I wanted to help her. "I don't think Rainwater would like it."

A book slammed against the wall, and everyone screamed. Richard's scream was by far the highest in pitch. My hand flew to my chest, and I could feel my heart thunder against my rib cage. I forced a laugh. "Faulkner! That's a very bad crow for scaring all of us."

"Faulkner threw the book?" Sadie asked. "I didn't see him leave the tree."

"He's fast," I said swiftly. "Sometimes he moves around the store so quickly, I don't even know it."

"How could he throw the book?" Simon asked.

"From his talons." My answer sounded lame to my own ears.

"Can he do that?" Richard asked.

"Oh sure," I said.

Overhead, Faulkner fluffed his feathers, "Not a day passes, not a minute or second, without a corpse."

"Your crow is a little a morbid," Renee said. "That's even worse than when he was reciting Poe all the time."

I laughed. "Well, he is a crow." I stood up and walked over to the fireplace. The book that I knew very well Faulkner *hadn't* flung against the fireplace wall lay open on the hearth. As I expected, it was *Leaves of Grass*. The book was open near the end.

To think of time—of all that retrospection!
To think of to-day and the ages continued
    hence-forward!
Have you guess'd you yourself would not continue?
Have you dreaded these earth-beetles?
Have you fear'd the future would be nothing to you?
Is to-day nothing? is the beginningless past nothing?
If the future is nothing, they are just as surely
    nothing.
To think that the sun rose in the east! that men and
    women were
flexible, real, alive! that every-thing was alive!
To think that you and I did not see, feel, think, nor
    bear our part!
To think that we are now here, and bear our part!

I realized Faulkner had been quoting Whitman as I read the next stanza.

Not a day passes—not a minute or second, without an
    accouchement!

Not a day passes—not a minute or second, without a
corpse!

Maybe Faulkner had thrown the book after all. I wouldn't
have put it past the troublemaking bird.

"Violet, what are you reading?" Simon asked.

I jumped. I hadn't realized he was standing next to me.

I scooped up the book. "It's just some poetry."

"Oh, let me see." He took the book from my hands.
"Whitman?" he asked. "Why, he's my very favorite. 'Song of
Myself' is one of the most profound pieces of poetry I have ever
read. It taught me what it is to be free with yourself, even living a plain and ordinary life. Whitman saw the beauty in the
everyday. The vulgar coachman in New York, the quiet woods,
and in the printed word." He blushed. "I'm sorry. How embar-
rassing for me to go on and on like this."

"No need to apologize. I think every writer can think of
the book or author that made them want to write something of
their own someday."

He nodded and looked over his shoulder. "I wanted to tell
you something before I leave. Something that I don't want
Sadie to overhear. It might upset her."

I hesitated. "I don't want to keep a secret from Sadie."

He nodded. "Neither do I, and I'm not asking you to. I'll
tell her what I am about to tell you. I just want to wait until
tomorrow. She will worry through the night, and I want her to
enjoy the day she held her book in her hands for the first time."

"What do you have to tell me?" I asked.

"It's about Danielle Cloud." He said this in a low voice.

I raised my brow. Danielle and Sadie were close friends, so I could understand why he wouldn't want to upset Sadie by telling her.

"What about Danielle?" I asked.

He looked over his shoulder again; Sadie was chatting with Richard and Renee. She held her book to her chest like it was a prized possession, which it most certainly was—not just to Sadie but to everyone who loved her, including Danielle.

"I saw Danielle at the bike race registration table."

I frowned. "So?"

"She was arguing with Joel Redding."

I remembered the scene in front of Le Crepe Jolie just that afternoon—Rainwater with his clearly distraught sister. Had she been broken up over Redding's death? "When was this?"

He looked over his shoulder again. "Just an hour before he died."

I stood dumbstruck in the middle of Charming Books. This must be why Rainwater had taken his sister away from the café today. It might be the very reason I hadn't heard from him since. If Danielle was in some way connected to the murder, he would want to protect her. He would also be looking for others to blame if she was a suspect. Others like Jo Fitzgerald. As much as I couldn't believe Danielle would kill someone, I knew Jo couldn't have possibly done it either. However, would Rainwater let his judgment be clouded in order to protect his only sister?

I shook my head. No, he wouldn't. I knew David Rainwater, and he was a better man than that. He was the most honorable man I knew.

"Please," Simon said. "If Sadie mentions it to you after I tell her, act surprised. I don't want her to know that I told you first."

I frowned. "Why did you tell me?"

"Because you're close to David Rainwater and Danielle is his sister. Whatever is going on with her is going to impact you." He paused. "And it might impact you a lot." He handed the Whitman book back to me.

I thanked him. I didn't know what else to do.

"Simon, are you ready to go?" Sadie asked, walking over to us. She smiled. "The two of you looked like you were having a very serious conversation."

I held up the book. "It was on Whitman."

"Oh." Her face brightened. "That's Simon's very favorite. It's funny that would be the book Faulkner decided to throw. What a strange bird he is."

I couldn't argue with her there.

I said good-night to the rest of the Red Inkers. After they left, I closed and locked the door to Charming Books. It was time to water the tree.

Chapter Nineteen

I'd once asked my grandmother why we had to water the tree every other day with water from the natural springs, and she'd said because every time a Caretaker forgot, the tree began to wilt. As an academic accustomed to rigorous scholarship, that didn't sit well with me. All I knew was that on the days I forgot the tree—I never claimed to be a perfect Caretaker—the tree wilted and its waxy leaves curled and fell from its branches. I'd also found that my shortcuts didn't work either. Like gathering extra water and saving it to water the tree another day. The tree still suffered when I did that. It seemed to me that the only way to guarantee the tree's health and the health of the essence was to water it every other day with fresh water from the springs. I hoped when I read the ledger my grandmother had given me that I would learn more about this.

Even though I was terribly worried about Jo and now about Rainwater because I knew his beloved sister was somehow involved in Redding's death, I still had to water the tree. If I waited until the next day, the tree would suffer, as would the shop's essence. I needed the essence to help me help Jo, so

I didn't see any choice other than to go after dark to lessen the risk of being seen. It was my duty, and one that I would carry until I passed it on to a daughter of my own, if I ever had one. No pressure.

I opted to walk to the springs along the well-worn path that led from our backyard to the edge of the park. I stopped at the garden shed before leaving the yard to grab the watering can I would need.

When I came out of the shed, Emerson was sitting by the gate with his skinny black tail whipping back and forth like a pendulum.

I put my hands on my hips. "Really?"

He smiled in the way only a mischievous cat can.

"Okay, fine," I said to the cat. "You can come along, but stay close and don't run off." There was really no point in arguing with him.

He purred a response that sounded like a lawn mower firing up in the quiet wood.

When Emerson and I walked into the woods, a calm fell over me. I hadn't realized how the tension of the day had affected me. Not that I was completely calm. I still didn't know where Jo was. She wasn't answering my text messages or emails. I promised myself that I would track Bobby down over the next few days. Jo worked for him. Maybe she'd told him where she'd gone and when she would be back. Or I could reach out to her brother again—but I didn't want to create added strain there.

My footsteps were noiseless on the mulch-covered path that led to the springs, located in a break in the trees.

An enormous boulder twice my height in the hillside marked the beginning of the springs. Evergreen shrubs and moss covered the rocky wall, where a tiny waterfall, no larger than the width of a man, trickled down it and filled the pool, where I gathered the water. The constant movement of water from the hillside and bubbling up from the aquifer that ran the length of the village and broke to the surface in this one spot kept the water clear and free of algae and pests.

Moonlight broke through the trees, playing on the hillside and then on the pool of water below. Birch trees encircled the springs, and an owl hooted softly from a pale branch. It was tranquil. It was where I needed to be to calm my spirit. Emerson sat beside me at the edge of the pond as I dipped my watering can into the clear water. The can filled quickly, and as much as I wanted to stay there, I stood up, cradling the container and the precious water to my chest. I looked down at the little cat. "Let's go home."

He whipped his tail, and I took that as agreement.

We were halfway down the path when a *snap* sounded from deep in the woods. Emerson jumped onto my back and climbed up my sweatshirt to perch on my shoulder. I almost dropped the watering can and all its precious water. That single ominous sound had displaced any sense of tranquility, reminding me that I was a woman alone traipsing along the woods at night with a killer on the loose.

I patted his head. "It's okay, buddy. It's probably just a deer."

He dug his claws into my skin.

"Emerson, that hurts. Get off of me."

He hunched down, digging in even harder.

I set the watering can down on the path and tried to remove the cat from my shoulder. He wouldn't budge. "Emerson, I'm not moving a step until you remove your claws."

As if he understood what I said, he retracted his claws. I let out a sigh of relief and hoped they hadn't drawn blood.

There was another snap of wood deep in the forest. Emerson's claws dug into me again. The cat's reaction had me thoroughly spooked. I didn't bother to tell him to calm down again. All I could think of was Dahlia Waverly in these same woods nearly a hundred years ago. She had died collecting this water. Was that to be my fate too? There were people who killed for far less in this village. I knew that from my own experience.

Another twig snap spurred me into motion, and I ran the rest of the way home.

I didn't feel safe until I was inside the shop and had locked the back door behind me. Emerson must have felt the same, because as soon as the bolt slid home, he retracted his claws and jumped from my shoulder.

"I'm sure it was just a deer," I said.

He meowed in response. I didn't think he was convinced, and neither was I. I walked through the swinging door that led from the kitchen into the main part of the shop. The shop was dark except for the moonlight coming through the skylight in the ceiling and through the front windows.

Faulkner flew from the sales desk to the top of the tree. He was a black shadow above me. Only when he was directly under the skylight could I make out his features.

Without ceremony, I poured the water into the dirt base around the birch tree, taking care to shake every last drop from the can. When I was done, nothing happened. It never did. With a sigh, I carried the watering can back into the kitchen. I would return it to its spot in the shed tomorrow. I wasn't going back outside tonight after getting spooked in the woods.

I decided to text Jo again. I knew it was a long shot that she would reply. Jo. This is Violet. I want to help you. Tell me where you are, and I will come to you. I know you are afraid. I'm here to help.

I hit send and paced around the birch tree for the next ten minutes. There was no response. I sighed and shoved the phone in my pocket.

As I came around the tree for what must have been the twelfth time, Emerson was sitting at the foot of the stairs, as he always did when he thought it was high time we went to bed.

I glanced at the door. Rainwater had said he would stop by that night and tell me what was going on.

My phone pinged in my pocket. I jumped like I had been hit by a dart in the back. I was convinced it was Jo texting back. I looked at the phone and saw that it was from Rainwater. Can't drop by tonight. Something came up. Will try to call if not too late.

My face fell, but I texted him back and told him I understood. I was starting to learn that this was just part of being in a relationship with a cop. You never knew when they would have time to see you.

Emerson was still on the step and meowed at me. "Okay," I said. "Let's go to bed."

Faulkner cawed agreement. He never could truly rest until I took Emerson into my apartment for the evening. The crow was convinced the cat would attack him in his sleep, which wasn't too far from the mark, if the way Emerson studied the crow with rapt attention was any indication.

Emerson and I headed up the stairs, and I let us into the apartment. In the middle of the sofa was another copy of

Whitman's poems that I knew I hadn't left there, and no one else would have been in my apartment since the Red Inkers had left for the night. I picked it up and found that it was open to the same poem the shop's essence had revealed to me when the Red Inkers had been here. My eyes fell on the lines in the middle of the poem.

> Have you guess'd you yourself would not continue?
> Have you dreaded these earth-beetles?
> Have you fear'd the future would be nothing to you?
> Is to-day nothing? is the beginningless past nothing?

Was this what the murder was about? Death? Fear of it? I frowned and took the book into the bedroom with me.

I went to bed with Emerson the cat and Whitman the poet. I read *Leaves of Grass* late into the night, hoping I would hear from the police chief before too long. Much to my disappointment, I didn't hear from Rainwater at all.

Chapter Twenty

The next morning, my body was not a happy camper. I had forgotten to take the aspirin Adrien had suggested. That had been a very poor life choice. Everything, and I mean everything, hurt, including my eyelashes. That's how bad it was. I could barely hobble to the bathroom.

The hot water from the shower soothed my aching muscles, but my mind raced as I tried to understand why the shop wanted me to read Whitman. The beginning stanza in 'To Think of Time' was most certainly about death, but I felt like that clue from the shop was coming a tad late. There had already been a death, Redding's death. If the shop's essence was telling me death was coming, it should have done that prior to the bike race. Unless . . . fate had another death planned. I shivered as the water in the shower ran cold. I didn't want to believe that. Perhaps it meant something else I wasn't getting just yet, but I knew I would. I had to.

I was moving slower than normal when I went downstairs and opened the shop for the day.

I unlocked the front door just as Richard was coming up the walk. The evening before at the Red Inkers meeting, I'd asked him if he would be able to work in the shop that day. I knew I wouldn't be able to be pinned down knowing that Bobby, Jo, Danielle, and possibly Rainwater might be in trouble.

"Thanks again for doing this," I said, stepping aside.

"I don't mind at all," he said in his affable voice.

"I promise not to ask you to watch the shop so much. It's just been a very strange start to the summer season." I held up my hand when he started to talk. "And I know that it's not exactly summer yet, but with the college out of session, I tend to think of it that way."

Richard smiled. "I can see that. I suppose it's less apparent to me, since I teach a few classes in the summer, but I'm very glad that I don't have class today, which allows me to help you out."

Faulkner flew down from the tree and onto his perch by the front window. "Off with her head," he cawed as he went. It was his very favorite catchphrase. I wished my grandmother had never read him *Alice's Adventures in Wonderland*.

At least it was a break from Whitman. My head was still spinning over his poems. Whitman was deceptively easy to understand, but only a close reader could recognize the deceit. Even his simplest poems had another layer or some other meaning that could be found there. Scholars had debated for over a hundred years whether or not that had been Whitman's intent or if the poems should be taken at face value. My guess was Whitman would want his readers to go deeper. He had been hoping to reach into the hearts of the common man with his poetry.

Like most great artists, Whitman didn't reach true fame and acclaim until long after he was dead. If Whitman had known this, it likely would have frustrated him to no end. He had been a proud man and wanted all the accolades he could get in life. It seemed to me that's why he had toted Ralph Waldo Emerson's letter so much. It was the encouragement he needed to keep going.

My cell phone rang in the back pocket of my jeans, shaking me from my thoughts about Whitman. I yanked the phone out, praying it was Rainwater. My grandmother's face smiled back at me on the screen. I put the phone to my ear. "Good morning, Grandma Daisy."

"Good morning, Violet. I have some exciting news for you." I could hear the satisfied smile in my grandmother's voice.

"What's that?" I asked hesitantly. Exciting news in my book and my grandmother's book could be two very different things.

"I solved the mystery of your necklace!" She said this like she was playing the game of Clue and had just caught Colonel Mustard in the conservatory with the candlestick.

"You have? What happened to it?"

"You will want to come down to the village hall to find out. I think it will be easier if you hear it firsthand. Can you come here?" she asked. "I know that you must have just opened the store, but you could close it for a little while."

"There's no need to do that," I said. "Richard is here. I asked him to work today."

"There's my girl. You were always good at problem solving. When can you be here?"

"Five minutes?" I guessed. "I'm leaving now."

"Good," she said, and ended the call.

When I got outside, Emerson was already sitting in my bicycle basket. I put my hands on my hips. "You aren't going with me. I'm going to the museum, and there are too many places there for you to hide."

He licked his paw and then swiped it over his ear as if he hadn't heard a word.

I grabbed at the cat to forcibly remove him from the basket, but he flattened his body against the wire mesh and curled his claws into the bottom of the basket. It didn't matter how hard I tugged at him, he wouldn't move. Emerson knew me well enough to know I wouldn't do anything that might hurt him. Game point, Emerson, again.

I groaned. "I guess we're both going to the museum."

He popped his head out of the basket and smiled. There was no winning with that cat. Shaking my head, I climbed onto my mom's old bike and strapped the violet helmet on my head. I coasted down the hill toward the Riverwalk. It was after ten in the morning, but the village was just waking up after the big race the day before.

Tourists quietly waited in line to get a breakfast table at Le Crepe Jolie, and others sipped coffee in paper cups as they strolled along the Riverwalk. I stopped my bike by the river. Emerson and I both stared at it.

The Niagara River sparkled this morning as the sunlight reflected off the small waves caused by the current rushing over the boulders and rocks, polished by thousands of gallons of water running over them for thousands of years. The wide river was like a beacon. I couldn't help but wonder what the runaway slaves had thought when they happened upon the shore, knowing that on the other side, one short but dangerous swim away, was Canada and freedom.

Those feelings and questions were what my grandmother wanted to preserve through the museum. Despite all the grumbling from the village council and a few villagers about how expensive it would be to open and run, the village was for the most part behind the idea. Cascade Springs was very proud of its part in the abolition movement, as it should be.

I was so stricken by the river's beauty, I didn't notice Fenimore approaching me.

"It's not often I see someone riding a bicycle with a cat in the basket," he said. He was dressed in his troubadour outfit of worn jeans and flannel shirt, his hair tied back with a piece of leather. His harmonica hung from a wire around his neck, and his guitar was slung over his arm.

I swallowed as emotions flooded my body. Hurt, anger, frustration, and confusion. They were all there. It was as if I was running through all the stages of grief in a matter of seconds.

Emerson braced his white front paws on the edge of the wire basket and cocked his head. He seemed to be studying Fenimore, trying to decide if he was friend or foe. Fenimore let the little tuxie smell his hand, and then he scratched Emerson between the ears. The cat leaned into the scratch. Traitor.

When I didn't say anything, Fenimore went on to say, "I heard that you were in the bike race yesterday, and there was an accident. I'm happy that you weren't hurt."

I bit back a sharp retort asking him why he would even care. He hadn't cared for me most of my life, so why the change of heart now that I was thirty years old? It seemed more than a little late for me. Instead I said, "Are you in the village for the race? I thought you would have gone home by now."

"I thought when I saw you yesterday . . ." He trailed off.

"What?" I asked as I removed my helmet and hopped off my bike. I wasn't making it easy for him, and we both knew it.

"I wanted to talk to you again. I didn't like how we left it last year. I was a coward. I should have tried to reach out to you." He adjusted his guitar strap on his shoulder. "I'm sorry for that. Did you read the letter?"

"I did."

"Did you tell anyone about . . . ?"

"Only Grandma Daisy."

He nodded. "That's right. She should know. She has a right to know." He looked out at the river. "She should have known a long time ago."

"We both should have." I cleared the lump from my throat. "I need to go. Grandma Daisy wanted me to meet her in the village hall." I turned toward the street, ready to walk my bike across. I would have run for it, but just then a horse and carriage with tourists inside clomped down the street, blocking my path. As the driver led the horses by, I heard him say, "The village hall was built in the 1850s, and now Cascade Springs is adding an underground railroad museum to it. You will want to come back for that. Let me tell you about the village before and during the Civil War . . ."

The carriage stopped me long enough for Fenimore to try again. "Violet, can we talk? There are things I need to tell you. Things you deserve to hear."

As if against my own will, I turned my head to meet his gaze. There were tears in his eyes, and I felt myself soften toward him. "Stop by the shop later today," I said, before I could change my mind. "We can talk there."

He nodded. I crossed the street and didn't look back.

Chapter
Twenty-One

When I stepped into the village hall, the great door closed behind me with a thud. Not that Grandma Daisy, Vaughn, and Bertie, who were standing in the middle of the hall staring at the hole in the marble floor, noticed.

"I don't know how the building has stayed up all these years," Vaughn said. "It was built over an aquifer."

Grandma Daisy stared down the hole. "Can you fix it? Can the aquifer be contained and the building made stable again? We don't want to lose this part of the building. It's part of our history. Runaway slaves hid underneath this spot prior to the Civil War. That makes the village hall the perfect place for the Underground Railroad Museum."

Bertie snorted at that comment.

"We can fix it," Vaughn said confidently. "But it's going to take a lot of money."

"I'll get you the money you need," Grandma Daisy said, and then spotted me standing with Emerson in the doorway. "There you are, Violet," my grandmother said brightly. "Why did you bring Emerson?"

"He wouldn't take no for an answer," I said. My brain was still occupied with seeing Fenimore outside the hall. Why had I told him to meet me at the bookshop later? I had nothing to say to him, and I seriously doubted I wanted to hear whatever it was he had to say to me.

"Pets aren't allowed in the village hall," Bertie said in her high-pitched voice. My grandmother's secretary scowled at me. Then again, I didn't know if she was scowling at me or everyone on earth. I suspected that Bertie found just about everyone on the planet equally taxing.

My grandmother laughed. "I don't think Emerson would consider himself a pet. He is more like a roommate. Wouldn't you say, Violet?"

"He likes to think so," I said, noticing that Vaughn stood off to the side with his hands in his pockets. He wouldn't meet my gaze. I gave my grandmother a questioning look.

"Bertie, I think that will be all. Violet and I would like to talk with Vaughn now."

Bertie didn't move.

Grandma Daisy didn't seem to be daunted by Bertie's lack of motivation to leave. "If you could just drop the notes that you took this morning on my desk before you leave, I would greatly appreciate it."

"Very well, Mayor Daisy," she said in a churlish tone, and then she made her way up the grand staircase.

Grandma Daisy shook her head. "She is very good at her job," she said, as if she was trying to convince herself as well as the rest of us.

I looked from my grandmother to Vaughn and back again. "Grandma Daisy, you asked me to come here. What's going on?"

Grandma Daisy smiled. "You told me about the necklace yesterday, and I took it upon myself to get to the bottom of it."

"You found it?" I asked, glancing at Vaughn. Had I been right in thinking he stole it from my pocket?

"Not exactly." She looked at Vaughn.

"Jo took it," Vaughn blurted out. "That's all I can think that happened to it."

"She took it from my pocket? That's not possible. I didn't even have it when I saw her. The only person I saw when I had it was you."

"I don't have it. I would never steal anything." He shook his head. "She took it originally, or at least that's my best guess. Daisy told me you found the necklace in the museum."

I glanced at my grandmother, and she gave me a nod. "It was on the scaffolding," I said. "I found it right before you showed up. Unless you saw me take it." I held up my hand. "Wait. You were there when I rescued Emerson? You watched the cat jump on my shoulders." I folded my arms. "Why didn't you say that yesterday?"

"I didn't see you take the necklace. I didn't even know about it until your grandmother asked me about it this morning."

"Then how did you know it was there?"

He sighed. "I didn't, but I know if there was a necklace at the top of the scaffolding, Jo put it there or dropped it."

"I'm not making the connection," I said.

"I hired Jo to work with me on the museum," Vaughn explained. "Mostly to do errands and other small jobs to save the guys and me some time while working on the project. It hasn't gone well. When she does show up for work, she usually climbs up in the scaffolding for hours at a time, daydreaming her day away."

I frowned. "Why didn't you fire her then?"

He rubbed the back of his head. "She's my sister. I was hoping that if I could give her some more time, she would find direction."

"How do you know the necklace is from her, then?"

"No one else could have dropped it up there. It had to be Jo."

"So it's hers?" I asked.

He shook his head. "I don't think so. Most likely she stole it from someone else. I know my sister, and that's what she does. It's a compulsion to . . . to take things. My guess is she stole it from you a second time when she visited your shop yesterday afternoon. Daisy told me that she was there."

I wished my grandmother hadn't told Vaughn so much about Jo. I knew she liked him, but I felt like something was off here. "Where is Jo now? It sounds to me like we need to ask her."

"I—I don't know where my sister is. I haven't seen her since yesterday morning. I went to her apartment near campus this morning, and she wasn't there."

I bit the inside of my lip. I told myself Jo was fine, but I couldn't discount that she was missing or at least appeared to be missing. What did she know about Redding? What did the garnet necklace I found have to do with any of it? My stomach sank, and I prayed she was safe. No matter what trouble she might be in, we could sort it out. I just needed her to be okay.

My grandmother clapped her hands. "See, I did solve part of the mystery."

I adjusted Emerson in my arms. The cat shifted. I knew he wanted to get down, but I wasn't going to lose him in the village hall again. "We don't know that for sure until we find Jo and ask her, and we still don't know where the necklace is now or who it belongs to."

Grandma Daisy shrugged. "I solved part of the mystery then."

I sighed. There was no point in arguing with her. "Vaughn, do you know where your sister might have gone?"

He shook his head. "Jo is a free spirit. She floats through life." He frowned. "I thought that was changing. The last few months, she had been so focused. She was going to class and most of her jobs. She said she was working on an extra project for class, which took her away from the museum, but I didn't mind it. I liked to see her have some focus, but in this last week it all fell apart. I don't know what happened."

Grandma Daisy patted his shoulder. "Violet will figure it out. She always does."

Vaughn's eyes narrowed just a bit when she said that.

"Won't you, Violet?" Grandma Daisy asked with a smile.

I frowned, wishing that my grandmother wouldn't make such bold promises on my behalf. If Vaughn didn't know where his sister was, I didn't know how I would be able to find her. "I'll do what I can." I swallowed. "I don't know if it'll be enough."

I needed to get away from the village hall to think. Emerson must have had the same idea, because after I said goodbye to Grandma Daisy and Vaughn, he jumped out of my arms and ran to the door. When I opened it, he ran down the hall's great stairs and jumped into my bicycle basket.

I walked down the steps at a much slower pace. "I think we are both ready to go home."

Emerson looked at me and meowed. As I was pedaling away from the village hall, I spotted my grandmother's secretary Bertie across the street standing alongside the river. It struck me as odd; I couldn't remember a time ever seeing her there. Part of me wanted to ask her if she was all right, but a larger part of me wanted to return to Charming Books. The only thing that might make it clear what was going on was the books themselves. I hoped they would talk to me.

Chapter
Twenty-Two

R ichard was with a customer when I came into the shop. I
waved to him as I ran up the stairs to the children's loft.
There were two little girls and their mother reading quietly. I
smiled at them and went into my apartment. Before I could
close the door, Emerson slipped inside.

The copy of *Leaves of Grass* that I had been reading the
night before was still on my nightstand. I picked it up and
walked over to my dresser. The scrap of verse Richard had written down for Redding to give me was there. I picked it up. "All
truths wait in all things." I knew this had to be part of a longer
poem. I sat cross-legged in the middle of my bed waiting for a
moment, hoping that the shop's essence would find the right
page for me. Nothing happened. I waited another minute. Still
nothing.

"What good is having access to magic if you can't control
it," I grumbled.

The shop didn't seem to care about my plight. Finally, I
did what I should have done in the first place—I flipped to
the book's index and looked for the verse. I found it quickly.

The line was from Whitman's most famous poem in *Leaves of Grass*, "Song of Myself." "Song of Myself" described a journey to uncover one's own identity and self-worth. The "I" in the poem was Whitman, but it was also everyman. It was also me. As I sat there flipping through the pages, I realized the "I" was also whoever had killed Redding.

I read the stanza aloud that contained Redding's quote.

All truths wait in all things
They neither hasten their own delivery nor resist it,
They do not need the obstetric forceps of the surgeon,
The insignificant is as big to me as any,
(What is less or more than a touch?)
Logic and sermons never convince,
The damp of the night drives deeper into my soul.

It didn't take a Whitman scholar to know that Redding, at least, had wanted me to know he would find out the truth about Charming Books. Redding had wanted me to know he would be patient. Now he was dead, and his promise and threat were unfulfilled.

My chest tightened. Or was it? I didn't know where Redding's guitar briefcase was. There could have been notes in there about Charming Books, and he certainly had taken enough photographs of the shop and of me. What would Rainwater think when he saw all those photographs on Redding's camera and on his phone? Had he seen them already, and was that the reason he'd been avoiding me?

I picked up my phone off the bed and sent Rainwater another text. Still I received nothing back.

Another thought hit me. If Redding had notes in his guitar case, there could be more notes about Charming Books in his office or on his computer or just about anywhere. But since I didn't wholly know Redding's motive—or his killer's—I couldn't allow myself to speculate too much on these things. His simply having photos of me did not automatically incriminate me or my shop. Well, that's what I told myself, anyway. Besides, any prying Redding might have done paled in comparison to Jo's safety, or Bobby's innocence, or finding the true killer before someone else got hurt. How could I possibly get rid of them all and erase whatever knowledge the private investigator had about my shop? It seemed like the search was hopeless, and the only one who seemed to know anything was Jo, and she was impossible to find. I dropped my face into my hands. I was on the verge of indulging in one heck of a pity party when I heard a shuffling sound. I lifted my neck and saw the papers of *Leaves of Grass* flutter in all directions. Then, just as quickly as it started, it stopped.

The book fell open to the middle of the poem called "Starting From Paumanok."

What do you seek so pensive and silent?
What do you need camerado?
Dear son do you think it is love?
Listen dear son—listen America, daughter or son,
It is painful thing to love a man or woman to excess,
    and yet
it satisfies, it is great,
But there is something else very great, it makes the
    whole
coincide,

It, magnificent, beyond materials, with continuous
    hands
sweeps and provides for all.

I frowned and read the poem again. What was the shop's
essence trying to tell me, and what was the thing greater than
love that Whitman was driving at? I read the next three stanzas
in the poem, and it didn't become any clearer as Whitman
waxed on about religion and democracy. So then, if it wasn't
Whitman's message the essence was trying to tell me, what was
the essence's message? I read the first line again. "What do you
seek so pensive and silent?" That could have been about me sitting in the middle of my bed trying—and it would seem
failing—to understand what Charming Books wanted me to
know.

The pages of the book started to move again. I lifted my
hands from the pages and let them flutter open on their own.
Finally, after what seemed like minutes, the book fell open a
second time. The poem in front of me was "Rise O Days From
Your Fathomless Deeps."

Rise O days from your fathomless deeps, till you
    loftier, fiercer sweep
Long for my soul hungering gymnastic I devour'd
    what the earth gave me,
Long I roam'd the woods of the north, long I watch'd
    Niagara pouring

This time the shop's essence wasn't pulling any punches. It
wanted me to go to Niagara Falls. I snapped the book shut and
jumped off the bed. I moved so swiftly I scared Emerson.

The tuxie leaped off the bed with a yowl. I couldn't sit there any longer and wait for the books to tell me something. I had to know for myself what Redding knew, and that meant going to his office in Niagara Falls.

When I came out of my apartment, the mother and her two little girls were gone from the fairy loft. I wondered how long I had been in my apartment pouring over Whitman. It was afternoon at least.

On the main floor, I found Richard engrossed in another arcane English text that the shop must have given him. He looked up from his book. "Truly, Violet, your selection in the store is mind-boggling. It's almost like I think of a book that I want and it appears."

"Huh," I said. "That's crazy."

"Crazy is as crazy does!" Faulkner cried from the tree.

I shook my head at the bird. "If you're okay here, I think I will go out for a little bit."

Richard waved me away. "Go ahead. I don't mind being here at all. I can read all day."

I smiled. At least Richard was happy. I wished he could stay on and work for us through the school year, but I knew that would be too hard with his teaching load.

I left the shop and was surprised Emerson didn't follow me. I really didn't know what the cat was thinking half the time, but maybe that was for the best. My Mini Cooper was parked on the street. Typically the only time I drove was when I had to leave the village.

I unlocked the car and climbed in. I yelped when I saw Emerson sitting on the passenger's seat.

"How on earth did you get in here?" I cried. "The car was locked! It was locked, wasn't it?" Now I couldn't remember if it had been or not. Sometimes my grandmother borrowed my car if she had an errand to run outside the village. She might have left it unlocked, but even so, the cat didn't have thumbs! How had he gotten the door open? I rubbed my forehead. I had the feeling of a migraine coming on.

I knew from past experience that I would have no luck removing the cat from the car. "Fine, you can come, but you are staying in the car when we get to the city. Understood? I don't want anything to happen to you. You might know your way around the village but not Niagara Falls."

Emerson placed his forepaws on the dashboard and smiled at me in that smug way cats mastered two millennia ago.

It was late on a Sunday afternoon, and the traffic getting into Niagara Falls was congested, as people had decided to visit the majestic landmark on such a beautiful day. I wasn't actually going to the Falls themselves. I had the address for Redding's detective agency programmed into my phone, and instead of taking me toward the tourist spots, the GPS took me into the city.

Redding's office was in a rundown part of the city. Trash cans lay on their sides, and a mangy-looking dog walked up the sidewalk. Emerson ducked low in his seat when he saw the dog. "You really do need to stay in the car."

He looked at me, and I think he actually listened for once.

There wasn't a parking lot in front of Redding's building as far as I could see, so I parked in a spot on the street. I didn't see a meter, so I hoped I wouldn't be there long enough to get a ticket. I got out of the car and locked it. Emerson watched me from the window.

Redding's detective office was in a nondescript three-story brick building with narrow windows. To me it looked more like a prison than an office building. There was a metal door that led into the building. Beside the door was a peeling sign that read REDDING, DETECTIVE AGENCY, INQUIRE WITHIN.

I wasn't so sure about the *inquiring within* part. All my senses were telling me to leave. It was an especially bad idea with my cat. I might have locked Emerson in the car, but I wasn't certain he wouldn't find a way out.

I started to turn and retreat when the door to the office opened. If I hadn't jumped back, the heavy metal door would have hit me in the face.

"Oh! Excuse me!" a large man said. "I didn't know anyone was here." I guessed he was in his thirties. He had black hair and wore jeans and a polo shirt. The polo was tight around his thick upper arms. He started to step around me and looked over his shoulder at me. "Can I help you with something?"

"I was looking for Joel Redding's office," I said. It was worth a shot, I thought.

The man turned all the way around now. "Why is that? Do you have a need for a detective?"

"No. I mean, I know that he can't help me." I trailed off.

The frown on the man's face deepened. "Are you a reporter?"

I held up my hands. "No. I'm from Cascade Springs, and . . ." And what would I say? I was trying to find out who killed him to get my former student off the hook for the crime?

"What's your name?"

"Violet Waverly," I said.

A strange expression crossed his face. "You're her."

"Her?" I asked.

"The woman he was obsessed with." He took a step closer to me.

"Obsessed with?" I didn't like the sound of that.

He took another step closer. "He thought you were keeping some great secret that, if he could prove was true, would make him rich."

"And did he tell you what that secret was?" I moved away from him, realizing that coming to this neighborhood in the city by myself had been a very bad idea. I didn't know this man or what he was capable of.

"No, he never did," the man said regretfully.

"You have my name. What's yours?" I asked, trying to sound a lot more self-assured than I actually felt.

"Scotty Jones. I worked for Redding to get in the required number of hours to earn my private investigator's license. I don't know what I will do to get those hours now that he's gone. I don't know if my hours will transfer to another PI's office or if another will even take me. Joel Redding didn't have the best reputation in the business. It might have done me more harm than good to work for him."

I wasn't surprised to hear that, but even so, Scotty sounded callous. He didn't appear the least bit upset about Redding's death, only inconvenienced.

He leaned in close to me, so close I could smell coffee on his breath. "So what is the great secret you were keeping from Redding?"

I took a big step back to get away from his breath. "I don't have one."

He laughed. "I don't believe that at all. If Redding said you had a secret, you did. He might not have been good at managing his money. If he had been"—he pointed at the brick building—"he wouldn't have been in this dump, but he was a darn good detective. He knew his stuff, and he knew when people were lying. He would tell me that you were lying right now."

"Then you would be wrong," I lied.

"Maybe I will take up the reins and try to find out if your secret is as good as Redding believed. He was usually right about that sort of thing. I haven't found it yet, but I might. Trust me, I have wanted to find out. I have torn that office apart looking for something that would tell me, but I've found nothing."

I supposed I should be glad Redding hadn't trusted his intern.

He narrowed his eyes. "Why are you here?"

"I—I know what happened to Redding, and I wanted to give my condolences."

"Who were those condolences to? No one cares that he's dead. He was a single man with no family to speak of, or friends, for that matter. No one will miss him."

Again, I felt terribly sad for the private investigator. How awful to die like you never even mattered at all.

He laughed. "I know why you're here. You wanted to come here and find out what kind of dirt he had on you. It must really be something good." He took a step toward me and grabbed me by the arm before I had time to react. "What is it? You can tell me."

I tried to pull away from him. "Let go of me." I looked up and down the street, but the block was deserted. All I could see were Emerson's two green eyes peering through the windshield of my car. What would become of my tuxie if this man hurt me? "Let me go!" I shouted, even though there wasn't anyone there who could hear me.

He pushed me toward the building. Was he going to try to take me inside? I wasn't going to let that happen. I remembered the self-defense training Rainwater had made me do. I stomped down hard on Scotty's instep, and he cried out. Before he could recover, I elbowed him in the gut, and he let me go. I leaped away.

"You—"

He didn't get to finish calling me whatever terrible name he planned to say, as two police cars careened around the corner and screeched to a halt in front of the detective's office.

Scotty swore and ran up the street.

"Police, stop!" a loud voice cried.

An officer in blue raced up the sidewalk and knocked into me, causing me to fall to the ground. About twenty yards away, he dove onto Scotty's back.

"Violet," a voice I knew all too well said.

I turned around and saw Rainwater standing in the middle of the dirty sidewalk. I sat there with my mouth hanging open.

Chapter
Twenty-Three

Rainwater extended a hand to me, and I took it. "Are you all right?" He helped me to my feet.

"I—I think so," I said, hating the fact that my voice shook. I cleared my throat, hoping to sound a bit more in control. "I mean, I'm fine."

He studied me. "What were you doing there with Jones?"

"I knew this was Redding's detective office . . ."

"And you thought it was a good idea to come here. Did you see the neighborhood? This is not a safe place for a naïve woman from Cascade Springs."

I put my hands on my hips. "I have spent most of my adult life living in worse neighborhoods than this as a grad student. I know how to handle myself."

He raised his hand. "Let's not argue about this here."

"So we are going to argue about it later?" I asked.

He gave me a look as the sprinting policeman who had catapulted himself onto Scotty's back walked the would-be P.I.

to us in handcuffs. The officer handed Scotty off to a female officer, who put him in the cruiser.

The first officer walked over to Rainwater and me. Rainwater held a hand to him. "That was a nice grab, Crump. If we ever have an interdepartmental relay competition, I want you on my team."

Crump laughed. "I only run to catch the bad guys. Well, that and if I'm chasing down an ice cream truck. I do love ice cream. I think after that snag I deserve a hot fudge sundae. I will get the fixings for my whole family on the way home. The kids love to hear about when I take down a bad guy."

"So Scotty is a bad guy?" I asked.

Crump nodded at me. "Who's this?"

"Violet Waverly. She's a citizen of Cascade Springs. She was visiting Redding's office when we came by."

The other officer's eyebrows went up, but he didn't say anything. I couldn't help noting that Rainwater didn't call me his girlfriend. I knew that it was to make things a bit easier for both of us. If the Niagara Falls police knew we were dating, there might be some complicated questions.

"Why did you arrest Scotty?" I asked. "I mean, I only knew him for five minutes when you all showed up, and I could tell he wasn't a great guy. But what did he do?"

The other officer raised his eyebrows at Rainwater again, this time the arch of his brow asking a silent question. Rainwater nodded. I must have passed some kind of unwritten cop test, because the officer said, "After looking at Redding's books, we saw that Jones was skimming money. Redding wasn't great at his bookkeeping and Jones took advantage of that."

"That's bad," I said. "But why did he run?"

The officer shrugged. "Because he's on parole for a similar crime to another company. He knew that if he violated his parole, he was going back to jail."

Maybe Scotty hadn't been interested in hurting me just before the cops arrived. Maybe he'd just wanted to know my secret so that he could make all the money Redding had bragged about if he learned the truth about me. Even if I didn't know that was true, it made me feel a bit better to believe it. Not that I ever planned to see Scotty again if I could help it, and it didn't sound like he would be getting out of jail anytime soon.

Crump shook Rainwater's hand again. "Hey man, I'm sorry I had to pull you into all of this, but you know with . . ." He trailed off when he glanced at me.

"You can speak freely in front of Violet."

Crump raised his eyebrows but didn't say anything against it. "Anyway, give your sister my condolences. She hasn't had an easy time of it."

"No, she hasn't," Rainwater said in a tight voice.

What did this have to do with Danielle? I bit the inside of my lip. I remembered that Simon Chase had said he'd seen Danielle arguing with Redding at the race registration table just an hour before the private eye died. Were the police trying to connect Danielle with Redding's murder? I'd have thought that if Rainwater was involved, he would have tried to do the opposite.

"It was a good grab," Crump said. "We'll take Jones to the jail and let him think things over. Any way you call it, he's in violation of parole. His officer is supposed to meet us there."

Rainwater nodded. "I would like a chance to question him about Redding." He paused. "And see what he knows about some other cases."

"Understood," Crump said. "Stop by the jail tomorrow, and we will give you the time."

Rainwater shook the other officer's hand.

"We picked you up. Do you need a lift back to Cascade Springs? I can get one of my rookies to take you back."

"We can take Violet's car back to the village," Rainwater said, hiding emotion from his face.

I knew him well enough now that I could see it. Rainwater was upset. I wasn't sure if I was in trouble with him or not, but I was certain I would find out when I was alone with him in my car.

Crump nodded and went back to his cruiser.

Rainwater turned to me. "Let's go, Violet."

He sounded so tired that my heart ached for him. Whatever was going on weighed heavily on the police chief.

I unlocked the Mini and was grateful to see Emerson right where I'd left him. "Hello, Emerson," Rainwater said, not surprised in the least to see my cat sitting on the passenger's seat. He picked up the cat, folded his long body into the car, and set Emerson on his lap as he buckled himself in.

I put the key in the ignition. Two thousand questions were running through my head at the moment. There were so many that I didn't know which to ask first.

"I know you have a lot of questions, and I'll answer the ones that I can. Let's drive to the Falls. It's pretty at night, and we need to talk."

"All right," I said.

It was early evening, but still a few hours before the Falls lit up for the evening light show. Tourists milled around the park at the American Falls, but not nearly in the numbers I'd seen when I'd driven by earlier.

I parked in the visitor lot, and Rainwater and I got out of the car again. For a second time, I locked Emerson in the Mini. Through the windshield, I watched as he curled into a ball and fell asleep. I found Emerson's behavior suspicious at best.

Rainwater took my hand. I stared down at it.

He laughed. "We aren't in the village right now, and I'm technically off duty. If I want to hold your hand, I can." He looked at me with those amber eyes. "And I do."

I squeezed his hand. "Okay."

The police chief led me through the park. We could hear the rush of the river and feel the mist of the Falls before we saw them.

Rainwater looked down at me. "You're being awfully quiet. I thought for sure the moment we got into the car, you would quiz me."

"I don't know where to start."

"How about I start then?"

I nodded. Just then, the path opened and we saw the Falls. The setting sun glistened off the water rushing over the side of the American Falls. Below, two *Maid of the Mist* boats bobbed in the channel. On the Canadian side, tourists going to the Under the Falls excursions shuffled down the steps in lines, two dozen deep, wearing blue disposable ponchos. Tourists from all over the world were scattered along the shorelines, snapping away and posing for the perfect selfie with the Falls in the background. A collection of street vendors hawked everything from hot dogs to stuffed animals. Commerce was alive and well at one of the eight natural wonders of the world.

I looked over the basin to Canada and could see just as much commotion on that side as on the American side.

"You shouldn't have gone to Redding's office today," Rainwater began. "The office is in a bad neighborhood, and you could have gotten hurt."

I pulled my hand from his grasp and stared at the Falls. I knew he was only worried about me and cared about my safety, but at the same time, it felt like a scolding of sorts. Knowing I wasn't on the moral high ground, I changed the subject. "Is Danielle okay? Is she involved in this mess with Redding somehow? And why was Scotty arrested? Do you think Scotty killed Redding because Redding found out about the missing money from his business?"

Rainwater threw back his head and laughed.

I stepped back and folded my arms. "I don't see what's so funny."

"It's funny that all your questions came out at once. I knew they were in there somewhere."

I cracked a smiled. "Oh, well, that's not all of them. I have many more."

He took my hand again. "I don't doubt it in the least." He took a breath, turning serious again. "But why did you go to Redding's office?"

"I thought I could find out some answers . . ." I trailed off. I couldn't tell Rainwater I was looking for answers related to my shop and to Jo. He didn't know the truth about the shop. Guilt ate at me at the thought. This man—this incredibly brave, self-less, good man . . . he deserved better than half-truths and prevarications from me. I knew one day soon I'd need to make a decision to bring him fully into my world or I'd have to set him free. A man like Rainwater deserved complete honesty. I glanced up at him and hoped that something of the way I felt—all those good feelings—was something he could see.

"Violet?"

Unsure what I could say, what I was ready to say, I changed the subject. "That self-defense training came in handy."

He grunted. "I wish you wouldn't put yourself in situations where you need those skills."

I didn't say anything. We both knew I wouldn't be promising I would do that. I wanted to be safe too, but I had a need to learn the truth, especially when I was helping a friend like Jo.

Rainwater led me to an open place at the rail around the American Falls. There was no one close enough to hear us over the rushing water. He stared down at that churning water like it might tell him something.

I placed my hand on his arm. "Are you okay?" I had never seen Rainwater so down. I had seen him irritated, mad, afraid, and stern, but never, in the time I'd known him, sad.

He took a breath and nodded. "The man who went over the Falls earlier in the week was my former brother-in-law, Aster's father, Bryant Cloud."

That was the last thing I had expected him to say.

Chapter
Twenty-Four

I covered my mouth. "Are you sure?"

"Positive. I went to the station in Niagara Falls and identified the body myself." He stared out at the water.

"Oh no! Is Danielle okay? Is Aster? Does Aster know?"
Again, I hit him with rapid-fire questions.

He shook his head. "No. Danielle doesn't want to tell her
yet. I don't know how she will tell her. Aster is only six. She
can't really understand, and her father hasn't been a part of her
life the last couple of years since they moved in with me. At
first Danielle had a restraining order to keep him away from
them, and then when the order was lifted and we didn't hear
from Bryant, Danielle and I were both relieved."

"Do they know what happened?"

"He was shot and fell into the water just north of the Falls."

"Shot? None of the news sources said that."

"The Niagara Falls police were keeping it quiet until the
body could be identified. He was badly beaten up in the water."
He grimaced. "And from going over the edge of the Falls.

Crump said they won't be able to hold the fact that it was murder back from the media much longer. The people in our tribe and who know my sister will know that Danielle was his ex-wife. There is a good chance I won't be able to protect her or Aster from the media."

Poor Danielle.

"What made the Niagara Falls police come to you for the ID?"

"Dental records." He sighed. "They asked me to come down to identify the body rather than my sister as professional courtesy."

"Why was he near the river?" I asked.

"He might have been fishing. They found his gear and truck upriver. He certainly was drinking. His alcohol levels were twice the legal limit when he was shot."

"Could it have been a hunting accident?" I asked.

"Not one I've ever heard of. The bullet that hit him was from a handgun."

"How awful," I said, but at the same time I wondered what any of this had to do with Redding.

"Even in death he manages to hurt my sister." Rainwater's face was a hard mask.

I felt the spray of the Falls on my cheeks. Ten yards up from us, another couple held on to each other as they looked at the Falls. They had that just-married glow, as Niagara Falls was a common location for a quick wedding. It was a romantic place. There was a reason so many people eloped here. I had wanted to come here with Rainwater, but our schedules were such that we had never made the time. I'd always thought we would visit during the summer when my classes were over. I certainly hadn't thought it would be under these circumstances.

"You were the one who told her," I said.

He looked down at me.

"When you took her from the café, it was about her ex-husband."

He nodded.

"I thought . . ."

"What did you think, Violet?" He was staring at me with those unique amber eyes again. Sometimes I felt I could melt into them, and other times, like now, I felt like they were hot pieces of glass reflecting myself back at me, not letting me peek inside his soul at all.

"I thought that it might have been about Redding. I know she and Redding had an argument before the race started."

"I'm not going to bother asking you how you know that."

"Good." I didn't want to have to bring Simon into this.

"What did they fight about?" I asked.

He looked out to the water again. "It was about Bryant. When Danielle first left him because he was physically and emotionally abusive to her and she was afraid he would do the same to her daughter, she and Aster went to New York City." He wouldn't meet my eyes. "She thought in the midst of all those people, she could hide." He gripped the railing. "She didn't come here to me first. She was too embarrassed." He took a breath and let it out. "Bryant wasn't going to let her go without a fight, so he hired Redding to find her."

I swallowed. All the words I wanted to say were caught in my throat.

"When Redding found her, she finally called me. She was afraid. Of course I dropped everything and brought her and Aster home."

I didn't say it, but that gave Danielle motive. It also gave Rainwater motive. I wondered if the reason neither of them was being questioned was because the man next to me was the one asking the questions.

"So you knew Redding before he came to Cascade Springs last year, before he tried to pin another murder on Lacey?"

He shook his head. "I didn't know that it was the same P.I. who had tracked my sister down. She didn't know his name and never saw him in the village. She wasn't in the café the times that he dropped by to speak to Lacey, so she didn't alert me it was the same man."

"Do you know why she would be talking to Redding before the race?"

"She was scared. She thought he was there because Bryant sent him after her again. She was asking him to leave the village, to leave her alone."

"But Redding denied that?" I was assuming things at this point and wanted David to provide the specific details instead.

He nodded. "According to my sister, he said his visit to the village had nothing to do with her. He said he hadn't even known she was in Cascade Springs. Danielle took his word for it and went back to the café."

"Danielle told you all that?"

He scowled at me. "Yes, and she doesn't have any reason to lie about it."

"Except that her ex-husband had died just a few days before."

"She didn't know that it was Bryant who went over the Falls. No one knew until after Redding was killed."

Obviously, Danielle would have known if she'd had something to do with Bryant's death and then maybe with Redding's too. I knew Rainwater must have seen the potential of trouble for his sister, even if he refused to admit it to me. He was a good cop, and even more, he was a smart man.

Rainwater ran his hand back and forth through his black hair. "I don't know how, but I have a feeling that these two deaths are connected. I just can't make sense of it."

"It seems to me that Redding is the tie." I almost added that it seemed to me his sister was the tie, but I didn't have to say it. I knew Rainwater already knew that.

He dropped his hand. "Do you know what the worst part of this is?"

I shook my head. The lights around the Falls were starting to blink on.

"The worst part of this is Danielle still loves him, and she blames herself that he's dead. Now she will have to carry that guilt with her, even if she did nothing wrong and even if the guilt is misplaced, which it is."

"But he hit her. He sent a private investigator after her," I said. "How can she still love him?"

He glared at me. "I'm not saying it's rational. But I know from watching my sister and being a police officer that whatever my sister's relationship with Bryant was, it wasn't real love, not selfless love. However, knowing that doesn't change how she feels about him."

I held up my hands as if in surrender. "I'm sorry. I can't know how she must feel."

He wrapped his arms around me. "I know. I'm sorry for becoming angry with you. I just want Danielle and Aster to be safe. I want all the women I love to be safe." He kissed the top of my head.

As we walked away from the Falls, I thought about who "all the women" Rainwater loved must be.

Chapter
Twenty-Five

Rainwater and I walked back to my car in silence, both lost in our thoughts. I didn't know what Rainwater was thinking when we walked through the park. His sister would be my best guess, but I was thinking of Walt Whitman. Whitman had visited the famous Falls on at least two occasions, once before the Civil War as a young man and once as an old man.

In the nineteenth century, Niagara Falls was one the most recognizable landmarks in the country. Travelers came from all over to see its majestic waters. In Whitman's day, the Falls were even more powerful than they are today. None of the water was dammed off to harness its power for electricity. The water poured undisturbed over the cliff, just as it had for thousands of years.

Whitman, with dreams of being the first great American poet, loved to wax on about the great vista and landmarks of the country to show its wonders and size. Naturally, Niagara Falls was on his list of landmarks to praise.

As we reached my car, Rainwater said, "I can drive."

I gladly handed over my keys. I was too deep in thought to insist on driving my car back to the village, and it would be nice to allow my mind to wander. Thankfully, when I opened the passenger side door, I saw Emerson just where I had left him. I picked him up and took my seat, settling the little tuxie on my lap.

The sun was starting to set. Charming Books would close soon. I shot my grandmother a text asking her to close up the shop for Richard and promised I would be there as soon as I could.

As we rolled out of the parking lot, Rainwater said, "You've been awfully quiet. What are you thinking about?"

"Dead poets," I answered honestly.

He chuckled. "I thought you were going to say murder, but that sounds about right."

He didn't know that, for me, many times dead poets are related to murder.

"You are thinking of Walt Whitman, aren't you?"

I started and turned to the police chief. "How did you know that?"

"*Leaves of Grass* was found with Redding's body."

I shivered. That was right. I didn't know how I could have forgotten. I knew, or hoped I knew, that the shop's essence didn't work outside the shop. The book was on Redding's person before he died because Redding had bought it at the shop, as Richard said. I didn't know why he had bought the title, the same title the shop's essence had revealed to me again and again.

"And," Rainwater went on, "we were at Niagara Falls, a place Whitman wrote about many times. He was fascinated with the power of the place. 'Under Niagara, the cataract falling like a veil over my countenance.' That's from 'Song of Myself.'"

"I know," I said, staring openly at him. "How do you know?"

"You know that I always wanted to be a writer, but I don't think I ever told you that I studied literature in school. I was an English major in college before I changed course and went into the police academy."

"I hadn't known that," I said. "Why haven't you ever told me before?"

He gave me a half smile. "It feels a little strange to admit you know a bit about literature to a person who has spent her entire life studying it. I suppose I didn't want to make a fool of myself in front of a scholar, especially a scholar I wanted to impress."

A flush crept onto my cheeks. Rainwater had wanted to impress me even when we first met? This caught me by surprise. The first time we'd met, he had thought I'd killed a man, or at least covered up the fact that Grandma Daisy had killed a man. We had both been proven innocent, of course, but still it seemed to me that would have been a rocky start. "And now you are all right revealing your education to me?" I asked, doing my best to cover my embarrassment, but I knew that with my pale skin and red-blonde hair, it was a pointless attempt.

He laughed. "I suppose I think you know me well enough now that you won't judge me as harshly."

"I wouldn't judge you at all," I said quietly, and stroked Emerson's back. The tuxie began to purr. As he did, he watched Rainwater intently. It was almost like he was following the conversation too.

"I know that now," he said. "You're not like some academics that I have known. Not counting Richard, of course. He's always kind."

I nodded. Truer words had never been said about the department chair. I supposed that was why I wanted so badly for him to tell Renee how he felt. They were both good people, and I wanted them to be happy. If they could be happy together, all the better.

"Do you have any guesses as to why Redding had that book in his possession?" Rainwater asked.

"There's nothing to say that the man didn't have a taste for poetry."

Rainwater shook his head. "Maybe, but he bought the book at your shop."

"Did Richard tell you that?"

Rainwater shook his head. "He didn't have to. Redding's credit card statements did the talking. That book was the last item he purchased before he died, and right after that purchase he went to the Riverwalk, had a heated conversation with my sister, got a bike from Jo, and took off in the race during which he died."

"So the question is, who tampered with the bike, knowing that Jo was going to give it to him."

"Jo Fitzgerald is the most likely suspect. She was the one who was there with the bike. She was also alone with the bikes while Bobby was away from the registration desk."

I frowned. "Bobby was alone with the bikes as well."

"Violet, I know that you don't want one of your students to be involved, but she had the best opportunity to tamper with the bikes."

"She's not just my student; she's my friend. Besides, she doesn't have a motive."

He frowned. "You have me there. Murder does usually come down to motive. It's the driving force."

I let out a breath. Maybe he wasn't completely sure that Jo was behind the murder. There was no practical reason for her to do it. "Who are the other people who might have wanted Redding out of the way?"

"The problem with Redding is he has a long list of enemies. The Niagara Falls police have been helping me follow leads as they can, but they have a big caseload and can't dedicate that much time to it."

"Who are his enemies?"

"Who wasn't? The man exceled in finding cheating spouses—that was where the majority of his cases came from. He was known in the region as the go-to guy if you wanted a divorce. There is a long list of former husbands and wives who aren't heartbroken over his death."

"Was he getting threats from any of them?"

He shook his head. "Not that we could find, but overall, Redding's files, both paper and digital, were very thin. It seemed that he kept most of his information about his cases in his head. That information is gone now."

That sounded like Redding to me. If he was secretive enough that he wouldn't tell his apprentice investigator why he was interested in me, then it was unlikely he'd recorded it anywhere Scotty could find it. This was a relief, but it was maddening when trying to find out who might have wanted to kill him.

Rainwater held the steering wheel until his knuckles turned white.

"What is it?"

"I want to tell you more about the case."

"I'm happy to listen."

He glanced at me. His amber eyes were the unreadable glass again. "I know, but it is my hope that when you hear how complicated it is, you'll let me handle it."

I didn't say anything.

Rainwater sighed, and I assumed that meant he wasn't going to say anything more about it. Then after a beat, he said, "Redding may be an expert on cheating spouses because he has experience in it personally."

I raised my eyebrows.

"His ex-wife had two restraining orders out on him over the course of the last year. There were countless domestic calls to their home when they were married."

"About what?" I bit my lip. "Did he hurt her?"

He shook his head. "The contrary, actually. She's a volatile person, and the calls were on her. From the police reports I read, she believed he was cheating while they were married."

"Was he?"

"He denied it. There was no evidence that he was. No woman ever came forward."

I thought about that for a minute. Could there be some scorned lover in Redding's past who'd tampered with his bike to exact her revenge?

"How long has he been divorced?"

"At least five years."

I frowned. That was a long time to wait to exact revenge, although it wasn't unheard of.

I shivered and touched my arm where Scotty had held me. "Scotty has to be a suspect too. I got the feeling in our brief encounter."

"Scotty is a suspect for a lot of things. He's not a good guy, but he has an alibi."

"What's that?"

"Part of his parole is living at a halfway house. Curfew was at eight. He was in the house until eight the next morning. There was no way he could make it to Cascade Springs and tamper with the bike before the race started at eight thirty."

"But couldn't the bike have been tampered with at any time? We keep thinking that it happened the morning of the race, but we don't really know that."

"We think that because Bobby insisted that he checked all the bikes to make sure they were in perfect working order before the race."

"That's Bobby's word, and Bobby is a suspect."

Rainwater sighed. "You aren't saying anything that I haven't already considered."

"There has to be something you haven't considered, something that we're both missing."

He glanced at me. "If anyone can figure out what that is, it will be you." He didn't say it like it was a compliment.

Chapter
Twenty-Six

The rest of the ride back to the village, Rainwater and I were lost in our thoughts. Emerson appeared to be contemplating something too, but it seemed to me the little tuxie was always considering what sort of trouble he could get into.

Rainwater parked my Mini under the gas lamppost in front of Charming Books. "I should go," David said.

"The lights are still on in the store. I think Richard and maybe Grandma Daisy must still be here. Why don't you come in and say hello?"

He smiled. "Since it might be Daisy, I will. She would never forgive me if I just snuck off without saying hi."

I smiled and opened my door. Emerson jumped off my lap and disappeared into the shrubs around the side of the house. I wasn't too worried about him wandering off here, since he was back in his element.

Before I could get out of the car, Rainwater grabbed my hand and held me in place. "Please, Violet, be more careful. If for nothing else, for me."

I stared into his eyes. This time the barrier wasn't up, and I could see that he meant every word. I swallowed hard. "I'll try to be more careful."

He kissed me softly on the mouth. "Thank you." He let go of my hand and got out of the car.

I took a deep breath and got out too.

When Rainwater and I stepped into the shop, I pulled up short.

"Violet, are you okay?" he whispered in my ear.

His strong hand was on my back. My grandmother and Fenimore were sitting in front of the quiet fireplace drinking tea. Fenimore's guitar leaned up against the hearth like that was where it belonged. Beside it on the floor were two black guitar cases. One was worn and the other looked new. I recognized them both.

Grandma Daisy looked up at us with a smile. "Violet, you didn't tell me you invited Fenimore over for a visit."

I swallowed and looked around the room for any sign of Richard.

As if she could read my mind, Grandma Daisy said, "Richard is gone for the day. I closed up the shop like you asked when you weren't back. Richard was very eager to return home and read all the books he miraculously found in our store. He is quite impressed with our collection."

I bet he was, I thought, resisting the urge to glance at the tree.

"We have a lot to talk about," Grandma Daisy said. "But I told Fenimore that we shouldn't begin until you were here. We have had a nice visit talking about his music in the meantime. You might be surprised that he's recorded an album."

Fenimore blushed. "It was over twenty years ago. I went to Nashville with high-minded dreams. It was just some folk music."

"I was just telling him he should release it on the Internet." She smiled. "I'm sure Violet knows someone from the college who can help you with that."

I did know people at the college who could help him with that, but I wasn't in the right mind-set to be helping Fenimore out with much of anything just yet. I needed a bit of time.

Rainwater looked at Fenimore and then my grandmother. "Should I leave? Is there some kind of problem here?"

"There's no problem." I grabbed his hand. "And please stay. I want you here."

Fenimore looked at our intertwined hands, and an expression of understanding dawned on his face.

"Violet, what's going on?" Rainwater whispered. He sounded so tired and concerned at the same time. I knew Danielle's situation with the murder investigation must be weighing heavily on him. I debated letting him leave so as not to burden him with my own troubles. Then I realized that would be the last thing he wanted me to do.

"You shared your complicated family with me. Now I need to share mine with you," I whispered back, and then I pulled him toward the fireplace. "David Rainwater, this is Fenimore James."

Rainwater nodded. "I know Fenimore from the times he's played his guitar in the village."

I gave him a half smile. "I know you do. What you don't know is Fenimore is my father."

Fenimore stood up from the sofa where he had been sitting and held his hand out to the police chief. "It's very good to officially meet you, David. Daisy here has been singing your praises." He shared his smile with me too. "Actually, she's been singing the praises of both you and Violet."

Rainwater smiled and seemed to have recovered from the initial shock of hearing who Fenimore was. "I'm sure she has, but Daisy is pretty amazing herself. The first female mayor of the village."

My grandmother grinned. "And over seventy too. Better late than never." She patted the seat beside her. "Sit, sit! Fenimore has something to tell us."

Rainwater opted to remain standing and leaned against the fireplace. My legs were shaking ever so slightly, not enough for anyone to notice other than me, but I didn't trust them to hold me up anymore, so I perched on the couch next to my grandmother.

She slipped her hand in mine and squeezed my fingers before folding her hands on her lap. "What was it that you want to tell us, Fenimore?"

The troubadour licked his lips. "I just wanted to say I'm sorry to both of you, Daisy and Violet, but to Violet especially. I should have come to you sooner and told you who I am and who I was to Fern. I suppose putting it off year after year was easier, and the longer I waited to tell you, the harder I thought it would be for you to accept who I am." He pulled his ponytail over his shoulder and tugged on it like it was some kind of comfort to him. "But Violet, when I saw you in the village last year and you looked so much life Fern, I couldn't stay away. Just like her, you had a presence about you. When you walk into the room, everyone notices, and by some miracle you have no idea that's happening."

"That's true," Rainwater said.

I looked at him in surprise.

Fenimore let go of his ponytail and sat up a little straighter in his seat. "I know I shouldn't have waited all these months to speak to you again, but I had to build up the nerve to ask you, and you too, Daisy, one question."

"What's that?" Grandma Daisy asked. She was holding my hand again. I hadn't even noticed that she had moved her hand back.

"Will you forgive me?" His voice was small, not much louder than that of a child asking forgiveness for stealing a cookie from the kitchen.

Grandma Daisy looked to me. It seemed I was the one who had to answer this question.

I felt my shoulders droop. Most of my life I had wondered who my father was, but I had never had the urge to find out. I didn't know how I could have, since my mother had left his name blank on my birth certificate. I'd put it out of my head until last fall when Fenimore had shown up on my doorstep with a letter. Since then, I had thought of him almost constantly, wondering where he was, whether if I should go and find him. It hadn't been until I knew I had a father that I realized I had missed having one, not just since seeing Fenimore but my whole life. I had buried that longing so deep that when it was woken up, it pained me.

I stared down at my grandmother's wrinkled hand over mine once again. She was all the family I had in the world, and Fenimore was giving me an opportunity to have more. I swallowed and looked up and found Rainwater watching me. He smiled at me, and I felt better. I did have other family. I had him, Lacey and Adrien, Sadie, and the Red Inkers. I had this village. Emerson, Faulkner, and this shop. That didn't mean there wasn't room for more. There was always room for someone else to love in your life if they will let you; not everyone lets you love them. How could I turn my back on that chance?

I turned to Fenimore, who was staring at his hands. "I forgive you," I said. There was no quaver of hesitation in my voice. It was strong and clear, and I meant every word of that brief sentence.

He looked at me as if in awe. I knew then that he'd expected my answer to be very different. I couldn't blame him for that. Months ago when he'd told me who he was, I had refused to believe him. It had been very brave of him to come back at all.

"Thank you, Violet," he said.

"Good, good," Grandma Daisy said. "Now that we got that over with, I will make some tea, and we all can have a nice chat." She smiled at Rainwater. "Have a seat, David. We can't have you standing in front of the fireplace like a statue."

Faulkner swooped down from the tree, and Fenimore jumped. The large crow settled next to Rainwater on the hearth. A moment later, Emerson materialized and jumped up next to me. He circled twice before settling himself onto my lap.

"Looks like the whole family is ready for a visit," my grandmother said cheerfully. "That seems fitting."

That's what I thought too.

Chapter
Twenty-Seven

The conversation with Fenimore was awkward at first, but it wasn't long before Grandma Daisy, with her tea and good humor, smoothed everything over. At one point, Emerson jumped off of me and sat on the sofa next to Fenimore. The cat stared at me with his yellow-green eyes as if to tell me everything would be all right. I believed him, if only for that moment.

Fenimore told us about his childhood growing up in Buffalo and how he'd met my mother that fateful summer she got pregnant while he was in the village for a summer job at the height of the tourist season. He smiled at the memory. "Your mother was so self-confident. I think that's what attracted me to her the most. She told me from the beginning that it would never last. She said she loved me, but her life was such that she couldn't have love. I was so hurt that at the end of the summer when she told me to leave, I did. I didn't know she was pregnant. I like to think, had I known, before she died things might have gone a lot differently."

So differently, I thought. I might not have grown up in Charming Books, I realized as I looked around the store. After my mother died, my father would have been within his rights to have me live with him. I would not have been there when my best friend Colleen died when we were seventeen. That was hard to fathom. Second only to my mother's death, Colleen's death had been the most life-changing event in my life. It made me run away from the village and stay away for twelve years until Grandma Daisy tricked me into coming back.

I've learned that death changes you like nothing else can. It doesn't matter if it's a long demise like my mother's or a split second like Colleen's passing. If you are the one left behind, you either come out better having survived it or worse. There is no in between.

Fenimore stood, opened the worn guitar case, and placed his guitar inside it. "It is late, and I need to be going back to Niagara Falls tonight. With all the festivities over in the village, it's best if I move on to the next place."

I felt my heart constrict. There were so many more questions I wanted to ask him. What were my mother's dreams? Did she ever want to leave the village? I knew now that since she was destined to be the Caretaker, she couldn't, but was there a time when she wanted to strike out from this small place? All of those questions were on the tip of my tongue and not one of them came out, but did he even know the answer to any of them? Instead I asked, "How did you get that other guitar case, Fenimore?"

Rainwater looked at the newer of the two cases.

"It belongs to Joel Redding, doesn't it?" I asked.

Fenimore straightened up. "I brought it here because I believe that it does."

"Where did you find it?" Rainwater asked.

"It was in the woods not far from the Riverwalk. It was just left there. No one claimed it, but it's a nice case, so finders keepers, you know." He licked his lips. "Then, with all I had heard about happening in the village, I thought I should get rid of it. I don't want to be tied to that murder. I didn't do it."

"Why do you think this would tie you to the murder?" Rainwater asked.

"I saw the man who died with the very same case earlier in the week. He was with another man."

"Who was the other man?" Rainwater asked.

"Don't know." Fenimore shook his head. "But he was Native American like you."

I stifled a gasp. It must have been Bryant Cloud. I glanced at Rainwater, but his stoic expression gave away nothing. At least now we knew Cloud and Redding were connected and what had happened to Redding's guitar case. I wondered if he'd stashed it in the woods before he got the bicycle from Jo. That made the most sense.

"I'm going to keep that guitar case," Rainwater said. He walked over and took it from Fenimore's hand. Then he set it on the floor. "Have you opened this?" Rainwater asked Fenimore.

Fenimore swallowed. "There's nothing in there but a bunch of papers."

"Did you remove anything from the case?" Rainwater's voice was sharp.

"No. I mean, I planned too, but I haven't yet."

Rainwater's eyes narrowed. "It's a good thing that you didn't. If you had, you would have been charged with tampering with evidence."

Fenimore's face grew red. "I wasn't tampering with nothing. And it's always been a rule of finders keepers."

"Not when there is a murder involved," Rainwater said. He removed latex gloves from his jacket pocket, put them on, and opened the case.

Both Grandma Daisy and I as well as Faulkner leaned in to take a look at the inside of the guitar case. Fenimore was right. It was full of a bunch of papers.

"Most of these are blank," Rainwater said in frustration.

Silently, I let out the breath I was holding. I had a fear that one of those papers would say, VIOLET WAVERLY LIVES IN A MAGICAL BOOKSHOP! That wouldn't do at all.

Rainwater moved the papers around and then said, "What's this?" He held up a black box cutter. He opened the blade, and it glistened in the lamplight.

"Why would a private eye need a box cutter?" Grandma Daisy asked. "Did he use it to break into somewhere?"

"Or," I said, "was this the tool used that cut the brake line in Redding's bike?"

Rainwater looked up at me. "I think you might be right about that, Violet."

Faulkner flapped his wings and cawed as his flew to the top of the birch tree. From there, he glowered down at us.

I found myself staring at Fenimore. Could he have something to do with the murder? I felt sick just thinking about.

Fenimore paled. "I—I didn't know that was in there. I just saw the papers and closed it back up. I don't want it. You can have it. I don't want anything to do with it."

"I will have my techs run it against the cut in Redding's brake line, but I'm betting this was the knife that cut his brake.

It might be difficult to prove, but if you look here, there is a nick on the blade. That might make it unique enough for a match."

*   *   *

Rainwater stood up in front of the birch tree with his back to us. He held his hands behind his back as he stared up at the tree. I could almost hear the wheels turning in his head. He had so many questions about the shop and the tree. I knew that he suspected something.

Fenimore looked at Rainwater. "I just took the case. I didn't know what was in it. I wouldn't have taken it if I knew that it was going to cause me so much bother."

"Let me walk you out, Fenimore," Grandma Daisy said. "I should be heading home too. I have a long day of meetings tomorrow. I've learned ninety percent of politics is sitting in meetings that seem to have no resolution at all." She smiled. "It's a miracle I got the museum through the village council the first time. If they knew all the issues we would have with the hall's foundation, it never would have passed."

"You're a force of nature, Daisy, just like Fern was," Fenimore said.

"You have no idea, Fenimore," I said, following them to the door.

He turned to me. "There's something else about the murder . . ."

"What about the murder?" I asked.

"I may know something about the man who died. You can't move through the village without hearing the whispers about it. I mean, I know something more than that that"—he pointed at the guitar case on the floor—"was his."

Rainwater turned away from the tree. "What else do you know?" His penetrating stare was on Fenimore now, and the older man seemed to cower beneath it.

"H—he spoke to me the day before the race."

"About what?"

"He asked me if I had seen anything odd in the village. Was there anything about it that didn't seem just right? He was especially interested in Charming Books."

I frowned.

"I told him that I was no help to him," my father continued. "I hadn't been inside the shop in decades."

"Anything else?" Rainwater asked.

"I—I think I saw the person who might have tampered with the bicycle."

Rainwater took a step forward. "Why haven't you come forward before?"

"I didn't feel right about doing it." He glanced at me. "I believe she's a friend of Violet's."

I felt my stomach twist in a knot.

"What did you see?" Rainwater asked.

"It was just after dusk the night before the race, and the bicycles were already at the Riverwalk, or at least some of them were. I saw a girl walking from bike to bike like she was checking them. One of the bikes she stopped at for a long time. I think it must have been the bike that the private detective rode."

"How do you know?" I asked.

"I suppose I can't be sure it was the same bike," Fenimore said.

"Was anyone else around?" Rainwater asked.

Fenimore tugged on his ponytail again. "There were a lot of people in and around the bikes before the race. It would be impossible to see what each one of them was doing. Almost all of them visited the red-and-silver bicycle."

"That means any one of them could have tampered with it," I argued. "It would only take a matter of seconds to cut the brake lines if you knew what you were doing, and these were serious riders. They all knew what they were doing."

Rainwater gave me a look as if to say, *That's a hollow argument, even for you.* "What did she look like?" the police chief asked Fenimore.

"She was small. Very small."

I felt my stomach drop. It was Jo.

Rainwater glanced at me. "What else about her stood out to you?"

"When she turned around, I saw that her eyebrow was pierced."

What had Jo gotten herself tangled up in? I needed to ask her, but I would have to find her first. Maybe her brother knew where she was.

"What times was this?" Rainwater asked.

"I would say about ten in the evening the night before the race."

"What were you doing at the Riverwalk after dark?" Rainwater asked.

"Waiting for the race to begin."

"The race was ten hours away," Rainwater said.

I cringed. I hoped Fenimore could see that his argument wasn't working with the police chief. However, all I could think was that I believed Fenimore was telling the truth that Jo had been alone with Redding's bike the night before he died. However, that didn't mean she'd done anything. She didn't have a motive. That was my saving grace in all of this. Without that, the police didn't have a case, or at least I hoped that was true.

"What were you doing at the Riverwalk?" Rainwater repeated.

Fenimore cleared his throat, and his Adam's apple bobbed up and down. "I was staying there for the night. I didn't have a sleeping bag or anything like that."

"Now, David," Grandma Daisy said. "Fenimore didn't know. Now that he knows, he won't do it again."

"I won't," Fenimore promised.

I was willing to bet Fenimore had known he'd been camping illegally, but I didn't say that. I was certain Rainwater was thinking the same thing.

"I thought you had a house in Niagara Falls," I said. "It's a short drive from the city to the village. Why didn't you go home for the night?"

He looked at me and then at the floor. "I sold that house. I needed money. I'm not home very much anyway. I live by my wits."

My goodness, my father was, what? Homeless?

"Did you see anything else while you were camping?" Rainwater asked.

"The next morning, that man Redding was one of the first men I saw at the Riverwalk. He was there right after sunrise, even before any of the race coordinators were there."

"What was he doing?" I asked.

Fenimore shrugged. "I think he was looking for something. He was snooping around all the bikes, even the silver-and-red one that he rode in the race. I think he would have kept searching until people started to show up for the race if he hadn't seen me."

"What did he do when he saw you?" I asked, feeling grateful that Rainwater wasn't telling me to stop asking questions.

"He asked if I saw anyone in the night around the bikes. I said that I did, and I described the girl to him just like I have to you. He seemed to know who I meant."

If Redding had known who Fenimore meant, that meant Redding and Jo had known each other. That wasn't a great thing to hear, because if she knew him, she might have a motive. If she had a motive, I didn't know what I could do to stop Rainwater from believing she was the killer.

"There is another thing," Fenimore said with his hand on the doorknob. "He asked me about you, Violet. He wanted to know what I knew about you." He glanced at Rainwater. "And then he asked me how long I had known I was your father. That's why when I saw you in the village again, I asked if you told anyone who I was. Somehow he already knew."

His words rang in my ears. *Somehow he already knew.* I shivered.

I felt Rainwater watching me.

"I didn't like the fact that he asked that," Fenimore said. "Every time that I would see you, he was nearby. He was watching you."

Fenimore's statement could mean only one thing. When Redding had been watching me, so was Fenimore. That wasn't creepy or anything.

After Fenimore finally left for the night, Grandma Daisy followed suit. But I knew she was just making herself scarce to give Rainwater and me time to talk. She gave me a hug at the door and whispered in my ear, "Tell him. It's time."

But how could I tell him about the shop's essence at a time like this? Wouldn't it be better to wait until the investigation into Redding's death was over, or at least until after we weren't at odds over Jo's involvement? Even though, after what Fenimore had said, I could see that things weren't looking good for my student.

"I need to talk to Jo. The problem will be finding her first." Rainwater ran his hand through his short black hair. "Someone has to know where she's staying."

I almost mentioned her brother but stopped myself at the last second. Instead I said, "Sure, it sounds like Jo, but it could have been someone else. She's not the only college student with an eyebrow ring."

"Violet, there aren't many people who are Jo's stature who would be around the bikes the night before the race."

"Well then, if she was there, she would have been there for her job. She has been working for Bobby."

"I know, and maybe you're right and it will be easy for her to explain, but nothing changes the fact that I need to talk to her. If she's hiding, she's not helping her case."

"Maybe she doesn't know you're looking for her," I argued.

"Violet, the entire village knows I'm looking for her."

He had a point there.

He rubbed his cheek. "It's been a long day, a long few days, and we're both tired. Let's talk about this again in the morning."

I bit the inside of my lip. He was exhausted and so was I. No matter what my grandmother thought, now was not a good time to tell him that he was standing in the middle of a mystical bookshop with flying books. He needed his wits about him to fully absorb that.

Just as I made this decision, a book fell at Rainwater's feet. The sound of the book hitting the old worn plank wood floor was like a gong going off.

Faulkner squawked. "Quiet. I need quiet," he said. "I'm sleeping!"

"You're not sleeping if you are talking," I said to the bird. I knew I was making a lame attempt to distract Rainwater from the book. I made a move to pick it up, but the police chief was fast. He was closer to the book, after all. Even before he said a word, I knew what the title would be.

He picked up the book and stared at the cover. He flipped through the pages. "Something is going on here."

My mouth felt dry. Part of me just wanted to tell him, but I couldn't get the words out. They were stuck in my throat.

"I have no idea what's going on," Rainwater said slowly. "But I know Whitman's involved." He glanced at the tree and looked around the shop. "I know all of this is involved."

I still didn't say anything.

Quietly, Rainwater placed the book on the nearest bookshelf and picked up Redding's guitar case. At the door he said, "Someday, I want you to trust me enough to tell me whatever it is you're holding back."

And then he was gone.

Chapter
Twenty-Eight

The next morning, the shop was quiet, and I felt at a loss. I was used to going a million miles a minute, rushing from class to teach to the library to study to Charming Books to help Grandma Daisy at the shop. Now I had only one of those to do, and it felt off-putting.

I should enjoy the quiet. Charming Books would be overrun soon enough with summer tourists and special seasonal events. I should bask in the fact that there was nowhere I had to be, but I wasn't very good at sitting still. I never had been. Since I was a child, I had been moving toward the next achievement, the next goal. A psychologist had told me once that it was because my mother was sick for much of my young life and died when I was just thirteen. Achievements and goals were something I could control, when all I wanted to control was my mother's health. Maybe there was something to that.

The shop might be quiet, but I still had goals I wanted to achieve. The first of those was finding Jo. As I walked down the spiral staircase from my apartment to the main floor of

Charming Books, I glanced at my phone. Over the last two days I had texted Jo a dozen times, but there wasn't one return text. But as long as she had her phone with her, I knew the texts were getting through. According to my texting app, they had each been delivered and read.

At the cash register, I texted her again. IF YOU NEED HELP, LET ME KNOW. I'M YOUR TEACHER—AND YOUR FRIEND—FIRST. I WILL HELP YOU.

I waited for a reply. There was nothing. I started to put the phone back in my pocket when it pinged, telling me a new message was there. It was from Jo. A tiny heart emoji. I still didn't know what she was doing or where she was, but seeing that tiny little heart gave me hope that she was okay. Part of me wanted to text back and ask where she was, but I stopped myself. Maybe I needed to give Jo time to come to me, and I realized I needed time to read *Leaves of Grass*.

Emerson jumped on the sales counter, his thin black tail whipping back and forth. Beside the cash register, books of Whitman's poems were stacked seven high. I glanced at the tree. "Subtle."

The page of the book at the top of the pile began to flutter, and then it fell open. Even though I had seen the essence work dozens of times, it still surprised me. Emerson, who was still on the counter next to the books, arched his back and hissed.

I ran my hand along his back and smoothed down his coat. Faulkner flew down from his perch in the tree and landed on a bookcase just a foot away from us.

I looked at the two of them. "I guess we're all curious about what Whitman and the shop want to tell us." With tentative hands, I picked up the book and carried it to one of the sofas in front of the fireplace. I perched on the coffee table and read "To Think of Time" again.

Frowning, I read on.

> Not a day passes—not a minute or second, without an
> accouchement!
> Not a day passes—not a minute or second, without a
> corpse!

The shop was reminding me that death was unavoidable. This I already knew. Perhaps, given my experiences, it was something I knew better than most people my age. However, what did this passage have to do with Redding's death? I reexamined the line. *Accouchement* was an old-fashioned word for birth. Birth and death happened every day. Did Redding's death relate somehow to a birth? I couldn't think of any recent births in the village, but that didn't mean I didn't know about any. I would have to ask my grandmother. I thought the village made an announcement when a new villager was born. There were so few who lived in the village full-time that any babies were worth noting.

I couldn't see how that line applied at all. I went back to the previous stanza. The line that struck me the most was:

> Is to-day nothing? is the beginningless past nothing?
> If the future is nothing, they are just as surely
> nothing.

It seemed to me that Whitman was asking the big questions that no one, not him nor anyone since, could give a clear answer to. I laid the book on my lap and waited. There had to be something else the shop's essence wanted me to read. This couldn't be all of it. This couldn't be the end of the clues, because I wasn't any closer to understanding what the shop wanted me to know.

But the pages didn't move again.

I frowned and opened the book to a different page and read. Perhaps if I read the poems on my own, everything would be made clear. It was worth a shot.

Throughout the morning, a few customers came into the shop. All of them left with a book or two. The shop's essence always knew what someone wanted or needed to read. I only wished it was clear about what it wanted me to understand from *Leaves of Grass.*

After the last customer left the shop clutching a cookbook to her chest, I went back to the couches and sat cross-legged in the one closest to the cool fireplace.

When the book didn't open on its own, I opened it to arguably Whitman's most famous poem in the book, "Song of Myself."

A hand tapped me on the shoulder.

"Ahh!" I scream and threw my arm out. It connected with something soft. I blinked to see Richard standing in the middle of the shop.

"What are you doing?" I cried.

"You said you needed me to work this afternoon." He rubbed his stomach.

"I'm so sorry. Did I hit you? Are you all right?" I jumped off the couch and let the volume of Whitman fall to floor. I scooped it up.

"That was the book the private investigator bought when he was here."

"I know. It made me . . ." I paused. I tried to put into words my intentions without giving away too much. "Knowing that he read it . . . made me want to reread it."

He rubbed his goatee. "I was surprised that he chose Whitman. Of course, Whitman was the poet credited with creating American poetry. On the surface, his writing is deceitfully simple. It's when you dig deeper, the challenge appears."

I arched my brow. "Richard, you teach Shakespeare."

He laughed. "Shakespeare in my opinion is a little more accessible than Whitman."

I groaned. If Richard, who had spent the last forty-some years immersed in literature, had trouble understanding Whitman, I was doomed.

"I would think that you would have a better handle on the poet, since he's a contemporary of Ralph Waldo Emerson."

"I wish I could say that was true." I read him the last poem that the shop had revealed to me, the poem about birth and death. "What's you interpretation of that text?"

He paced back and forth in front of the fireplace, just like he did in the classroom in the middle of a discussion. Richard was a very good teacher and cared very much about connecting the great writers to the students in his class. "Of course it depends on what form of literary criticism you apply. With my students, I like to apply readers' responses to start. It shows them that literature is something to feel and to be experienced. I would ask you, then, what this means to you, Violet?"

I looked down at the passage again, feeling a little irritated that he wouldn't just give me the answer, but that wasn't

Richard's way. I almost didn't answer. "It's about life and death. Mortality and immortality."

"Is he telling the reader what to believe?"

I shook my head. "No. I wonder if he's talking about another death."

"What death?" Richard asked.

I didn't answer and simply stared at the pages in front of me. Was the shop telling me that Redding and Bryant Cloud's deaths were connected? Did I just want them to be?

"I have to go. Is there anything that you need?"

He blinked at me. "But I thought you wanted to discuss this piece of literature."

"Maybe another time, Richard. I promise." I headed to the door.

Chapter Twenty-Nine

Even on a slow weekday in the village, Le Crepe Jolie was busy between the lunch and dinner crowds. I didn't think I had ever been to the café when there wasn't another customer there. It was the most popular restaurant in the village and typically was included in the list of top places to eat for the region.

Lacey smiled at me when I walked in the door. "Here for a late lunch, Violet?"

"Maybe in a bit. Is Danielle here?"

Lacey's eyes went wide. "Is something wrong?"

There must have been something in my tone to trigger her concern.

I smiled. "Nothing is wrong."

She didn't look convinced. "She told us about her ex-husband. It's just horrible, and poor little Aster. I have no idea how she is going to tell her."

"She hasn't told her daughter yet?"

Lacey shook her head. "No, and I can't say that I blame her."

I didn't either.

"Right now, she's on her break. Usually if the weather is nice, she goes to the Riverwalk. You can look for her there," Lacey said, not looking any less worried than she had when I first walked in the café.

I smiled my thanks. "Okay, I'll go look for her, then."

"Would you like a baguette before you go?" she asked.

I would, but I didn't have time to waste if the poem was telling me there was a connection between Redding and Bryant. I had to find out what that connection might be. I left the café and walked across River Road to the Riverwalk.

Danielle was on a bench with her back to me, watching the rushing river. Her long black hair hung over one shoulder.

"Danielle?"

She turned, and there were tears in her eyes. Unlike her brother's, Danielle's eyes were a warm chocolate brown. "I have been wondering when you would come talk to me. I thought you might not because of my brother."

I smiled. "I don't want to upset David, but I need to know. One of my students from the college is in a lot of trouble. I have to help her."

She smiled. "I know you're a good teacher, Violet. I have overheard students studying in the café say how much they like you. They said you're hard but you make class fun."

"That's one of the best compliments any teacher can have."

"The student you're talking about is Jo Fitzgerald, right?"

I nodded.

"I know Jo," she said. "She's a good kid, just a little confused, and . . ." She trailed off.

"And what?"

She shook her head, and I decided to let it drop for the moment. It seemed to me that several people in the village knew something about Jo that I was missing.

"Can you tell me about Redding?"

She turned away from me and stared out at the churning river. "I guess it's better to start with Bryant. He was the most handsome man on the reservation, and he picked me. Maybe I was flattered at the beginning. Bryant and I got married very young. David told me that I shouldn't marry so young, but I didn't listen. I felt like I had been preparing to marry Bryant my whole life. We met as children, fell in love as teenagers, and it made sense to me that we would marry at the end of high school." She looked at her hands. "But it was never easy. Bryant was angry a lot of the time. To others he was kind and charming, but with me at home, he could be harsh. Nothing I did was right, and if I really made a mistake, he would hit me."

I squeezed her hand. "There is no mistake that you could ever make that warrants that. Ever."

She squeezed my hand back before she pulled hers away. "Then I got pregnant. I was so excited, but scared too. I didn't know what would happen when I had a baby. Bryant was so sweet to me while I was pregnant. He doted on me. He didn't hit me once. I thought that he had realized his mistakes and was cured. It wasn't long after the baby was born that I learned I was wrong, and he was back to the way he was before, maybe even worse. But he loved that baby and only looked on her with love. When the baby cried and woke him up, it was never her fault, only mine, and I was happy to take the blame for that. I loved her like I've never loved anyone else. I didn't know what true love was until Aster was born. She loved me back. I knew it.

"Things were fine for a while. Hard, but I found ways to not give him reasons to be upset, but as Aster grew older, that became more difficult. I saw that he was beginning to give her the angry looks that he first gave me. He started to speak to her harshly, and she would shrink away from him. I knew it wouldn't be long before he would hit her too. I left for Aster. He never hit her," she said quickly. "Only me."

I felt a lump in my throat. Those two words, *only me*, held so much weight.

"David knew none of this. He never liked Bryant, but he didn't know what he was really like. When I decided to leave, I was too scared to tell my brother. I was afraid he would be disappointed with me for staying so long. To me, that was almost harder to take than all the blows Bryant had given me over the years."

I cringed as she said this. I knew Rainwater would have dropped everything and run to his sister's defense. He would have dropped anything and run to anyone's defense in that situation. That was just the sort of man he was.

"So instead I ran away to New York City. I thought Aster and I could hide there. There were so many people, and there is a large Native American population there that I thought could help us get started. They did. I found a waitress job and a tiny studio apartment for us. My new friends watched Aster while I was at work. I was happy and I was free until Joel Redding showed up."

"Bryant had hired him to find you," I said.

She nodded. "'You weren't that hard to find.' That was the first thing he said to me, and I knew Bryant had sent him. I knew he would tell Bryant where I was, so I called David.

"David and Bryant showed up at the same time. It was a bad scene. The police arrested Bryant. David, for the next year, helped me navigate everything that I needed to do to get a divorce and full custody for Aster. It was awful." She looked at me with tears in her eyes. "Never once did David blame me for what happened. Never once did he complain he was being saddled with my daughter and me."

"He loves you both. He's happy that you're in the village. He wants you to live with him."

She wiped at her eyes. "I know that, but I want to be out on my own too, and David needs his own life. Now that he has you, I know things will change."

I wanted to ask her what she meant by that, but stopped myself. This conversation was for Danielle and what she needed to say, not about what he might have said to his sister about our relationship. "Tell me about when you saw Redding here in the village."

"He came into the café. I was carrying a tray of food to one of the tables. I was so shocked to see him that I dropped the tray, which was the worst thing I could have done. He saw me, and I know he recognized me. I cleaned up the mess the best I could. Lacey helped. She's so kind. Both she and Adrien are. I couldn't ask for better bosses." She looked out to the river again. "By the time we cleaned up the mess, Redding was gone."

"Did you tell your brother?"

She shook her head. "Maybe I should have, but I wasn't thinking straight. He had never met Redding. When he came to New York City to get Aster and me, I didn't tell him everything that happened. I couldn't bring myself to do it. As time went on, there didn't seem much point to telling him everything. Aster and I were in Cascade Springs; I started to work at the café. We were happy. I didn't feel the need to remember hard times."

I could understand that, but I wondered how much damage Danielle had done to herself by not talking about it. I wished she and I had been better friends and she had felt comfortable telling me about her past. Or that she had tried to talk to Lacey. Lacey had her own traumatic history. The two of them could have healed together, but that was an opportunity lost now.

"Seeing Redding here in the village made me ill. This was the place where I rebuilt my life, and he had no business being here."

"Did you see him when he was here in the winter?" I asked. "Redding was the investigator on the case involving Lacey's sister."

"When Lacey was accused of murder? No. I never saw him at the café, and Lacey never wanted to talk about what was happening. I knew what it was like to have secrets, so I didn't press her."

I nodded.

She rubbed her hands up and down her bare arms as if she felt a chill. "The next three days were horrible. I didn't see him again, but I was a mess. I kept thinking that Bryant would show up at any moment at the café, at our home, or even at Aster's school. In my head, I had it worked up that he was going to take my daughter away from me. I couldn't eat or sleep. David asked me again and again what was going on, but I couldn't bring myself to tell him. I wanted to pretend this wasn't happening." She gave me a wan smile. "But since I wasn't eating or sleeping, it was clear that I wasn't doing a very good job of it. Just when I was going tell my brother, I saw Redding again."

"Where?"

"Here at the Riverwalk. It was the day before the race. He was talking to Jo. Whatever he was saying clearly upset her. She ran away from him."

"Did you hear any part of the conversation?" I asked.

She shook her head. "No. I was in front of the café and they were across the street. I couldn't hear them."

I bit the inside of my lip. Danielle was the second witness to mention seeing Jo and Redding together. It was clear that she knew the private detective. What had she gotten tangled up in? The little heart emoji she'd sent me earlier in the day didn't seem as encouraging anymore.

Danielle took a shuddering breath. "After Jo left, I couldn't take it anymore. The worry I had over knowing Redding was in the village was too much. I went across the street and confronted him." She closed her eyes for a moment. "He seemed surprised that I would come at him in that way. I think most people who have met me don't think of me as a confrontational person. I'm usually not, but I had to do this to protect Aster. I love her."

I squeezed her hand. "I know you do. What happened next?"

"I asked him if Bryant was in the village, and he seemed surprised. I would even say that he seemed scared. Like me mentioning Bryant was not what he expected. I don't know what he thought I would say. He said Bryant wasn't here.

I asked him if Bryant sent him to find me, and he said no, he wasn't in the village because of me."

"Did you believe him?"

"I did because I wanted to, but I don't know if he was lying or not. He could have been. I'm sure that, because of his line of work, he was very good at lying."

I knew he was from my experience.

"Then when I heard Bryant had died, I was so confused. How could he happen to die when I had just seen Redding, and Redding was dead too? I can't believe that the two weren't connected. When you saw David speak to me at the café, he told me about my ex-husband. I was sad. I thought after all this time, after everything that he did, that I wouldn't be sad to learn he had died, but I was terribly upset. I suppose I still loved him in a way. He was my first love. I had loved him since I was a child. I'm not sure if I ever let him go."

I could understand that. I had been in love with the same man most of life until I met Rainwater. It had taken a very long time for me to let go.

"I can't believe the deaths aren't somehow connected to me, too. I was the only person in the village they both knew, as far as I know."

"Did he say why he was in the village?"

"He was on another case. He said the case was much bigger than mine."

A knot formed in my stomach. Could that reason be Charming Books?

"My people have said that this river is so powerful that it can give life and take life," she said in a soft voice. "That it can heal. These were the stories that David and I were raised on.

I think David has grown out of those stories. He is too much of a logical police officer. But I believe them. I like to think that there is a spirit in all things, just like our people have taught us. David might deny that, but I think deep down he still believes it too."

A snippet from the end of the last Whitman poem the shop had revealed to me came to mind.

> I swear I think now that every thing without exception
>   has an eternal soul!
> The trees have, rooted in the ground! the weeds of the
>   sea have! the animals!
>
> I swear I think there is nothing but immortality!
> That the exquisite scheme is for it, and the nebulous
>   float is for it, and the cohering is for it!
> And all preparation is for it—and identity is for it—
>   and life and materials are altogether for it!

Maybe that was the part of the poem I was supposed to read. Maybe Danielle had to be the one to show me that. If that was the case, what did it tell me about Redding's death? I didn't know.

Chapter Thirty

The next day, I asked Richard to open the shop, and he was more than happy to do so. Grandma Daisy was busy with meetings, and I didn't want to ask her.

No one had seen Jo Fitzgerald in days. I was worried about her. I knew she was an adult, but after seeing the calendar in her apartment with all those shifts to work and classes to attend, it concerned me that she would blow all that off. Jo was too organized just to walk away from her responsibilities like that. She had a reason to stay away, and I was afraid it was because she knew who had killed Redding. But why wouldn't she go to the police if she knew?

I needed to clear my head, so after Richard arrived, I went for a walk to the Riverwalk. As I was leaving Charming Books, Faulkner squawked at me and Emerson made a dash for the front door. For once in my life, I was faster, and I beat him out of the bookshop before he could escape. I had a feeling I would pay for that later. I usually did when it came to Emerson—and to Faulkner, for that matter. The two creatures were assertive about their importance at Charming Books.

New white tents were in the process of being put up on the Riverwalk for the coming weekend. During the tourist season, it seemed that the village celebrated one festival after another. Many of them had no historical context or reason. They were simply planned and held to attract more tourists from Niagara Falls to our little village.

"No, you can't go into the village hall today," a strong baritone voice rang out along the street. "The mayor is doing very important work." Charles Hancock a bald, eightyish man, stood at the foot of the village hall steps, stopping the path of village councilman Cameron Connell. My grandmother's golf cart was parked next to him on the sidewalk. I was certain that was some sort of parking violation, not that Rainwater and the other police in the village had time to deal with such a small infraction right now.

"Like hell I can't," Cameron shouted back. "I'm on the village council. Get out of my way!"

I hurried over to them. "What's going on?"

Charles smiled at me. "Hello, Violet."

"I'm going in," Cameron said.

Charles jumped in front of him. He could move pretty quickly for a man of his advanced age. "No, you shan't."

Charles, with his old-fashioned mannerisms, was one of the few people on the planet who could say *shan't* without sounding ridiculous.

"It is my duty as her knight to protect Mayor Daisy Waverly at all costs. I'm sorry if you are offended," Charles said, not sounding sorry in the least. "But she's very busy going over the museum budget right now and asked not to be disturbed."

"Charles, what are you doing here? Isn't Bertie supposed to be Grandma Daisy's gatekeeper?"

"I am at your grandmother's service whenever she has a need. She mentioned to me that Bertie requested the day off, so I came here quick as a flash and offered my services as her gatekeeper."

I blinked. "She did?" I didn't know that Bertie ever took time off. The mayor's office was her whole life.

"This is ridiculous!" Cameron removed his cell phone from the inside pocket of his sport jacket. "Do I need to call the police to get you forcibly removed from my path?"

Rainwater didn't need this with two murders on his hands, so I stepped in. "Charles, just let Cameron go in. He is on the village council. Grandma Daisy won't mind."

Charles looked at me.

"Don't you trust me when it comes to what my grandmother wants?" I smiled.

He stepped aside. "I suppose so."

Cameron stomped around him, muttering curse words as he went. I had a feeling Grandma Daisy was about to get an earful about her guardian knight.

Charles watched him go. "I'll make sure he doesn't stay too long and fatigue Daisy with his complaints."

"I'm sure you will." I turned to go.

"Violet?" Charles called after me.

I turned.

"Are you still looking for the Fitzgerald girl?"

My eyes went wide. "How did you know that?"

"Daisy told me."

Of course she had. I sighed.

"Have you seen her?"

He shook his head sadly. "No, but I'm praying for the child. I just want you to know that."

Unexpected tears sprang to my eyes. "Thank you, Charles."

He nodded and turned his attention back to the street, looking for unwelcome visitors to my grandmother's office.

I wiped the tears from my eyes as I walked around the side of the café where I had stashed my mother's bike with the intent to ride it over to campus. My hope was that Renee could use her super librarian skills and help me find the connection between Walt Whitman and this case.

My grandmother had told me that during construction of the museum, they had discovered that the hill had been man-made. The building and all the buildings on River Road, including Charming Books, had been built on limestone. Beneath that limestone was the aquifer, the source of the natural springs that gave power to Charming Books. I hadn't thought much about how the water must affect other places in the village. Why was Charming Books the only place with magic? Then again, perhaps there were other Caretakers in town and other unique elements I had yet to learn about. Were there others in the village hiding their gifts, as my family had, out of fear?

I shook my head. These deep questions were too much. I needed to focus on finding Jo and finding out who'd killed Redding.

Shovels and a pickax sat behind the village the hall. There was also a battery-powered lantern. The basement window stood open—I wondered if my grandmother knew. If it rained, water could get into the building. Given the unstable foundation, water was the last thing we wanted in the village hall.

I was about to peer into the space when Vaughn Fitzgerald struggled out of the opening. He had blueprints in his hand that were streaked with mud. "What are you doing here?" he asked.

I stepped back. "I was just taking a look. I wanted to tell my grandmother the window was open."

The surprise on his face smoothed over. "She already knows. I told her this morning I would be on-site today."

"Has construction resumed on the hall?" I asked as I peered through the open window. It was so dark all I could see were the first few feet of limestone wall. The little kid in me wanted to go in there and explore. When I was a child, Colleen and I had made up fantastical stories about hidden treasure and a Native American princess that must have lived in Cascade Springs before the Europeans settled in the area. A place like this would be a perfect spot to hide such a treasure. Although I had to remind myself that the village hall had been built long after the Europeans settled in the village.

"Not yet. It will soon. Your grandmother told me how well the race did in raising funds. I don't have any doubt that we will get this project back on schedule with Grandma Daisy at the helm."

I laughed. "I don't have any doubt either. She's determined to make this happen. How's it looking under there?"

He squinted in the afternoon sunlight. "The sun sure does a number on your eyes when you're underground for so long."

"I bet."

"The site is mostly stable. I like to check on it every few days. We're supposed to have a big thunderstorm tonight, and I want to make sure everything is secure. There's nothing we can do right now to keep the water out until we have the money to do the extensive repairs. I just want this building to make it through until the repairs can be permanent."

I looked up at the sky and it was perfectly blue, but I knew powerful storms could roll in off Lake Ontario with very little notice.

"It would be terrible to lose the village hall," I said.

He smiled at me. "Don't worry. I won't let that happen."

I nodded. Vaughn was the best at his job. My grandmother and the village council wouldn't have hired him otherwise.

"I see you have a passenger on your bike." He laughed.

I looked behind me and groaned when I saw Emerson grinning at me from the bicycle basket.

"It seems to me that he thinks he's going wherever you are."

"He definitely believes that." I narrowed my eyes at the little cat before turning back to Vaughn. "I'm headed to campus to visit a friend."

He nodded, and then a sad expression crossed his face. "Have you heard from Jo?"

I shook my head. "Have you?"

"No, and I'm becoming worried. It's been three days since I last heard from her. It's not unusual for me to go a day or two without hearing from her. She's my sister and an adult. I'm not her keeper. She can do what she wants, but she's not responding to any of my text messages or calls."

I thought of the little red heart I had received. I could tell Vaughn about it, but instead I said, "She's not replying to my texts either."

"I suppose it should make me feel better that she's not singling me out to be ignored, but I'm worried about her." He brushed dirt off his sleeve.

"I'm worried too," I admitted.

Vaughn let out a great sigh. "If you hear from her, will you let me know?" he asked.

"Of course," I said.

He bent over and closed the window. "That should hold through the storm."

I nodded. "Do you need help putting your tools away?"

He shook his head and laughed. "You know what I think, Violet Waverly? You're always trying to be overly helpful. It might get you in trouble someday." He winked.

Chapter Thirty-One

I wondered about Vaughn's comment until I got back to my bike, and then all I could worry about was Emerson. When I was in front of the cat, I put my hands on my hips. "You aren't going to campus with me."

The cat hunched down in the basket. I knew I would have a terrible time getting him out.

I rolled my eyes. "You're lucky Renee likes cats."

He popped up again and braced his forepaws on the front of the basket. He knew that he'd won the argument. He almost always won. I didn't even know why I bothered to argue with the tuxedo feline anymore.

I climbed onto my bike and pushed off. On the sidewalk in front of River Road, I waited for a white horse and carriage to pass. The back seat of the coach was empty, and I guessed the carriage driver was practicing his route for the height of tourist season that really began on Memorial Day, just a week away.

After the carriage passed, I crossed the street on my bike and turned left onto the Riverwalk along the river and into Cascade Springs Park. When I was under the trees in the park, the village seemed to fade away, and I felt I was in the Cascade Springs that my ancestress Rosalee must have known, the one that was wooded and had a mixed community of Native American tribes and white settlers. Some of those white settlers were French fur traders, and other were new settlers like my ancestress who had been displaced by the War of 1812.

As I rode deeper in the woods, the pavement stopped and I began to ride on just packed mulch and dirt. The pungent smell of the mulch assaulted my nose. The parks department must have just put down new mulch, as they did every year at the beginning of the tourist season. The village was getting ready for the crowds.

Emerson lifted his nose in the air. He smelled the mulch too. The little cat sat back in the basket and looked at me with those bright-green eyes. His mouth was turned up into a knowing smile. I rolled my eyes. "You make it very hard to stay annoyed with you."

He settled down into the basket as if he was happy with that knowledge. I shook my head.

We rode by the spring where I collected the water.

"Come out!" a hushed voice called.

I slowed my bike to a stop and listened.

"I can help!" the voice called again.

I got off my bike and pointed at Emerson. "Stay there," I whispered. "I'm going to see who's in the woods."

The little tuxie hunched down in the bicycle's wire basket.

I followed the shouts to the other side of the springs. I spotted Bobby thrashing his way through the bushes. If he was trying to be quiet as he searched the woods, he was doing a poor job of it.

Bobby jumped. "Violet! What are you doing here?"

"I could be asking you the same."

"I—I'm out on a hike."

I frowned. "I didn't know you hiked. I thought you were strictly into cycling."

He forced a laugh. "It's always good to cross-train. You can't get too used to an exercise."

"Have you seen Jo?" I asked.

He looked in every direction except at me. "No, not since race day."

"Aren't you worried about her?"

He laughed again. "She will turn up. Jo lands on her feet."

I wondered how he knew this, and then it hit me. I was alone in the woods with a possible killer. Even I knew this wasn't good.

"Don't look at me like that, Violet." Bobby sounded hurt.

"Look at you like what?" I asked as casually as possible.

He studied my face. "Like I killed someone."

I took a step back. I needed to get back to Emerson and my bike and pedal out of there. Even knowing that, I asked, "Did you kill Redding?"

"No, of course not." Perspiration gathered on his forehead.

"Can you prove it?" I stepped back a few feet, putting a large maple tree between us. It made me feel better to put something between Bobby and me. Hopefully, it would be all I needed to get away.

"Y—you aren't the police. I don't have to prove anything to you."

"Can you prove it to the police?"

He took a step toward me. "How dare you!"

"What about Bryant Cloud?" I asked. "Did you kill him?"

"Who?" he asked, honestly confused.

It was clear to me that Bobby didn't know who Bryant was. He might not have killed Danielle's ex-husband, but it didn't put him in the clear for Redding's murder.

"Do you know Redding?"

"I never spoke to the man."

That answer seemed vague. "Had you ever seen him before the race?"

Bobby took two steps back, and I let out a small sigh of relief. The more physical distance I had from him, the better.

"When the police showed me his photograph, I recognized him. He had come into the bike shop once, a month or so ago. I had been with another customer and Jo had helped him, but I don't think he bought anything. Spring is our busiest season, as so many people bring their bikes in for a tune-up or are ready to upgrade to a new bike. That's something that you should really give serious thought too, Violet."

I wasn't going to get distracted from my line of questioning by the fact that Bobby thought my mother's bike was out-of-date. I knew it was, and that was one reason I liked it. Besides, it had held its own during the bike race. I couldn't ask for much more than that. "Did you see him again?"

He shook his head. "He just came into the shop the one time. That's all I know. I have already told the police this."

Why hadn't Rainwater told me this? I knew he couldn't tell me everything about the investigation, but it might be a help to me to find Jo if I knew Redding had visited the bike shop where she worked.

"When was this?" I asked. "Do you have it on security cameras?"

"I don't have any security cameras. They are too expensive."

That was a shame. The police could have looked at their body language to see if it appeared they knew each other.

I thought security cameras were something Bobby should rethink with a killer on the loose in the village. As long as he wasn't the killer.

"Do you think Jo killed Redding?" I asked bluntly, because I wanted his honest reaction. As much as I didn't want to believe that Jo could kill anyone, I knew she was the police's number-one suspect for a reason.

"N—no . . ." But it took him too long to answer to sound the least bit convincing.

"What are you really doing in these woods, Bobby?"

He scowled at me.

"Are you looking for Jo?"

He didn't say anything.

"Because I'm worried about her too. I want to find her and make sure she's all right. I think she might be in trouble and someone might want to hurt her."

"No one is going to hurt Jo," he said through clenched teeth.

Not even you? I wanted to ask, but I held my tongue.

"I have to go." He turned around and headed into the underbrush. As much as I wanted to follow him and make him talk to me, I knew that was a bad idea. I didn't want to believe Bobby could hurt anyone, but I didn't know he was innocent. My only comfort was that I believed he really did care for Jo like a father, but it was a small comfort. Did that mean he would have been willing to kill Redding to protect her?

He thrashed his way through the undergrowth to the path on the other side of the woods. I followed him just long enough to see him reach the path. There was a mountain bike parked on the path, and he climbed onto it. So he had been lying about the hike.

He climbed onto the bike and sped off toward the Riverwalk.

Chapter
Thirty-Two

As much as I wanted to stay near the quiet spring and think about all I had learned, I knew I had to get to the library.

Knowing Renee, she wasn't going to keep the building open one minute past closing time, which was four o'clock in the summer. It was already three thirty. I increased my pace.

The path out of the park opened onto the Springside Community College campus. It was a beautiful, small campus nestled in wine country. Across the main road from campus was a vineyard that stretched for acres with row after row of vines. In May, there weren't any grapes on the vines, but the bright-green leaves pointed themselves toward the sun. A handful of students walked across the quad, but there were so few classes during the summer that the population on campus had dropped dramatically. I parked my bike in front of the library and locked it to a nearby tree. Emerson let me take him from the basket without any fuss, confirming my suspicions that he'd intended to come with me all along. I walked up the steps into the library building.

"No cats allowed in the library," Renee said in a loud voice, but she was grinning. "I just have to say that if administration happens to come by. If the VP stops in, I can say I told you the cat was against the rules."

"What's the likelihood of the VP walking into the library during summer term?"

She chuckled. "Nonexistent, but I like to cover my bases."

I set Emerson on the reference desk, and he walked up and down it like he owned the place. "I can respect that."

"Shouldn't you be at the bookshop with Daisy running the village?"

"Richard is at Charming Books right now. He's been a great help. I'm not looking forward to the fall semester when he can't work for me anymore."

"It seems to me he's spending most of what he's earning on books at the store." She pulled out the three books Richard had bought for her. "He delivered these the other day. I don't know how he knew these were the books I wanted for my collection."

"Speaking of Richard . . ."

"Violet, don't you start. I get it from everyone else on campus. I'm not going to take it from you too.'

"What?" I asked innocently.

She glowered at me as only a librarian can glower. "Don't play dumb. You're too smart for that."

I laughed. "He did bring you those books."

She rolled her eyes. "What he needs to do is grow up."

"What do you mean?"

"I'm not an idiot. I know that Richard has had a crush on me and has for a while now, but has he done anything other than buy me books and visit the library every single day because he 'keeps remembering there is more research' that he needs to do? Yeah sure, no one researches that much, and I'm saying that from the perspective of a college librarian."

"You want him to ask you out," I said, understanding for the first time.

"Yes. It's the principle of the thing."

I arched my brow.

"If Richard can't get up the nerve to ask me on a date, how is he going to work up the nerve to do anything else? We have to be equal partners, and I can't be equal with someone who is too scared to ask me to coffee, let alone dinner. I'm not scared to ask him, but he has to prove to me that the same is true for him."

"I can respect that," I said.

She gave me a thumbs-up. "And that's why you're my friend, Violet. I doubt that Rainwater has ever been vague about his intentions with you."

That was true. Rainwater had been very clear from the start how he felt about me. I'd been the one who'd treaded lightly, but not nearly as lightly as Richard. He was going on years of pining for the outspoken librarian.

"I'm not going to wait forever, Violet," she said. "I have a life of my own to lead. I don't need Richard to complete it."

"Spoken like a true feminist."

"You'd better believe it." She straightened a stack of papers on her desk. "Now, I know you didn't come to campus to talk to me about my love life."

I smiled. "It's a great topic."

There came the glower again.

"I was wondering what you might have on *Leaves of Grass*. I feel like I have exhausted all the research databases from home. I've looked at the Whitman archive online too."

She arched her brow. "What's the sudden interest in Whitman? I thought you were taking a break from serious reading for the summer to recover from your dissertation. Whitman doesn't seem like light reading." She snapped her fingers. "I know—you're reading it because a copy of the book was found with Redding's body."

"You heard about that?" I asked.

"I think everyone in the village heard that. It was a very odd thing to be carrying through a bike race."

I thought about this a minute. "Everything about Redding's participation in the bike race was odd."

"I do have a theory why he was reading Whitman. It was because of the village connection."

I frowned. "What do you mean?"

"I thought you knew." She paused. "Walt Whitman visited Cascade Springs."

Chapter Thirty-Three

"What?" I stared at her.

She nodded. "Oh, you didn't know that, I take it."

I shook my head. "I knew he visited Niagara Falls, but never Cascade Springs. How would you know that?"

"Because there was a small mention of it in one of the journals from the mayor at the time, the one who had the village hall built. He hadn't been too impressed with Whitman, but Mayor Hodge, who was in office from 1850 until 1881, was a fussy man. I think he had heard about Whitman."

I blinked at her. "Why hasn't anyone written more about this? Whitman was credited to be the founder of American-style poetry. It would be a big deal in literary circles that he came to the village." Then I added, "Why didn't you tell me?"

She shrugged. "You have never been interested in Whitman before, so it's never come up."

I opened and closed my mouth. I might not have been researching Whitman in particular, but he had been a contemporary of Emerson, Thoreau, and the Alcotts. All of these transcendentalists had been a main focus of my research. It would have been nice to know that someone who actually knew them had visited my village.

"I can show you the entry in the journal, if you'd like to see it."

"Yes!" I almost shouted.

"Jeez, girl," she said. "You're going to have to calm down at least a little bit. I know no one is in here right now, but this is a library." Then she laughed to take the edge off her words. "It's almost four, so let me lock up the building, and then we can go down to the archives and look at it." She shook a finger at me. "If you tell the stodgy archivist that I showed you this without him present, I will deny it to my death."

I nodded and crisscrossed my finger over my chest. "I promise."

Her eyes narrowed as if she didn't quite believe me.

After Renee locked the front door and turned off the main lights, I followed her down the back staff stairs. The college archives were in the basement of the large library. Although the space was underground, it was clean and finished and smelled faintly of disinfectant and whiteboard markers.

My hands tingled as we walked. I could barely contain the excitement inside me. I knew I was about to learn something important. The only problem was, I didn't know how it was important. It was how I'd felt when I'd gone down any little tangent in my research for my dissertation. I'd always felt like my skin was crawling, that all the nerves in my body were on high alert as I was about to learn something that would change everything I'd known before.

I had visited the college archives on one occasion before, and at the time the archivist had been there. He was a bear of a man who didn't like anyone to come into his lair. Well into his seventies, he wasn't showing any signs of retiring, and I thought that the college was too scared to send him packing. He would get along famously with Bertie, now that I thought about it.

Renee removed a large ring of keys from her pocket and unlocked the door. The moment we stepped inside, the comforting smell of old books and papers welcomed me into the space.

Renee turned to me. "The journal is in the vault. You can't go in there. The archivist would kill me if I let anyone in there. He is organized like you wouldn't believe, so it should only take me a second to find the journal." She took another key from her ring, unlocked another door, and disappeared inside.

While she was gone, I looked at the display cases. There was a display about the village on its bicentennial last year. There were drawings and hand-written descriptions of what the village looked like at the time. I peered closer to one of the hand-drawn maps, which was dated 1817. I could clearly see the house that would become Charming Books on River Road. Rosalee had still been living then. She didn't die until right before the Civil War. She would have been living alone in that house with her daughter, LillyAnn. I realized I didn't know much about LillyAnn, and I promised myself I would look in the ledger my grandmother had given me as soon as I could. What had her gift from the essence been? There might be something here in the archives about my family too—if I could work up the nerve to ask the archivist. Probably not. I would just come back another time when Renee was here alone and ask her to look for me.

The thick fire door to the vault opened again, and Renee stepped out wearing white gloves and carrying a small, light-blue cardboard box. I recognized it immediately as a phase box, used to house fragile artifacts.

There was a long, antique table in the middle of the main room, surrounded by heavy wooden chairs. The whole set looked like it dated back to the time of Rosalee, but it was much more likely just from the turn of the twentieth century. Renee placed the box on the table and sat in one chair. I sat next to her. The wood was cold, as everything in the archives was kept at a constant cool temperature to keep the artifacts safe.

She opened the box and peered inside. Then she removed an old, cracked, leather-bound book that looked just like the ledger my grandmother had given me but was a third its size.

She removed the gloves. "Here. If you want to touch it, you have to put these on."

I nodded, knowing the oil from my hands could harm the delicate pages.

I held the journal and read aloud.

June 13th, 1880. Today, the village received a visitor. The poet Walt Whitman is here. He carries with him his abhorrent body of work, which he calls Leaves of Grass. He tried to give me a copy, but I have no use for scandalous drivel. He said that he was visiting our village because of his aliments and he had heard that the springs could heal those pains. My, he is an old man and waxed on about the days of the war when he would see Mr. Lincoln in Washington. I do believe that he was trying to impress me when he told me this. It was to no avail. There were many who knew Mr. Lincoln. After leaving me at the village hall, he, of course, went to the Waverly home. It is no surprise to me that a man who would write such questionable text would be drawn to the women living in that house.

My breath caught as I stared at the words THE WAVERLY HOME. My home. It must have been LillyAnn Waverly with whom he had visited. I stared up at Renee. "Did you know about this?"

She leaned over the book and read over my shoulder. "I had no idea he had visited your family. I never read directly from the journal. I had just known what the archivist had told me verbally. Admittedly, I don't listen to half of what he says. The man is a bit of a bore."

I wasn't listening to her myself as I read on.

He will go to the springs with the Waverly women. I hate to think of the scandal it will bring down on our quiet village.

I set the book back on the table. "I need to ask Grandma Daisy about this. I'm sure she didn't know. She would have told me. She knows about my interest in *Leaves of Grass*." I almost added, *She knows the shop wants me to read it to solve the murder.* Instead I asked, "Can I take a photo of this journal entry?"

She nodded. "No flash."

I removed my phone from my pocket and turned off the flash before snapping five photographs of the page. I could hardly wait to get back to Charming Books and show my grandmother. Maybe she would be able to help me sort out what this revelation meant.

Renee carefully replaced the journal in the phase box and closed it up. She then stood and went back into the vault.

As I followed Renee back upstairs, I was deep in thought. What was the shop telling me by having me read Whitman's work? Was it trying to tell me the shop's connection to the poet? Was all this reading completely unrelated to the murder? No, I knew that couldn't true, because the shop had given Redding a copy of *Leaves of Grass*, and it would not have done that unless he wanted or needed that. That's how the shop's essence worked—or at least that's how it worked as Grandma Daisy and I understood it—when it was sharing books with anyone who was not the Caretaker.

While I often pondered on the magic, its significance and how it worked, there was one thing I'd never doubted: the kinship it shared with literature. Both the shop's essence and all great books had the power to change lives. What was Redding's kinship with Whitman? Maybe if I could answer the question, I would be able to solve the murder.

In the time that we had been in the basement, the skies had darkened. Renee opened the door that led onto the library steps. She looked up at the clouds. "Looks like it's going to be a nasty one."

It seemed that Vaughn had been right in his forecast of bad weather. There was a crack of thunder far off, but no lightning.

Renee grimaced. "Do you want me to give you a lift home, Violet? I don't like the idea of you riding your bike if a storm breaks."

I didn't like the idea of that either, but my brain was swirling with everything I had learned about the village, Whitman, and my own family. I had no idea how this all related to Redding's murder, but I knew it must somehow be connected to it.

I hugged Emerson to my chest and shook my head. As much as I wanted to take Renee up on her offer to avoid getting wet, I wanted to be alone more. I had a lot to think about. Besides, the storm was still a ways off. I could outrun it. "I'll be fine. I'll go straight back to Charming Books, no stops."

She sighed. "When you and your cat get soaked, don't say I didn't offer."

I grinned. "I would never. Should I tell Richard about our earlier conversation? Maybe he just needs a nudge?"

"No. No nudges. He needs to ask me out on his own."

I nodded and hoped he would. Like Renee said, she wouldn't wait forever.

Chapter Thirty-Four

Emerson and I were on the trail that led through Cascade Springs Park when the skies opened up. The little tuxedo hunched down low in the basket. The rain was coming down so hard, I could barely see. Deep in the woods, it was black as night under the trees.

I thought of the village hall and hoped what Vaughn had said was right about the building holding strong through this storm. It would be a great loss if the village hall didn't survive until there was enough money to make the necessary repairs on the foundation.

When I was pedaling past the springs, I thought I saw movement by the water. I slowed the bike and stopped.

Emerson lifted his head a fraction of an inch and yowled.

"Shhh, Emerson," I said. Rain poured down, and I didn't know how I hoped to see whoever or whatever was on the other side of the springs. I lifted my hand to shield my eyes from the worst of the downpour.

There was a streak of lightning, immediately followed by a crack of thunder. When the light flashed, I saw the clear image of a person on the other side of the springs, and I gasped as I recognized the slight figure.

"Jo!" I cried.

But the sky went black again, and I could no longer see her.

I stood there and waited for the lightning, but when it flashed, she was gone.

Emerson yowled once more from his spot in the basket, and I climbed back onto the bike. I would do more good riding back to the bookshop and reporting what I saw than forcing my way through the woods in search of Jo Fitzgerald on foot.

But I hated to leave knowing she was out there.

I started to pedal back to the bookshop. I rode hard and felt mud from the path splash all the way up my back as it was kicked off my back tire. I didn't care. I wanted to hurry home so I could help Jo. When I reached the back garden of the bookshop, I parked my bike under the overhang by the back door, grabbed Emerson from the basket, and ran through the kitchen door just as another crack of thunder rumbled through the sky.

"Violet, where have you been?" Grandma Daisy asked. "I just got off the phone with Renee. She said you insisted on riding your bike home in this terrible weather. She called to make sure you were okay." She froze in the middle of the kitchen. "Girl, you're soaked to the skin, and look at poor Emerson."

The little tuxedo cat yowled as if to agree with her assessment.

"Can you dry Emerson off?" I asked, and handed her the wet cat.

"Oh, you poor little creature," she cooed, and grabbed the dish towel from the stove handle. She set Emerson on the stool next to the kitchen island and began drying him.

"Violet, you need to get out of those wet things, too."

"I will in a minute," I said. "I need to call Rainwater."

My phone was in the back pocket of my jeans, and I took it out. Without explaining to my grandmother, I made the call. A glance in their direction showed me Emerson was mostly dry; it appeared the tuxie was enjoying the extra attention.

"David," I said.

"What's wrong?" he asked. He immediately could tell from my tone that this wasn't a social call.

"It's Jo."

"Did you find her?"

"Not exactly." I told him what I had seen in the park.

"We'll search the woods for her. Did she look like she was okay? Was she hurt?"

"I only saw her for a few seconds during a flash of lightning. She was standing. I know that, and then she was gone. I should have gone after her."

"No," he said quickly. "You did the right thing. My officers and I will find her. This is a fast-moving storm, and according to the radar it should be out of the village in twenty minutes. We'll search every inch of those woods to find her."

"I know." But even as I said this, I couldn't expunge my guilt for leaving Jo in the park alone in the middle of the storm. "I want to come with you."

"No. I can't have two people lost in the woods. If she's there, we will find her. I'll get a couple of park rangers to help. They'll know all the places someone is likely to hide."

I wanted to argue more, but I knew that by keeping Rainwater on the phone, I was keeping him from finding Jo, and finding her had to be the first priority. "I understand. Thanks, David."

He assured me he'd let me know the minute they found her. Trusting him and his ability to do his job, I ended the call.

"Violet, what is wrong with Jo?" Grandma Daisy's forehead crinkled with concern.

I told her just what I'd told Rainwater.

"That poor girl," Grandma Daisy said. "What is she thinking by hiding out in the woods? I know she is resourceful—she has had to be—but why hide out in the middle of the storm? She'd be safe with us and a whole lot warmer."

"I know, and I have told her as much in so many text messages over the last several days."

Water dripped from my hair and my clothes. I started to shiver.

"Violet," Grandma Daisy said. "You need to go upstairs and get cleaned up. You're not any good to anyone if you catch a cold."

"How's Emerson?"

Grandma Daisy smiled. "He's fine, and he'll be even better once I make him a bowl of warm milk." The tuxie purred loudly in anticipation. She glanced over his head at me. "Then I'm sure he plans to lord his adventure over Faulkner."

I rolled my eyes. "You don't think they really talk to each other, do you?"

"They might not speak a language we can understand, but make no mistake, those two can communicate with each other just fine. Go upstairs and change so you will be ready when David brings Jo here."

"Will he bring her here?" I asked. "She's a suspect in a murder investigation."

"If he knows what's good for him, he will. I'm the mayor of Cascade Springs."

I stopped short of rolling my eyes. I knew Rainwater hadn't gotten along with the last mayor of the village, Nathan Morton. A lot of that had to do with the fact that Nathan had been my ex-boyfriend, but I couldn't say for certain that the police chief thought things had improved much since Grandma Daisy's election. Sure, the two of them respected each other and got along much better than Rainwater and Nathan ever had, but Grandma Daisy certainly kept Rainwater on his toes. She kept everyone on their toes.

When I stepped into the apartment, I half expected to see a stack of Whitman's poems in the middle of my bed, but there was nothing there. I wondered if Whitman had stepped in this very room when he visited LillyAnn. I guessed probably not, since these would have been private quarters even back then. If LillyAnn had met with Whitman, it would have been in the main room of the bookshop. I wondered what he'd thought of the birch tree growing in the middle of the house.

After changing my clothes and giving my own hair a brisk towel-drying, I hurried back downstairs. I found my grandmother in the main room of the shop starting a fire in the massive hearth. "It may be May, but there are still chilly nights, and you could have caught your death of a cold. I want to have this fire going for when David brings Jo here."

I pressed my lips together. My grandmother was so certain Rainwater was going to find Jo, but I wasn't so sure. The college student had been able to hide for days without being detected. What were the odds that the police could find her in the middle of this terrible storm?

As if to make my point, there was a flash of lightning through the skylight window that was almost immediately followed by a crack of thunder.

Grandma Daisy stood up, and as if she could read my mind, she said, "If Jo is in the woods, David and his team will find her."

I nodded absently. Perhaps I should have left Emerson and my bike and gone after Jo. If she'd fallen and hurt herself in the time that it took me to ride back to Charming Books and alert the police chief, I would never forgive myself.

Emerson walked into the main room from the kitchen, licking milk from his lips. His fur still appeared to be a bit damp, and he jumped onto the stone hearth, walking up and down in front of the fire to warm himself. Finally, he curled up as close to the fire as possible without burning his tail.

"At least wet cat doesn't have a smell like wet dog does. That's the worst." Grandma Daisy shivered as if just the memory of the smell was too upsetting to recall.

I went back into the kitchen and grabbed my shoulder bag from the island. I spread the contents on the counter so they could dry, but what I was really looking for was the damp copy of *Leaves of Grass*. The pages of the book were already curling as they dried. I wasn't too worried about losing this particular newly printed edition of the book. If I did, I knew the shop would send me another copy, which was why Grandma Daisy's less-than-accurate filing and inventory system worked for Charming Books. Because, really, if the shop could manifest books at whim to suit the needs of a reader, even the most detail-oriented filing system would fail to compensate for the magic.

I carried it back into the main room of the shop.

"Where did you go?" Grandma Daisy asked. "Did you hear anything from David?"

"Not yet." I held up the book. "I went to go get this."

"Oh, I hate to lose a book to the elements like that. Place it in front of the fire; maybe it will dry out."

I did as she asked, opening the book to the very middle. I wasn't sure if would do much good.

"Have you discovered why the shop wants you to read Walt Whitman?"

"Maybe," I said. "At least for the first time in all of this, I feel like I'm finally getting somewhere, and it might be more tied to this shop than we ever knew."

She arched her brow at me. "I think I might need to sit down for this." She perched on the arm of one of the sofas near the hearth.

The heat from the fire radiated into my back and was so soothing. It felt like the warmth was burning away all my aches and pains from my fast ride through the woods. I wished too that it could burn away my worries, especially those worries I had for Jo. I hated to think that my student was out there in the cold and rain. I closed my eyes for a moment. It probably would be better for me if I didn't think about Jo at the moment, so instead I concentrated on a long-dead poet. "Did you know that Walt Whitman visited Charming Books?"

"What?"

"Walt Whitman was here in this very room."

She blinked at me. "Where did you hear that, my girl?"

I removed my phone from my pocket and showed her the photos I had taken at the college archives.

She whistled. "My. That is something. I think we should make a plaque or something to advertise that Walt Whitman was here. It's quite a feather in our literary cap."

"Is it mentioned in the ledger?" I asked.

She smiled. "You are the Caretaker. You are the one to answer that."

I frowned and walked over to the sales counter. Crouching down, I remove the ledger from the safe. It was the best place I could think to keep it. I carried it back to the couches in front of the fireplace and sat down. Carefully, I opened it. The pages crackled. I realized I should have been wearing white gloves as I had in the archives when handling the old mayor's journal.

On the first page, there was a list of all ten Caretakers, ending with my own name. I recognized that it had been added in my grandmother's hand. Each entry had the birth and death dates next to the Caretaker's name. Only Grandma Daisy and I had no death date. My fingers hovered over my mother's name and her date. I bit the inside of my lip. I couldn't let the old and familiar grief overcome me now; I had to help Jo.

I flipped quickly through Rosalee's entries of helping people to LillyAnn's. It seemed from what I read that LillyAnn had the gift of calming others with her touch. She helped many people with nerves by doing this. I flipped to 1880, which was the year I knew Whitman had visited Niagara Falls.

There was a short entry that caught my eye. "The poet had pain of lost love and pain of the stomach. I did what I could for him, giving him the herbs my mother taught me for his stomach. The broken heart is much more difficult to heal, but he said my touch soothed him to see happiness in this world."

There was no mention of the poet's name, but it was June 1880, when Whitman would have been at Niagara Falls. Had LillyAnn purposely left his name off, when the names of so many others were clearly written in the ledger? Had she known that the mayor didn't approve of Whitman's visit and omitted his name just in case the ledger was ever found by someone outside the family? These were questions I would never know the answers to.

I told Grandma Daisy what I had found. "But what does it mean in relation to Redding's murder, and not only that, what does it mean in relation to the tragic death of Bryant Cloud?"

"Who is that?"

I told her about Danielle's ex-husband and the conversations I'd had with Rainwater's sister.

"This is a tangled case and seems to be affecting everyone you hold dear."

I hadn't thought of it that way, but she was right. Was I the connecting person in all of this? I shook my head. That couldn't be. I'd never met Bryant before he died.

The front door banged open, and a very wet Rainwater, followed by Officers Clipton and Wheaton, came inside. I jumped out of my seat and looked for any sign of Jo. She wasn't there.

Rainwater shook his head ever so slightly.

Chapter Thirty-Five

"We tore the park apart, but we couldn't find her. The rain washed away any tracks."

"I know she was there."

"And I believe you." His face fell. "I'm sorry, Violet."

My heart ached. He looked so crestfallen. All I wanted to do was give him a hug, but Clipton and Wheaton's being there held me back.

Grandma Daisy didn't have the same qualms, as she gave Rainwater a hug. "Chin up, my boy. Jo will reveal herself when she is good and ready. I'm sure she has a very good reason for hiding in the woods. When the time is right, all will become clear." She stepped back from him. "You all look like a group of drowned rats. Here, warm yourself by the fire before you head back out into that weather."

Wheaton shook out his coat, sending water specks flying all over the room, even on the books. It was all I could do not to say something, but I held my tongue. It wouldn't do much good as far as Wheaton was concerned. I was certain the police officer liked to get a rise out of me.

Clipton scowled at him. "Watch you what you're doing, Wheaton." I liked her a little better for saying that.

Grandma Daisy held out her hands. "I'll take your wet jackets and hang them to dry. Violet, can you start a pot of tea?"

"Of course," I hurried into the kitchen, happy to have an assignment. I didn't think I could have sat there any longer just looking at Rainwater's down-turned face.

In the kitchen, I put the kettle on and gathered the tea tray, just as my grandmother had taught me when I was a little girl. I stacked it with teacups, saucers, cream, and sugar. I selected English breakfast tea, even though it was the afternoon. It was my favorite.

Then I added a plate of cookies from Le Crepe Jolie. It seemed that we always had some on hand from Lacey and Adrien. We could never pay them back in books with the amount of food they gave us on a daily basis, and they refused to accept any money. But I did try to return the favor and kept their cookies out at busy times in the shop. The moment I saw a shopper reach for one, I was quick to tell them just where they could purchase more. I liked to think that the "advertising" benefited Lacey and Adrien.

The swinging door to the kitchen opened, and the kettle whistled at the same time.

I picked the kettle up from the stove and poured the boiling water into the waiting teapot. "The tea is almost ready." I looked up, expecting to see my grandmother there, ready to help me take the tray into the shop.

"I'm glad to hear it," Rainwater said.

I smiled at the police chief. "I thought you were Grandma Daisy."

He laughed. "I hope you weren't disappointed."

"Never." I finished filling the pot with hot water, set the kettle back on the stovetop, and placed the lid on the teapot. When I turned around, Rainwater was standing directly behind me. I wrapped my arms around his waist and hugged him tight. His police uniform shirt was damp against my cheek, but I didn't care. "I wanted to do that the moment you walked into the shop. You looked so upset."

He hugged me back. "I could tell. I can always tell when you want to say more, Violet."

"Am I that l obvious?" I asked in a lighter tone, and stepped out of his arms.

"Your forehead wrinkles, and you press you lips shut like you are trying to physically keep the words in."

"Hmm, how very telling. I'll have to work on that."

He smiled briefly and then sighed. While I enjoyed our banter, I wasn't the only one with a tell. I watched David's lips turn down and his jaw clench, and I knew I wouldn't like whatever he had to say next.

"Out with it, David."

"There is some information about Jo that I need to tell you."

I raised my brow. "I thought you didn't find anything."

"We didn't. At least we didn't find anything in the woods. Earlier today, I learned something else . . ."

"David, you are making me nervous. Whatever it is, just spit it out." I took a step back and fussed with the tea tray.

"She was watching you."

"What?"

"I found a file. I went back to her apartment after we searched it."

"How did you search her apartment without a warrant?"

Rainwater pressed his lips together. "The apartment lease is actually in her brother's name and he agreed to let us in, so we didn't need a warrant. He gave us free rein over the place. He's worried about his sister and hoped that we would find something there that would lead us to her."

"And did you?" I asked.

"Not the first time, but I found something interesting when I went back on my own. I don't know what made me do it, but I felt like Jo must be hiding something."

"Okay." I waited.

"What's more, she'd been hiding her research. Something about this whole case has never sat right with me, and I scanned her apartment with a particularly critical eye. Some well-worn scratches on the floor suggested that the bed had been pushed to one side, and on multiple occasions. That's where I discovered a loose floorboard under her bed. I would never have found it if I hadn't moved her bed."

I swallowed. "What did the file say?"

He looked away from me and ran his hand through his head. "It was all about you. There were notes about what you did every day. She was keeping a daily log."

I placed a hand to my forehead. This couldn't be true. Jo was my friend.

"And how is Redding involved in this?" My voice sounded higher than it should.

"In the file there was a note from him that told her she would get paid when the job was done."

"She was working for him," I said.

"Looks that way. She was working with him on a case about you." Rainwater was quiet for a moment as he let that sink in, but it didn't sink in. It couldn't sink in. It didn't make any sense at all.

"And this all leads back to Redding's murder. That's what you think," I said.

He ran his hand down the side of his face. "I don't have any choice but to consider that as a possibility. Redding is dead. Jo is missing. You're the only one here who can make this a little bit clearer to me."

"So you think the murder has to do with me because Jo and Redding were spying on me?"

"You're the only person that holds the two of them together. Without you, I doubt they would have even known each other."

I felt dizzy, but I didn't want to show Rainwater or anyone else how much this upset me. "What did her notes say?"

"For the most part, they conveyed that you lead a quiet life, at least when you aren't in the middle of meddling in a murder investigation. She observed that you mostly went to the college, taught, studied at the library, worked here at Charming Books, and spent your free time when you had any with me." There was a slight blush to his tawny complexion when he said that.

"That's all?" Relief flooded my chest. Jo painted me as boring, which is exactly what I wanted.

However, my relief was short-lived when he added, "There was one more thing. Her main observation was that you go to the springs every other night to gather water in a watering can. It didn't matter where you were or what you were doing, you did this faithfully every other night, and then would take the water into the bookshop. She didn't see what you did with it from there."

I felt very cold. The cookies on the tray no longer looked as appetizing as they had a moment ago.

"What is the water for, Violet?" Rainwater asked in a quiet voice.

I didn't know how to answer him.

He sighed. "It's against my better judgment, but I haven't shared this with anyone else, not even my officers. You are the only person I've told."

Why was he telling me that? Did he not intend to share all that he'd learned with his team? If they'd gone into Jo's apartment, then I was pretty sure all the evidence had been properly collected and documented. So if David was suggesting that he might somehow remove that bit of evidence—I swallowed hard—that would be a huge concession for a man of his character to make. And, as much as I didn't want to be cast dead-center into the middle of this investigation, I didn't want David to compromise his integrity for me.

"You have to tell your officers."

He nodded. "I plan to."

I let out a sigh of relief. "I'm glad."

I was kicking myself for not going and searching Jo's apartment when I had the chance. The trip to the detective agency in Niagara Falls instead had been a complete waste of my time. I took a breath. "You need to tell your officers, even if it makes Jo or me or both look bad. I would never forgive myself if you were reprimanded, or worse, lost your job on my account."

He nodded. "I wanted to tell you first."

I chewed on the inside of my lip. He was going to tell the others in the department. Would they then believe I was tied to the murder?

Grandma Daisy poked her head into the kitchen. "Violet, what's holding up the tea? I think Officer Clipton might be frozen through." When she saw my face, she entered the kitchen. "What's wrong? Is it more bad news about Jo?"

I nodded. "David can tell you." I sat on the stool then, not caring what either of them thought. My brain was reeling.

They talked quietly for a few minutes while I replayed what I'd learned about Jo—the betrayal simmering beneath my skin and making my stomach twist painfully— and what I'd learned about Rainwater. For as much as Jo's actions hurt me, there was such comfort in knowing how far David might go to protect me. He was the most honorable man I knew, and to think that he'd even momentarily considered compromising those morals for me—it was very humbling.

"I'm quite sad to hear that Jo was working for Redding to spy on Violet, but there is nothing to worry about when it comes to that water."

"What do you mean?" Rainwater asked.

Grandmas Daisy laughed. "Oh, you silly man. You can't possibly be thinking there is anything sinister in Violet gathering water? I can assure you that there is not. She's doing it for me."

Rainwater arched his brow. "For you?"

"Yes, for me," she said. "How do you think I stay so fit and look so good for my age? I have been drinking water from the springs since I was a little girl. You, because of your heritage, should know the stories surrounding the water in the springs.

I believe it too. It's made me young and vital. Do you think I could be the mayor of our lovely little village when I am over seventy years old without a little boost?"

"I think you can do anything, Daisy."

Grandma Daisy smiled. "I appreciate the confidence, my boy, but it's just not true. The spring water is sort of my answer to vitamins."

Rainwater narrowed his eyes. He still wasn't buying it.

"That water, without being purified, wouldn't be safe to drink. There is algae and microbes even in the cleanest freshwater. Not to mention the animals and birds that drink from it. How is it that you're not getting sick from drinking the spring water?"

"Oh, I know that. I boil it for my tea, which makes it safe to drink." Grandma Daisy smiled.

Rainwater shook his head. "Why is it in a watering can?"

Grandma Daisy shrugged. "It seems to me a practical way to carry water. If you would like Violet to collect water for me using another receptacle, we are all ears."

I cringed. Everything inside me wanted to tell Rainwater the truth, but I couldn't, not yet.

Rainwater looked at me. "Why didn't you just tell me that the water was for your grandmother when I mentioned it?"

"I—I didn't want to give away Grandma Daisy's secret. I don't think any woman wants people to know all of her secrets."

"That is too true," Grandma Daisy said. "Maybe it's vain, but women want others to think they come by their beauty and health naturally. I do, in my way. I suppose I didn't want to give the water the credit." Grandma Daisy picked up the teapot from the tray. "I'll take this out first. I like to always carry it separate." She laughed. "I suppose I've broken too many teapots in my day not to be careful."

After my grandmother left, I smiled at Rainwater. "I'm glad we were able to clear that up for you."

"Violet, it still doesn't clear up the fact that Jo was watching you for Redding. Why would Redding want to keep tabs on you?"

"You know he followed me when Lacey's sister was murdered in January. My guess is he thought I would lead him to another big case, which I clearly haven't, if the most interesting thing she learned was that I gather water from the springs. I mean, it seems kind of silly when you think about it. I'm just gathering water—not gold. And this whole region is known for its water. Tourists come from all over and fill their own containers at the spigots in town."

I grabbed the handles of the tray. "Let's take the tea to the others. I hope you and your officers like English breakfast." I started to pick up the tray, but Rainwater put his hand over mine, stopping me.

"What is it you want to tell me, Violet?"

"I said I wanted to give you a hug about not finding Jo."

He shook his head. "There's something else you want to tell me. You've wanted to tell me for weeks. At times I thought you were on the verge of saying it, but then you'd press your lips together and stop yourself."

I chuckled, but the sound was hollow even to my own ears. "I not sure what you are talking about."

"Violet." His voice was quiet.

I wouldn't look at him. I was afraid my face would give too much away. After a beat, he removed his hand, and I picked up the tray. "Grandma Daisy and your officers will wonder what happened to us, and we can't let the tea get cold. There is nothing Grandma Daisy hates worse than cold tea." I carried the tray to the door.

"Violet?"

I turned, holding the tray and with my back pressed up against the swinging door ready to push it in.

He stared at me with those mesmerizing eyes. "You are going to have to tell me eventually or this isn't going to work."

I swallowed hard. Unable to speak, I went into the other room. I plastered a bright smile on my face. "Hot tea and cookies from the café."

Clipton grabbed one of the chocolate-chip cookies. "This is just what I need. Nothing makes a tough investigation easier than chocolate."

Wheaton grunted but refrained from comment.

I examined them both, and they each appeared to be in a better mood since they'd warmed themselves by the fire.

Clipton took another cookie. "What's the plan now, Chief?"

Rainwater sighed. "After you two finish your tea and cookies, I want you to go back to the station and file the report from the search. I also want you to hit up all of Jo's friends again. Widen the net. Even go to classmates. Anyone who might have any idea of where she would go to hide."

"I'll talk to Bobby again," Wheaton said. "He was the last one to see her before she disappeared. He might know something if I press him a little harder."

"Not too hard, Wheaton," Rainwater warned.

"Don't you think it would be easier to find Jo if we knew what sent her into hiding in the first place? And are we sure she ran away on her own accord?" Grandma Daisy asked.

"There is no evidence of kidnapping or anything sinister, but of course we consider every possibility," Rainwater said.

Wheaton grunted. "She's hiding because she killed a man. It doesn't take a genius to figure that out."

"We don't know that," I said.

Wheaton stood, grabbed two cookies from the tray, and marched to the door. "But don't we? All the evidence points to her."

Wheaton, unfortunately, had a point. Good officers, like Rainwater, followed the evidence. They didn't make assumptions or presume to trust or judge people—they went by the facts. And, if Rainwater's search of Jo's apartment had proven anything, it was that she was, in fact, closely tied to the murder victim. A fact that none of us could ignore.

"I know that she's your friend," Wheaton went on.

Rainwater scowled but said nothing.

"And because of that, we've been instructed not to jump to conclusions," Wheaton said. "But this is the only theory that makes any sense in this confusing case. Let's go, Clipton. I would like to get home at a decent hour tonight." He went out the door.

The female officer rolled her eyes at us as she followed her partner out into the rain.

Chapter Thirty-Six

Grandma Daisy and Rainwater left shortly after his officers. I leaned back against the door. The day had not gone as planned. Not that most of my days did, but every once in a while it would be nice.

"I thought they were never going to leave," a small voice said.

I jumped and pushed myself off the door. "Jo?"

She was standing at the foot of the birch tree. She had her bare arms wrapped around her thin body, and she was shivering.

"You're soaking wet."

"That's what usually happens when you're caught in a thunderstorm," she said.

"Go stand by the fire and warm yourself up."

She walked over to the fire and held her hands out to the warmth. "That feels good. I wasn't sure I would ever get warm again."

"I'm just glad you are okay."

I started to remove my cell phone from the back pocket of my jeans. I needed to tell Rainwater Jo was safe and sound, if a little wet. He would be so relieved. But then I stopped myself. Given the evidence, Wheaton's attitude . . . would they be relieved to find her, or to have a break in the case?

She looked over her shoulder at me. "You aren't going to tell the police chief I'm here, are you?"

The phone froze halfway to my ear. "I have to tell them. They had a search party for you. Everyone in the village is so worried about you."

"Not everyone," she said bitterly.

Before I could ask her what she meant, she asked, "Can I have one of those cookies?" She looked longingly at the tray.

"You can have all five. I can make you something more substantial. I do most of my eating at Le Crepe Jolie and don't take that much time to cook, but I can make you a grilled cheese."

She stacked the cookies on top of each other. "These are fine."

"Where have you been? I mean, before you were hiding in my storage room," I asked.

"I can't tell you that," she said around a bite of cookie. "I just came here to show you that I was all right. I could tell by your many text messages that you were worried, and I've felt bad about that. I never wanted to make you worry. You've done so much more for me than any other teacher has. I wanted to tell you thank you and that I'm all right."

"Of course I was worried. A man is dead and you went missing. Everyone is worried."

She swallowed. "I didn't kill him. I know that's what the police think, but I'm telling you I didn't."

How could I even believe her? As much as I wanted to believe Jo hadn't killed Redding, how could I know that when I'd found out she had been working for him to spy on me? I didn't say any of these thoughts yet. For all I knew, she could've been in the shop the entire time and heard everything Rainwater and his officers had said. A chill tracked up my spine. Had she been spying on me? Again?

The words were on the tip of my tongue, but I bit them back, my lips pressing together. No doubt, had Rainwater seen my expression, he would've known there was more I wished to say.

Rather than barrage her with questions, I managed a semblance of a smile for Jo. I wanted to understand why she did what she did, and accusing her wasn't the way to go about it. She would clam up, or worse, she would run away again. I couldn't let her leave. Rainwater would be so upset if he found out.

"We have a lot to talk about, but before we do, at least let me get you something else to wear. Even with the rain stopping, you can't go out again in those wet clothes. You'll get sick if you do."

She thought about this for a minute, then said, "All right." She popped another cookie in her mouth, and I wondered when she'd last had a decent meal.

"Let's go up to my apartment."

When we reached the second floor, I unlocked the door to my apartment. Inside, Jo followed me into the bedroom and froze. On the bed were five copies of Whitman's *Leaves of Grass*. The books hadn't been there when I had gone upstairs to change an hour before. Apparently the shop's essence wasn't happy with me for ignoring its instructions to read the book over the last several hours. In all fairness, I had been a little busy.

Jo stared at the bed. "Why do you have all those copies of Whitman on your bed?" Her face was pale.

"Is something wrong?" I asked.

"N—no, it just seems odd that you would have so many copies of that particular book when it was the book that Redding had when he died."

It was a fair question, just not one I was prepared to answer. "Where have you been, Jo? The po—I have been looking for you for days."

"I've been around. Sometimes even when people are looking for me, they don't notice me." She played with the damp hem of her shirt.

I wondered what she meant by that. "I was just reading through the poems because I was curious why Redding had the book on him, too. I wanted to compare the different editions. Do you know this collection?"

She ignored my question and said, "They're all the same edition."

I forced a laugh. "My mistake. I must have grabbed the wrong stack from the poetry shelf in the shop. I'll get the right ones when I go back downstairs." I gathered the books off the bed and set them on the corner of my dresser.

Her forehead wrinkled.

"Now, let's find you something to wear." I frowned. It wasn't going to be easy. I was nine inches taller than Jo and outweighed her by at least thirty pounds, and that was being generous to my ego. I opened the dresser drawer and pulled out an old college sweatshirt that no longer fit but I hadn't been able to part with yet. Then I found a pair of leggings. I handed the clothes to her. "You can double the leggings over a few times at the waist, and they should work. The sweatshirt will still be a bit big. I have a scarf and gloves, and I believe one of Grandma Daisy's pea coats in the closet downstairs, and those should fit better, keep you warmer."

She smiled at me and accepted the clothes.

"Can I ask you one more question?" I asked.

She sighed. "Sure."

"Do you know why Redding was killed?" I search her face. "Is that why you're hiding? You're hiding from whoever killed him?"

She wouldn't look me in the eye. "That sounds a bit dramatic, doesn't it? You make it sound like I'm in the middle of a spy movie."

"Are you?" I asked.

She frowned. "What do you mean by that?"

"I know that you were watching me for Redding. Why were you doing that?"

Her eyes went wide. "How do you know?"

I let out a breath. I thought she might deny it, but as painful as it was to hear from her, I was grateful she didn't. "The police found your file."

She shook her head. "I knew I should have taken it with me or burnt it. I didn't have enough time to go back to my apartment to do either."

"Why? What are you running from? Jo, I'm your friend, but I'm your teacher first. I can help you."

"Why would you want to help me after what I did?" she asked bitterly. "I wouldn't in your place."

"Because I know people make mistakes when they are your age—we all make mistakes—but only a few mistakes can truly ruin a person's life." I paused. "One of those is murder."

"I told you I didn't kill anyone." Her voice was sharp.

I noticed that a puddle was forming around her feet and sighed. "We can talk more when you get cleaned up."

She nodded and held the clothes I gave her so tightly that her knuckles turned white. "Thank you, Violet. No matter what, you are a great teacher and friend. You don't deserve what I've put you through, and I'm sorry for all of it."

"I just want you to be okay, and I think the best way for you to do that is to turn yourself in to the police. They can protect you from whatever it is you are so afraid of. Chief Rainwater is a good man. I'm not just saying that because he's my boyfriend, either. When I was in trouble with the law, he listened to me and believed me. He will believe you too if you give him a chance."

She nodded. "All right. I'll do that if you go with me to the police station."

"Of course I'll go. The bathroom is just there." I pointed to the closed door on the other side of the room. "I'll leave you to it." I picked up the stack of Whitman's poetry and went into my small living room.

A moment later, I heard the shower turn on. I couldn't blame Jo for wanting to take a shower if she had been in the woods these last few days; she needed one. I shivered at the very thought. I would have made a terrible camper if I'd ever tried it, which I never had.

I waited in the living room for five minutes and then removed my phone from my pocket. I didn't know for certain that Jo wouldn't change her mind about going to the police station. Maybe it would be better to have the station come to her, and, I told myself, she would be more comfortable talking to Rainwater by the fire in Charming Books than she would in a sterile interrogation room.

Even with my rationale in place, I felt like a traitor texting Rainwater. However, I didn't have much choice. I knew Jo needed more help than I could give her. If she really was in trouble and hiding from whoever had killed Redding and probably killed Bryant Cloud too, she needed protection, more protection than I could give her.

I texted Rainwater. Jo is here

Where

Bookshop. She was hiding in the shop the whole time you were here.

I'll be there in two minutes. Don't let her leave.

Okay.

I waited another minute. I could still hear the shower going in the bathroom, and then a feeling of dread fell over me. I knocked on the door to my bedroom. "Jo?"

There was no answer.

I knocked and repeated her name again. When there was still no answer, I went inside. The bathroom door stood open and the shower was on. There was no one in it. I went back into my bedroom, and she was gone. Her wet clothes were on the floor and the window was open.

Chapter
Thirty-Seven

I realized my mistake. I'd never thought Jo would go out my second-story window. I peered out the window.

The Queen Anne Victorian had a wraparound porch under the window. My guess was that Jo had lowered herself out the window to the porch roof and then shimmied down one of the porch posts. It would be at least a six-foot drop from my window to the porch roof. A risky move on a night with good weather, and this wasn't good weather. The roof was slick with rain. I would never have tried it for fear of breaking an ankle.

She must have been desperate to do that. Jo was afraid. I should never have left her alone. Guilt washed over me. I felt like I'd betrayed my student for telling the police she was there, and I felt like I'd let Rainwater down for letting her get away. There was no way I was going to come out on top of this.

There was a knock at my apartment door, and I jumped, hitting my head on the widow frame.

"Violet." Rainwater came into the bedroom with his hand on the hilt of his gun. He was dry and in civilian clothes.

"How did you get inside the house?" I asked.

He blushed. "Your grandmother gave me keys in case of emergency years ago. I thought she would have told you that."

"No, she never mentioned it." My eyes narrowed. "In all the time that we've been dating, you've never told me about the keys."

"I've never had a reason to use them until now," he said. "I never thought to mention it. She didn't give me a key to your apartment."

Like that was supposed to make me feel better.

"I can give them back if you don't want me to have them."

"No, no." I closed my eyes for a moment. "It's fine, but a little warning next time; you startled me. I almost fell out the window."

"What are you doing with your head out the window?" He took a step forward.

I frowned. "I was looking for Jo."

"She left?"

I nodded. "I'm sorry. I left her in the bedroom so she could change out of her wet clothes. I thought she was taking a shower."

Rainwater went into the bathroom and turned off the shower. I hadn't even realized it was still running. He came out of the bathroom again. "That's the oldest trick in the book."

"Well, it's never happened to me before, so it's new to me."

He moved to the window. "The rain is tapering off, but I'm in no mood to go back into those woods tonight and look for her. She's very good at hiding and could be anywhere. Tell me everything you learned from her. Where's she been? Where she's staying? Why she ran away? I don't believe it's because she knows we think she's the killer. There's something more to it."

I walked out of my bedroom into the living room and to the door. "Grandma Daisy would say that we need some tea for this. Let's go downstairs so we can talk."

"I need a lot more than your grandmother's tea, if that's what you're thinking," Rainwater said.

"I have harder stuff, at least I think so. Renee brought wine to the last Red Inkers meeting. There's an unopened bottle. She would understand if we broke into it."

He followed me down the spiral stairs. "No, I need to keep my wits about me. I never drink when I'm working a case. I need to be able to think clearly and to act at a moment's notice." He stood by the fireplace. Without being stoked, the fire was starting to die down.

Faulkner stood on the hearth with his wings out. Apparently he liked the feeling of the heat on his feathers. Emerson had finally fully recovered from his soggy ride through the park and watched Faulkner with narrowed eyes from the sales counter.

I perched on the arm of the sofa.

"Tell me everything Jo told you," he said in his best cop voice.

I tried not to take his cop voice personally and told him what I knew. "She's definitely hiding from someone. She didn't say as much, but I think she knows who the killer is."

"Then she should come to the police. We can protect her."

"That's what I told her, but I think she's too afraid to do that or she thinks the police won't believe her."

He made a face.

"I tried to convince her otherwise."

"I know you did." He sat on the couch. "This case is the most frustrating of my career, because I know Jo holds all the answers, but I can't get to her. If I just had a shot to talk to her, I know it would be solved quickly."

"She's just a scared kid."

"I know that, believe me, I do. And I have compassion for her. But we can't forget, if she doesn't turn herself in, others could be hurt or worse. She could be hurt."

I gasped.

"She's alive, but if she is this afraid, for how long will that be?"

I shook my head. I couldn't bear to think of real harm befalling the girl. Rainwater, too, frowned as if already contemplating Jo as the next victim. And it was true. While I'd been so focused on finding Jo, protecting the shop, and figuring out how Walt Whitman tied into this entire mess, there was one big, glaring fact I'd steadfastly refused to acknowledge. There was a killer on the loose, one who had killed not one person but two.

"Why was Jo watching you for Redding?"

"If I told you, I'm not sure you would believe me."

He rubbed his hands through his hair in frustration. "Violet, you either tell me or I'm leaving. You can't push me away like this forever. If you want to be with me, I have a right to know what's going on."

I stared at him and realized that in all this time I had been worried about tell him about Charming Books, I'd never considered giving him a chance to understand. That wasn't fair to him or to me.

I walked over to the tree and ran my hand up and down its white trunk. "Once you asked me how the tree healed so fast after being shot. You wanted to know why there wasn't any mark. I never answered your question."

"No, you didn't." His voice had an edge to it.

"I healed the tree." I dropped my hand from the trunk.

"You?"

"It wasn't me specifically. It was the water, from the springs." I turned to look at him.

"So you don't collect the water for Daisy." His voice was mild, like he was trying to remain calm to process everything I was saying. I didn't blame him for taking it in slowly. It was a lot to digest. When I'd heard it the first time, I hadn't believed. I didn't want to believe. I was perfectly happily with the boring life I had before I knew about my inheritance as the shop's Caretaker. Some days, when the shop's essence was quiet, I still didn't think I would believe if the tree weren't there as a constant reminder to me of my responsibilities.

"No. I collect it for the tree and the shop." I placed my hand on the tree again. The tree's smooth bark was cool to the touch. "This tree is over two hundred years old. If you look it up in any nature guide, birch trees aren't meant to live that long, and honestly, it's probably older than that, but my ancestress Rosalee found it just after the War of 1812 and built this house around it. She was a mystical healer and knew of the power of the spring water in the village, which wasn't even a real village then, only a collection of Native American and white settlers. In any case, she knew of the Seneca tribe's tales of the springs, so she moved here from Cleveland after her husband was killed in the Battle of Lake Erie. At some point after she built the first, much smaller version of this house, she started watering the tree with water from the springs.

"We will never know the reason she started it, but she watered the tree every other day from water collected from the spring. The water went directly from the spring to the tree. Every daughter in the family after that has done the same."

Rainwater was quiet, but I felt him watching me. I didn't look to see if the feeling was correct.

I cleared my throat. "The Seneca said that Niagara water was special, and Rosalee believed that too. It became more apparent over time, as the water and the tree were able to give gifts or to send messages to Rosalee's descendants. To me."

I turned around to face him. Rainwater was watching me. He had his mask up. I couldn't read his expression. I couldn't tell if he believed me or thought I was crazy.

I looked away from him. "That's why Grandma Daisy had me come back to the village. It wasn't just to be closer to her. She wanted that too, but I had to come back to become the Caretaker of this shop and the tree. She knew that it was time to pass on the responsibility that she had carried for so long." I took a breath. "My mother should have been the Caretaker now, but since she's not here, it had to be me."

"There's more . . ." David prompted after a minute.

"My grandmother's mother turned the family home into a bookshop because she didn't want to be a Caretaker; she refused her gift. Grandma Daisy didn't. Now it does the same with me."

"How?" Rainwater asked.

"The shop will tell me passages to read from books."

He glanced at the pile of *Leaves of Grass*. "Like Whitman?"

"The shop has been putting Whitman in my path ever since before Private Investigator Redding died. I knew something was going to happen, but I didn't know what. I know that somehow Whitman's poems are connected to Redding's death. I have been trying to find out why Redding took the book with him on his fatal bike ride. I was especially curious because he had been following me. I know this. I saw him around the shop, and you told me that he hired Jo to follow me too. She admitted to that, by the way. Well, technically, not that she was being paid, but she admitted to following me and keeping a file. She said she regretted not destroying the file." The thought of her trying to cover her tracks or destroy the evidence of her spying on me hurt as much as discovering she'd done it in the first place.

"How does this connect to Redding?"

I drew a deep breath. "I think it was the shop's secret that he was after. I think that's why he had Jo watch me. He so desperately wanted to know what was happening inside Charming Books. If he learned what it was, he might get a lot of attention or even money for revealing my family and me to the world. Not that I really know how he would profit much from it after the initial curiosity wore off. He might have spent months trying to figure out what was going on and be disappointed when he finally learned the answer."

"Does Jo know your secret?" His voice was low.

I shook my head. "I don't think so. Grandma Daisy and now you are the only ones who know for certain. Jo may suspect something odd is going on, but nothing more than that. She surely suspects something about why I gather the water from the springs." I took a breath. "I'm sorry I didn't tell you before. I was afraid to. Everyone before me, my mother, my grandmother, going all the way back to Rosalee, ended up without love in their lives. It seems to be the cost of the gift for the Waverly women. I expected the same to happen to us, so I've held you at a distance. Now you know everything. I'm not holding anything else back. You can decide what you want to do with that. You can decide if it's too much and you want to leave." My voice caught.

He shook his head. "I need to process this. It's a lot to process."

"I know," I said. "I felt the same way when I returned to Cascade Springs last year and Grandma Daisy told me about my inheritance. It wasn't something I wanted to hear. I didn't even want to stay in the village." I felt tears gather in my eyes. "Now I can't imagine leaving, and a lot of that has to do with you. I can't imagine leaving you, and now that I've told you the truth, you're going to leave me. It was all for naught." A single tear slid down my cheek, and I dropped my chin to my chest.

"Violet, look at me."

I couldn't look into those amber eyes that might judge me. It was too painful.

"Violet." He lifted my chin with his finger and made me look at him. "Violet," he said again. "This is a lot to take in. Basically, you are telling me you can magically talk to books."

I shook my head. "I don't talk to them. I interpret the passages the shop reveals to me."

He smiled. "Okay, talk was a bad word. But you are telling me that some kind of mysticism is behind this, that the shop, the tree, whatever it is, communicates with you, and it is your inheritance to accept those communications."

I nodded and looked away from him.

"Look where I'm at. I'm still here." His voice was soft. "It's not going to chase me away from you. Nothing can."

I met his eyes.

"I've known that this shop, the birch tree, and you were special. I knew there had to be something more going on here than you wanted me to know. I knew you would tell me when you were ready. That doesn't change how I feel about you. I loved you before this and I will love you after."

His eyes were soft and reminded me more now of warm honey than of amber. I was fairly sure I was crying with happiness and with relief, but I was too much in awe of his reaction to know for certain.

"Nothing can change that," he said. "Nothing."

Then he kissed me.

Chapter
Thirty-Eight

The conversation about the shop essence with Rainwater had gone nothing like I had expected it to go. I'd thought it would chase him away, but it had had the opposite effect. He loved me. I was one of the women he loved like his sister and Aster, but very different too. If I'd known that was going to happen, I would have told him a lot sooner. I would have told him I loved him too instead of burying it deep inside my heart for fear of what he would say when he learned the truth about Charming Book and about me.

I woke up the next morning before dawn breathing easier. I hadn't known until that new morning what a weight my secret put on my shoulders. There were no more barriers between Rainwater and me. I felt lighter, and then I remembered Jo. The girl was still missing, and there was still a killer on the loose, most likely trying to find her. I had to find her first.

Whitman was on my nightstand. Still wearing my pajamas, I picked it up and carried it into my living room. I sat on the couch and started to read, hoping the answers would become clearer. I thought of the line of poetry Redding had left for me again. "All truths wait in all things." But what were the truths when it came to Redding's death?

I kept reading, and when I looked at the clock again, it was after ten. Charming Books should have been open by now. I dashed into my bathroom and got ready.

By the time I ran down the spiral staircase, I saw the front door of the shop was already open. Faulkner sat on his perch by the front window, ready and able to greet shoppers with a verbal insult or a line of poetry. Which one he would use really depended on his mood. Nine times out of ten, though, he fell on insult.

"I opened for you today, Violet," my grandmother said, coming into the main room of the shop from the kitchen. She had a teacup in her hand, and she wore a butterfly scarf around her neck.

"You should have woken me up." I rubbed my eyes. "I was up reading and lost track of time. You should have knocked on my door."

"Don't be silly. You've been up late so many nights dealing with Redding's death that I thought it was high time I pulled my weight around here."

I shook my head. "Grandma Daisy, you have always pulled your weight. You took care of this shop long before I moved back to the village."

She held up her teacup. "Maybe so, but I believe I've been so wrapped up in this museum that I have been shirking my duties here."

"You have responsibilities. The village needs you."

She patted my cheek. "And none more important than you. Besides, there isn't much I can do at the village hall while it's in disarray. The rain did a real number on the foundation, and Vaughn said no one should go in there until he's sure it's stable. I can work on mayoral things remotely." She shook her head. "Despite everything, I still believe that this museum will be the crown jewel of the village when it's done." She handed the teacup to me. "For you, dear."

I sipped and found that she had made my favorite English breakfast tea.

"You're going to need your strength if you are going out there to find Jo."

I raised my eyebrows.

"Don't you think I would know that's what you were planning to do today?"

"Well, yeah."

She took the teacup from my hand. "Then go, girl."

I left the bookshop a few minutes later, going to the only place I thought I might find someone who knew where Jo was.

I rolled into the parking lot of Bobby's Bike Shop, and the owner greeted me at the door. "Ready to trade in that old thing for a hybrid? They ride like a dream."

"No, not yet." I removed my bike helmet.

He grinned. "It was worth a try. I am having a sale on helmets." He looked at the violet-painted helmet in my hand.

I hung my helmet on the handlebar of my bike. "My grandmother made that for me. No matter how much I might look ridiculous wearing it, I can't get a new one."

He laughed. "I can respect that. If you aren't here to buy something, it must be about Jo."

I nodded.

He sighed and rubbed the back of his head. "I knew you would come back, and I have been struggling with what to do when you did."

"What do you mean?"

"You had better come inside."

I followed Bobby into his shop, which was one giant room full to bursting with bikes and bike parts. Bicycles even hung from the rafters above our heads. Bobby wove through the bikes to the back corner of the store, where there was an oil-stained drop cloth on the vinyl flooring. On the cloth was an upside-down bike, clearly in the middle of repairs. It had no spokes in its wheels or tires. The seat was missing, too. Bobby kneeled behind the bike. "I found this beauty sitting on the lawn in front of one of the swanky houses in the bird neighborhood. It's amazing what rich people will throw away. This bike can be as good as new with a little TLC."

The bird neighborhood was the expensive artist colony in Cascade Springs. Rent there started in the thousands per month.

He turned the pedal closest to him and watched as the chain click-clicked forward and then caught and stopped.

"You know where Jo is." It was a statement, not a question. I felt odd looming over him while he worked on the bike, so I perched on a nearby stool.

He shook his head. "I knew where Jo was a day ago. I don't know where she is now."

"Where was she hiding?"

He tried to turn the pedal again. It wouldn't give. "I let her stay here."

It was what I'd expected him to say. "She came to my shop last night."

His eyes went wide. "She did? Is she all right? Was it before or after the storm? I was worried about her being out in that."

"During the storm," I said. "She had been hiding in the park."

"I'm not surprised to hear that. I haven't heard from her in at least a day. I'm glad to hear that she was all right."

"Why did you help Jo hide from the police?"

He sighed. "I see myself in her. We have a lot in common in our pasts."

"What do you mean?" I set my feet on the high rungs of the stool.

"I was a kid who got in trouble too. The only attention I ever got was from getting into trouble. I thought after some time that's who I was. It wasn't until I was sent to juvenile hall that I got scared straight. I didn't want something like that to happen to Jo. At the core of it, she's a good kid who's made some bad choices."

"You mean the stealing."

"You know about that?"

I nodded. And while I hadn't truly counted the free coffees at the campus as stealing, her "gifting" of free beverages did in fact deprive the campus of income.

"I've been trying to help her, and she's been doing so well too, ever since she started working for me, but I've noticed in the last few months she has been more guarded again. Secretive. I know from my own troubles that it was a sure sign she was falling back into her old ways."

"What happened over the last few months?" I asked.

He removed the gears from the bike and laid them on the drop cloth. "She's been calling out from work more often. She's been jumpy. She seems to be always looking over her shoulder. When I asked her about it, she told me that she was fine, only stressed out about school. When the semester was over and she didn't seem to get better, I knew something else was going on, but she still wouldn't tell me what it was."

I wrapped my arms around my waist. I wished Jo had been comfortable enough to trust me. I could have helped her too. I wondered if my relationship with Rainwater was what had kept her from trusting me like she had Bobby.

"Did she come to you for help after the race?"

He spun the gears on the bike in front of him.

"Bobby, Jo's in danger. Please tell me what you know."

He sighed. "She did. She told me that she was in some kind of trouble. She didn't say what it was. This was before I knew Redding was killed. I didn't know anything about that."

"What did you do for her?"

"I offered her a place to stay, like I told you. I said no one would be at the bike shop because it was closed for the race, and all my customers were in the race besides. I gave her a lift back to my shop."

"So that's why you weren't around after the bike race."

He nodded. "I didn't even get out of the car when I dropped her off here. I had to get back to the race."

"Was she here after you learned about Redding?"

He nodded. "I told her the police were looking for her and asked what she had done. She bolted after that. I regret my questions now. I should have handled it differently."

"Did she ever come back to the bike shop after that?"

"No. She was here only one night as far as I know." He held the chain up to the light and examined it. "I know that she left because she wanted to protect me. She didn't want me to get in trouble too. She left me a note telling me that."

"Do you still have the note?"

He sighed.

I cocked my head. "Can I see it?"

He frowned and then stood up. He opened the drawer of a tool cabinet and pulled out a scrap of paper. "It's not much." He held it out to me.

I took the note from his hand. In hasty cursive, it read,

Bobby
Thanks you for help. I had to leave. It's not safe for me to be here. I'll be fine. I know how to take care of myself.

The note wasn't signed, but I had no reason to doubt it was from Jo. "The police need this."

"You can have it," he said.

"I can give it to them, but they will want to talk to you about it." I folded the note as carefully as I could and put it in my pocket.

"I know," he said with resignation, and knelt in front of the broken bike again. He put the chain back on the drop cloth. "Like I said before, she's a good kid, even if she's made some really bad choices in the past."

"Why didn't you tell the police or me any of this before?" I asked, holding on to the stool with both of my hands on either side of my legs.

"I thought maybe that she killed him. I didn't want to believe that it was possible, but it is possible, and I didn't want the repercussions for her. If she killed him, I knew she would go to prison, and I didn't want that. I thought it would be better if she could get away. I've made mistakes too. That's why I left Atlanta all those years ago. I had to get away and start in someplace new. After a while, I ended up here in Cascade Springs, and I never looked back. I was hoping that Jo would leave and find her own Cascade Springs. Although I would miss her, I thought that was what was best for her."

I realized that Bobby cared about Jo a lot. Her saw her potential and didn't want her to ruin her life. I didn't want that either, but if she'd murdered Redding, didn't justice have to be served? I mean, there were crimes, and then there was the deed of actually taking a life . . .

I shook my head as if to chase the thoughts away. I couldn't believe she had killed him. It just wasn't possible. Because if she'd killed him, did that mean she'd killed Bryant Cloud too? And if that was true, where had she gotten the gun to shoot Danielle's ex-husband?

"Where else might she have gone after leaving the bike shop? Do you know any of her friends? Did they ever visit her in the shop?"

He shook his head. "No, Jo is a loner."

I nodded. That had always been my perception, too. "What about her brother? He's in Cascade Springs working on the village hall. Would she have gone to him?"

He replaced the gears on the bike and picked up a can of oil and oiled them. It reminded me of the tin man oiling his joints in *The Wizard of Oz*. He looked up from his work. "I doubt it.

I never got the impression that she was close to anyone in her family. She told me once she and her brother grew up in the foster system. They were separated and didn't reunite until she was eighteen and out on her own."

My heart broke from hearing that. No wonder Jo had a problem with authority like the police.

"Bobby, I want to help her. I don't believe she killed Redding, but I do believe she knows who did. We have to protect her from that person. The only way to do that is to find her."

"If she knows who killed him, she never told me. I told her not to tell me why she needed to hide. The more I knew, the harder it would be to protect her." He replaced the chain back onto the bike's gears. His hands were covered in oil.

"I don't think she told anyone, which might be even worse for her. If she is the only one who knows the identity of the killer, all the killer has to do is kill her to get clean away."

Bobby sat back on his heels. I could see the wheels turning in his head like the gears on the many bikes in his shop.

"Please, Bobby. I care about Jo too. I just want her to be safe. She can't run from whoever she's so afraid of for the rest of her life."

"There's one more place that she might have gone. It was the place she talked about the most since she started acting strangely."

"Where?"

"The village hall."

Chapter Thirty-Nine

As I rode back to the village on my old bike and wearing my ridiculous helmet, I debated telling Rainwater what I knew before going to the hall. In the end, I decided against it. I thought that if Jo was there, she was much more likely to speak to me alone.

River Road was quiet. There were a few tourists in the village, and it was near lunchtime. My stomach rumbled. I hadn't stopped to eat breakfast that morning.

My footsteps echoed in the hall. I looked around the wide-open rotunda, taking care not to step into the hole in the floor. If I was hiding in this building, where would I go? Not the rotunda, that was for sure. I could see every inch of it from where I stood. I wouldn't go into the hole, either. It was too creepy and too dirty. I glanced at the plastic sheet that led into the part of the building that would be the museum. That's where I would go.

Before I entered the museum, I heard the *click, click, click* of heels on the curved marble staircase. "What are you doing here? Your grandmother isn't here," Bertie said.

"I know that. She's at Charming Books."

The secretary came at me at a brisk pace. "She should be here. The village budget is in a crisis because of this museum that she insisted we build. It's been a disaster from beginning to end."

I stared at her. It wasn't her words that caught my attention; it was the garnet necklace hanging from her neck. The same necklace I had found in the museum the day of the race. "Where did you get that?" I pointed at the necklace.

She wrapped her hands around it. "I've had it for years."

I frowned. "Did you lose it recently?"

She narrowed her eyes. "How did you know?"

"When did you lose it?" I asked.

"The day before the race. I was so distraught, but not a soul seemed to care because they were so caught up in Daisy's great plans for the village. A whole lot of rubbish, if you ask me."

"Where was it when it went missing?"

"I had it on my desk in my office, and it just disappeared. I assumed one of those terrible bike people nicked it."

"Did you tell Grandma Daisy?" I asked, wondering why my grandmother hadn't mentioned that the necklace belonged to Bertie.

"Why would I tell Daisy? She thinks the people involved in the museum and her precious fund-raisers can do no wrong. I know she has been trying to push me out. She doesn't include me in meetings. She claims that she doesn't need someone to take minutes—she'd rather have Councilman Connell click on his laptop and record the whole event. She doesn't need me. Why would I talk to her at all?"

I pressed my lips together. I knew my grandmother thought she was being kind to Bertie by not including her in anything to do with the museum, since it upset the secretary so much.

"Who else was there? I assume Bobby from the bike shop."

She nodded. "And that girl who works for him. I do not like facial piercing at all. The only place earrings should be is in your ears."

"Anyone else?"

"There had to be at least a dozen volunteers, plus Vaughn. Your grandmother can't say enough good things about him. In her eyes, he can do no wrong." She snorted.

"Vaughn is Jo's brother. The girl with the piercings."

She wrinkled her nose. "I wouldn't have known it. The pair of them didn't even talk to each other at the meeting."

"And one of these people took your necklace?" I asked.

"It had to be one of them. I was heartbroken to see it was gone. It's very precious to me. It was a gift of my late husband. I didn't move it, and there weren't any others in the mayor's office that day. I may not care for your grandmother, but I would never accuse her of stealing."

"How did it come back?" I couldn't help but think this necklace was in some way related to both Redding's and Bryant's murders, but I didn't know how.

"It just appeared. It was right in the middle of my desk two days later like it had been there all the time. I know that it wasn't there before. I looked everywhere for it."

Someone had put it back on her desk, but why? And it had been after I'd found it. So they stole it from me to return it?

She shook her head. "You tell your grandmother that she will have no luck running me out. She may have term limits, but I don't." With that, she spun on her heel and marched out of the hall.

I watched Bertie go and felt confused. Why would someone take the necklace, hide it in the museum, and then return it? And what had happened to it after it was in my pocket? Was it really connected to Redding's and Bryant's deaths like I suspected or just a strange coincidence?

I shook my head. I would worry about the necklace later. I had to find Jo. I pushed the plastic away and stepped into the museum. "Jo?" I called.

There was no answer.

"Jo, I want to help. I just spoke to Bobby, and he told me how he helped you. I want to be there for you too. I know you're scared."

There was a squeak that sounded like a sneaker's tread catching on the marble.

"Jo, please stop running! This has gone on long enough."

There was another squeak, and then she appeared from around the ceiling support. Tears were in her eyes. "Violet, I'm scared."

"Let's go to Charming Books and you can tell me why."

To my surprise, she nodded. Jo had finally grown tired of running.

Chapter Forty

I dropped my bike off by the garage and took Jo in through the back door of Charming Books. I had texted Grandma Daisy that we were on our way, and she was waiting for us in the kitchen.

"Oh, you poor thing." Grandma Daisy wrapped her arm around Jo's shoulders. "We need to find you something to eat. How about cake? Lacey just dropped off a chocolate torte from Le Crepe Jolie."

Jo sat on the stool by the island. She was so petite her legs couldn't reach the foot rail below but swung freely back and forth. She sat cross-legged on the stool as if self-conscious about her small stature.

Grandma Daisy cut a large piece and put it in front of Jo. She cut a much smaller piece for herself and for me.

Jo dug into her cake.

"Jo, can you tell me from the beginning how this all started?" I asked.

She swallowed a bite of cake. "I—I take things. That's how I got into this terrible mess. The stealing started when I was younger. My brother and I were foster kids and we were moved from home to home. We were separated. We didn't have anything, so I started taking things. It made me feel better at first. I would steal T-shirts and shoes from the mall. I soon moved on to wallets and money. Then I got caught more than once. If I did it again, I would have gone to juvie. I promised myself I wouldn't, and I didn't for the rest of high school."

"But after high school?" I asked.

She nodded. "It started again. There was a petty cash drawer at the college student union where I worked during the school year. No one counted the money out of it. The supervisor just had it in case something was off about the drawer and we had to make up money at the end of the night. I ignored it all my first semester at Springside, but as the classes got harder and my stress increased over working multiple jobs and going to school, I started taking money. At first it was just a couple of dollars. I wanted to test it to see if anyone would notice. No one did, so I took more." She licked her lips.

"When I was alone in the coffee bar, I wouldn't report some of my sales in the cash register. I would make the coffee and put the money in this petty money drawer so it always looked like there was money there. It was going so well." She rubbed her forehead. "I became braver, and started taking other things like I did before."

Something dawned on me. "Like Bertie's garnet necklace?"

She nodded. "I took it from her desk when we were in the middle of the meeting about the bike race. After I pocketed the necklace, I thought better of it. I knew Bertie would make a big stink about it being missing, so I left it in the museum on the scaffolding, hoping that it would get back to her."

"That necklace was Bertie's?" Grandma Daisy asked. "I never even noticed she wore a garnet necklace."

I bit my lip.

"Did it get back to her?" Jo asked.

"It did," I said.

"I'm glad." She let out a breath. "I should never have taken it and do feel bad if she was upset over it."

"How is Redding involved? This involves him, doesn't it?" I watched her face closely as I asked. I knew now that Jo was a gifted liar. How could I believe anything she said? At the same time, I wanted to believe her.

"He had been around campus. He knew that I'd had a class with you, and he would ask me questions about you all the time. I blew him off, but then he was in the coffee shop in the evening. It was a busy night in March. All the students were chased inside because of the awful weather. The girl who was supposed to work with me called off. I was alone and doing lots of sales. It was the perfect night to do my scheme. I remember selling Redding a coffee at some point that night. I was so busy, I honestly don't know how long he was there after I gave him his drink. Apparently, it was long enough to see what I was up to. When I was locking up at the end of the night, he confronted me."

Grandma Daisy cut another generous portion of cake and put it on Jo's plate. "You are going to need it. I can always tell."

Jo nodded and continued her story. "Redding said he wouldn't report me if I did him a favor."

My heart sank. I knew what that favor was. "To spy on me."

Her eyes went wide, and she nodded. She took another bite of cake. "The more I worked with Redding, the more I enjoyed the private-eye thing. He wasn't that bad of a guy after a while. He started paying me to report back to him. It was an easy job, and he said I would make a good investigator because no one ever notices me. I'm so small and quiet. I can move easily from place to place without being seen."

I wondered how many times this had been true for me. How many times had Jo been following me back and forth to the springs and I had no idea?

Grandma Daisy touched a napkin to the corner of her mouth. "So you've explained how you started working for Redding, but why was he killed?"

"Because of something I stole." She looked at each of us. "And I still have it."

She set her backpack on the island and opened it. She pulled out a tin box that was encrusted with mud. Grandma Daisy peered more closely at it. "Has this box been dipped in wax?"

Jo nodded. "It's super old. You can open it."

Grandma Daisy nodded to me. "Violet, you do the honors."

I took a breath, having no idea what I would find inside. The lid creaked as I opened it. Inside was a stack of thin paper. I moved the paper aside, and at the bottom of the box was an envelope addressed to Walt Whitman. The return address was the White House.

I stared at the envelope for a long time. This was why Redding had been carrying *Leaves of Grass* with him. This was the reason the shop had kept putting his poetry in front of me with conflicting passages, and why I hadn't been able to sort out what those passages meant. It wasn't the words that the essence wanted me to pay attention to. It was the author. My hands shook, and I set the envelope back into the tin box.

It was then that I saw the similarities between Jo and Walt Whitman. Maybe the shop's essence all this time had been pointing me toward that connection. Both Jo and Whitman were hard workers when they wanted to be, but they hated to be penned in. They both had dreams of greatness, too. Whitman's greatness was his poetry. Jo hadn't discovered hers yet, but I knew she wanted something more.

"Where did you get this?" My voice was hushed.

She pressed her lip together.

I looked at her. "Jo, if this is real, it is priceless. I couldn't imagine what a letter written in Lincoln's hand would be worth. It's made even more valuable because it was addressed to Whitman."

"Read the letter," she said.

I took care opening the envelope. I did so slowly. I could only imagine what Renee's archivist would have said if he saw me touching such an important document with my bare hands.

Dear Mr. Whitman,

I have enjoyed your work *Leaves of Grass* very much. Your words have been a comfort to both my dear wife and me during the loss of our son, Willie. Especially when you talk about the hereafter.

Even in these difficult times in our nation, I encourage you to pursue your art. We cannot let the war deter us from having a vibrant America, and this includes the arts of which Mrs. Lincoln and I are quite fond.

I have heard of your fine service to the sick and wounded here in Washington. Thank you for your service in the hospitals, tending and reading your great work to our wounded, both from north and south. Both are our sons. The causalities of war pain me. Every life lost in the divine pursuit of preserving the union is precious and not lost in vain.

Truly yours,

A. Lincoln

The letter was brief, but I couldn't help but think what Whitman would have thought when he opened it. He loved Abraham Lincoln and saw him as the man who would restore peace to the country. He referred to him often in his work and eulogized him in the famous poem "O Captain, My Captain" when Lincoln died. It was, in a word, priceless.

"Jo." I stared at her. "Where did you get this letter?"

"I can't tell you that, but you should have it, Daisy, for your museum."

My grandmother read the letter. "This would be the crown jewel of any museum, but I don't know if ours is the right place."

Jo stood up. "I want you to have it. I don't want it anymore. I thought I could . . ." She shook head. "It doesn't matter anymore what I thought. I'm glad that I gave it to you. Even if you don't keep it, you will know what to do with it." She turned as if to go.

"Jo, you can't leave." I jumped out of my seat. "Whoever killed Redding is still out there."

She nodded. "I know. This is why you two should keep the letter. It's not safe with me any longer." She ran to the back door and was outside in a blink.

By the time I made it to the back door, she'd disappeared into the woods. Again.

Grandma Daisy shook her head. "That girl can really move when she wants too."

And it seemed to me that she always wanted to.

Chapter
Forty-One

When Rainwater walked into Charming Books ten minutes later, his expression was thunderous. Grandma Daisy's eyes went wide. "Yikes, you'd better talk to him, Violet."

"Me? He's not mad at you. You should be the one to talk him down." I pushed her in front of me.

"I can hear you," Rainwater said in an irritated voice. He folded his arms and leaned against the sale counter. He looked to me. "You let Jo get away again?"

I grimaced. "I'm sorry, but I honestly thought she would stay this time. She left something with us. Something very important, if it is authentic."

"It's authentic," Grandma Daisy said. "I can feel it in my bones." She placed the tin box on the sales counter. "Read it."

Rainwater sighed and read the letter. His eyes widened. "Is this real?"

"We will have to have it authenticated," I said. "But I think it might very well be real. David, what if the box the letter was in was found near the foundation of the village hall? It's encrusted with dirt and it clearly was protected from the elements by dipping it in wax. What if Whitman lost it here in the village? Whitman visited Cascade Springs on his second trip to Niagara Falls late in life. He even visited this shop. There's proof of it in the college archives. Also proof that Mayor Hodge didn't care for him in the least. What if Hodge had the box with the letter buried in the foundation of the village hall?"

Rainwater's eyes went wide. "There are a lot of ifs in there."

"Maybe there are, but if I'm right"—I took a breath—"I think I know who the killer is."

Rainwater cocked his head. "Did the shop tell you who it was?"

Grandma Daisy clapped her hands. "Oh! You told him. I was so wishing you would." She hugged Rainwater. "This is wonderful!"

I frowned. You would have thought I'd told her Rainwater and I were getting married by the way she reacted.

"Hear me out," I said, ignoring my grandmother's outburst.

"All right," he said.

"I think it's Vaughn."

"Vaughn! No, never!" Grandma Daisy cried. "He's been working so hard on the museum. He's there every day."

"Right, so he would have an opportunity to put the garnet necklace that I found back on Bertie's desk. He was the last person I saw when I had the necklace. He must have stolen it from my pocket and put it back on Bertie's desk."

Grandma Daisy opened her mouth, as if she were about to protest.

"I know it doesn't seem to be connected, but he would know his sister. He would know she was the one who took it because of her history of shoplifting. But moreover, he's working with the hall's foundation. He would be the one who found the letter. What if she stole the letter from him, and he thought she was going to give it to Redding?"

Rainwater frowned. "It's a loose theory, but it's worth bringing Vaughn to the station to talk it over. At the very least, we can say it has to do with his sister. We've already talked to him a number of times since her disappearance. He's been upset, to say the least, that we haven't found her."

"Was he upset you hadn't found Jo or that letter?" I asked. I knew I was right. "It has to be him. Who else would she protect other than her brother?"

"Okay, you have me convinced that we should talk to him." He pushed off the counter and removed his cell phone from his belt. "Clipton, I want you and Wheaton to track down Vaughn Fitzgerald and bring him in . . . yes, again . . . I think he might know more about the case than he's leading on. Check his home, office, and the village hall. Right." He ended the call.

"I'm ready to go," I said.

Rainwater shook his head. "You aren't going anywhere. I want you and Daisy to stay here in case Jo comes back, and I can't take the letter just yet. Keep it safe for me."

"Of course," Grandma Daisy said.

He looked at me again and said, "Stay here. Please."

I wanted to promise him I would, but I couldn't manage to say the actual words. "You will keep us in the loop?"

"If that keeps you here, I will," he said.

"It's your best shot." Grandma Daisy smiled at him.

Rainwater sighed and left the shop.

The rest of the afternoon dragged on, and I didn't hear anything from the police chief. The entire time, I was a ball of nerves. What if I was wrong and Vaughn wasn't the killer? Would I be just like my accusers all those years ago when Colleen died? I didn't want to be like that.

"Violet," my grandmother said. "If you pace anymore, you're going to march right through those floorboards and be in the basement, and we all know how you feel about that."

I stopped pacing. The basement in Charming Books was a dirt floor, dank and dusty. I avoided going down there as much as possible.

"You aren't going to settle down until you do something. Let's go to Le Crepe Jolie for an early dinner."

"It four thirty."

"Then think of it as a late lunch. Did you eat anything other than that chocolate cake today?"

I tried to remember. "The shop doesn't close for a half hour. Maybe we should wait until shop hours are officially over."

"And let you fall into the basement? I don't think so." She shook her head.

"What about the letter? Should we be here to guard it?"

"I hid it in the perfect spot. No one could possibly find it."

"Where's that?"

"If I told you, then you might find it."

"Are you asking me to go to Le Crepe Jolie because it's next to the village hall and that might be where Vaughn is?" I narrowed my eyes.

She shrugged. "Would your grandmother do something like that?"

The short answer was yes.

In the end, I followed my grandmother out of the shop and we walked to Le Crepe Jolie. We passed the village hall. It stood quiet and resolute.

"He must not have been here," Grandma Daisy said. "I'm guessing that David already took him to the station for questioning. I'm sure everything will be settled soon." She sighed. "I still can't believe that Vaughn is responsible."

I nodded, starting to think she was right. My theory had been pretty farfetched. I prayed I hadn't accused an innocent man.

"Violet! Daisy!" Lacey cried as we walked into Le Crepe Jolie. "This is a fun surprise for you to stop by so early. Take your usual table by the window."

Grandma Daisy and I sat, and as we did, I spotted Richard and Renee at a table in the far corner of the dining room. Renee waved me over to their table.

I walked over with a smile, despite all my worries over Jo and Vaughn.

"Violet," Renee said. "It's nice to see you."

Richard fumbled with his knife and fork.

"It's nice to see the two of you, too. Enjoying a late lunch?"

"Just coffee." She pointed at the cup in front of her. "Richard asked me out on a coffee date. Isn't that sweet?" She smiled at Richard.

"Very sweet," I agreed.

Richard swallowed hard. "I knew Renee and I both had a fondness for coffee. We've had a very nice conversation on books."

"I'm sure you have."

Renee winked at me. I smiled back. It seemed that Richard had finally gotten up the nerve to ask her out. I was glad to see something happy on such a difficult day.

I backed away. "I will leave you two to it."

Renee held up her hand. "Wait, Violet."

I stopped and turned around.

She pressed her lips together, and her excitement of finally being on a real date with Richard seemed to fall away. "I was planning to stop by Charming Books after Richard and I were done here."

"Something up?" I asked.

"After you left the library, the next time I saw the archivist, I asked him about Whitman's visit to Cascade Springs. He was more than excited to talk about it, and he talked and he talked and he talked. I swear the man could wax on about dryer lint. Finally, when I had a chance to get a word in, I asked him if anyone had been in the archives recently to ask about Whitman. I don't always know who the archivist meets with, especially in the summer when the library has odd hours." She took a breath. "He said that over the last month he'd actually spoken to two different men about it on two different occasions. He was quite excited to tell me about. I know that it can get pretty boring down there alone with all those old papers and books."

Richard cleared his throat. "I would be happy to go down and visit with the archivist from time to time to keep him company. Now that I have heard about the village's connection to Whitman, I am curious about the rest of our literary history. It might be the good start of a book for me, perhaps a nonfiction book as well as a fiction book."

Renee smiled at him. "Thank you, Richard. I'm sure the archivist would appreciate that. There is nothing that he loves more than for the archives to be used for publications. Although I wouldn't tell him you were writing fiction. He doesn't see much value in that."

He blushed.

I held my arms at my sides. "And who were the men?"

"Well," Renee began. "I asked the archivist for the registry, because anytime anyone uses the archives, we are supposed to record it. The archivist is a bit lax on this and claimed he forgot. I believe him. He can remember minute details about the history of Cascade Springs but would lose his own head if it wasn't attached to his neck. Let me tell you, I will be putting more procedures into place after this so that I know exactly who has been in and out of the college archives."

"Could he describe the men, then? Even if he didn't know their names?" I asked.

She nodded. "I'm getting to that. He said the first man—"

"Had a blond mustache and a guitar case," I interrupted.

"Right."

Redding. I should have thought of it earlier. Redding was a detective. He was trained to follow the facts. Of course if there was a letter written to Whitman from President Lincoln found in Cascade Springs, he would want evidence to prove that Walt Whitman had actually visited the village.

My hands felt cold. He would have seen the entry about the Waverly house, just like I had when I visited the archives.

Perhaps I had been wrong about him to some extent. Perhaps he hadn't been watching Charming Books just because of me but had wanted to understand the connection to Whitman. Maybe he'd even thought Grandma Daisy and I knew something about it. He wouldn't have come right out and asked me. If he had, he knew, I would have researched the question myself. He knew enough about me to know I was a tenacious researcher too.

I shook my head, trying to control the thoughts whirling inside it. "And who was the second man?"

She licked her lips. "It was Jo's brother."

Vaughn. Maybe I had been right that Vaughn was the person behind the murders. It made sense, then, as to why Jo would be hiding. She wouldn't want her brother to get arrested, but at the same time, was she afraid of him too?

I thanked Renee and went to sit with my grandmother. Grandma Daisy, Lacey, and Danielle chatted while I stared out the window. I was too distracted by not hearing from Rainwater to pay attention. Was Vaughn innocent? Had I gotten it all wrong? Would Jo forgive me if I wrongly accused her brother even if I honestly thought I was helping her?

Through the window, I saw a small figure walk by.

"That was Jo!" I jumped out of my seat. "Grandma, call Rainwater."

"Girl! What are you doing?" my grandmother shouted after me.

"This time I'm not going to be responsible for her running away." I ran out the door.

Jo disappeared around the side of the village hall. As I came around the side of the large building, I saw her slip in through the basement window. This must be where she had been hiding.

I hesitated at the opening of the window. There was a loud crack and a shout deep under the building. It sounded like a gunshot. I hoped my grandmother had reinforcements here soon, because I was going in.

Chapter
Forty-Two

The windowsill was slick with water. The heavy rain from the night before had flooded the space beneath the hall. From outside the window, it was impossible to see what a large drop it might have been to the earth below. It might have been three feet or a hundred. I didn't dare turn on the flashlight on my phone to guide my way. There was too much of a risk of being seen.

I slipped through the window, and my feet hit the ground with a splash. I stood in at least four inches of water. I didn't think Vaughn had been totally honest with my grandmother about the condition of the village hall. I was no contractor, but standing water on the foundation couldn't be a good thing.

The smell of mold and decay permeated the close space. I wondered what it had been like to be a slave trying to reach Canada. What would it be like to sleep in this dark, dank place during the day, knowing that the mighty Niagara River was just across the road from you, knowing that freedom was just across the road for you? I doubted any of the slaves caught a wink of sleep that last day. Tomorrow would have been too important to miss one millisecond of it.

The sound of the running water was chilling. Where was it coming from? I bummed into a steel support, which had to be one of the new additions Vaughn's team was installing to shore up the foundation. My eyes adjusted to the only light, which came from the window behind me.

As I inched forward around the support, the window light faded. However, a new light became clearer. There was another basement window on the back of the village hall. It was open. Warm evening air flowed from it into the space.

To the right of that window, I saw the source of the rushing water. There was a pipe with a hole in it. As I stood there, the pipe cracked in two, and the water came out in a waterfall that seemed as powerful as the great Niagara Falls themselves.

"Where is it?" a sharp voice asked, which I immediately recognized as Bertie's. Bertie. How could I have been so wrong?

I squinted and saw the outline of two figures standing thirty feet from the broken pipe. The pipe was behind Jo's head. I guessed that the gunshot had hit the pipe. We had to get out of there. The foundation would fill up quickly. The water pumps in the space couldn't keep up with the onslaught of water.

"Where is it?" Bertie repeated, completely ignoring the water filling the room.

"Where's what?" Jo's voice quavered.

"The letter. Tell me what you've done with it."

"What letter?" Jo asked.

There was a smacking sound, and someone fell to the ground. "Don't lie to me, girl. I need that letter. I've already killed two people to get it. I don't mind killing a third."

I stifled a gasp. Bertie had killed Redding and Bryant.

"I—I don't have it."

I inched forward. The toe of my shoe caught on something, a stone or maybe a brick. I windmilled my arms to keep myself from falling and held my breath. I was certain my gymnastics would catch their attention. I regained my balance and froze, listening with every part of me to hear if they'd noticed.

"I still don't know what you're talking about," Jo said. Her voice sounded muffled, like she was speaking through swollen lips.

"Yes, you do," Bertie snapped. "You were there when your brother told Redding about the letter. You were the one who connected them. Redding was the one who had a connection to Cloud, who could sell it. I had to get rid of both of them. They knew too much about it."

"But what about Vaughn?"

She snorted. "He doesn't even know the letter is missing. You did a good job of stealing it from him and leaving an identical box behind in its place. Now, hand it over."

"How do I know you won't kill me if I do?"

Bertie laughed. "I'll surely kill you if you don't. Is that a chance you're willing to take?"

I let out a breath. They didn't know I was there, at least not yet. Taking more care with my steps, I moved forward again. I could see them now in the light coming in from the hole in the rotunda's marble floor. The floor was six feet above my head in this part of the foundation.

I took three more tiny steps forward. Now they were completely in my view. Jo was on the floor, and Bertie stood over her with the gun.

"But I thought Vaughn . . ." She trailed off.

"You thought your brother killed those men. You don't have much faith in your family, do you?"

"He found the letter. He and Redding were going to sell it with Cloud and split the money three ways. He must have killed them to keep it for himself," Jo insisted, as if she didn't believe Bertie in taking credit for murder.

"So what if they had that plan? I had a plan too. I heard them discussing it one night in the village hall rotunda. All three of them had no idea I was there. They hatched their plan, and I hatched my own. I just had to get the letter from them. I tried. I tried very hard, and each time they didn't give it to me, one of them had to die. They never expected it. No one notices me. No one pays attention to me."

"Listen," Jo said. "I'm the same way. I understand. No one sees or pays attention to me either. It's always been like that. I was raised in foster care and never was anywhere long enough for anyone to know me or what I could do. I can understand why you're upset."

"I don't want to hear your sob story. I don't care that you were in foster care. I don't care that life dealt you a bad hand. I don't care that it dealt me a bad hand. You still choose what you do with that hand. I've spent my life working for this village for nothing. I've just been cast aside. I will get what I deserve, and that letter will get it for me. Now, hand it over, or I will have to kill you like I have the rest of them."

There was scraping behind me. There was someone else there. Was it Rainwater?

I took another step, and my ankle turned as I came down on a stone. For a moment, I wobbled in place. I took care not to cry out and willed myself to be silent. I regained my footing, but my ankle ached. It wasn't broken, but I had twisted it good on whatever I'd nearly fallen over. I squatted and brushed my hand along the dirt floor under the rising water. My hand connected with a stone. I picked it up, and when I did, I realized it wasn't a stone at all but a piece of brick.

I weighed the heft of it in my hand.

"I'm sorry that I have to do this. I could have used your skills." She leveled the gun at Jo's chest.

Her apology was my cue. I lifted the brick and threw it with all my might at Bertie's head. I was only five feet from her, but she couldn't see me in the shadows. It would be more of a miracle if I missed than if I hit my mark.

The piece of brick connected with the side of Bertie's head in a sickening crunch. I felt ill just hearing it. Like a felled tree, Bertie crumbled to the ground, her face in the water.

I'd thought Jo might drown, but so could Bertie. I pushed myself through the muddy water to her. I grabbed her and pulled her out of the water. "Jo! Run! Go!"

The girl spun and ran for the window.

I heard shouts soon. Wheaton and Rainwater were there.

"The ceiling is going to cave in! Wheaton, get Bertie. Go!"

Wheaton scooped up the murderous secretary and took her out.

I took Rainwater's hand, and he pulled me up. Stones fell onto our heads, and we ran for the window. Rainwater tripped and fell. I hear a sickening crack like a broken ankle. The portion of the ceiling where I had just been fell in. The building groaned.

"Violet!" Rainwater shouted. "Go!"

More of the ceiling and the marble flooring from above fell into the foundation. We were going to die under the village hall after all. Rainwater gave me a boost out the window. When I was clear, I turned back to him. "David!"

There were more crashes and splashes from inside as the water wreaked its havoc on the old foundation. Rainwater's hands and the top of his head appeared in the widow. I grabbed those hands and pulled for all I was worth. He came through just as the window crashed to the ground behind him.

On the grassy hill, I rolled on top of him. Dirt and stones hit my back as I did my best to protect him from any of the flying debris.

Finally the roaring of the falling building stopped. I looked behind me. The village hall sat precariously on its foundation, or what was left of it. The crash hadn't hurt the buildings on either side.

"How did the foundation fall like that and not take out the entire building?" a voice asked. I couldn't identify where it was coming from. My ears were ringing too badly.

"It's like it was magic," someone else said.

Magic. I thought of the aquifer below the village hall, the aquifer that was part of the same system that supplied water to the natural spring. Magic.

"Violet," Rainwater said. "You're crushing me a bit."

I looked down at him. Mud streaked his face and there was a cut above his eyebrow, but he was smiling at me, and the look in his amber eyes was something I couldn't identify.

I rolled off him. "Are you all right? Are you hurt?" I checked his body for wounds.

"Violet," Rainwater said in a gentle voice. "I'm okay."

I stopped fussing over him and stared at him. "I love you." I kissed his muddy forehead. It tasted like dirt, but I didn't care.

"I love you too," he said.

Then I threw my arms around him and hugged him tight. "I've loved you for a long while."

Epilogue

Three days later, Rainwater and I were sitting at Charming Books on the couches in front of the fireplace. Jo was upstairs in the children's loft reading a book, and my grandmother was outside showing Charles and Fenimore her garden.

"How did the letter get under the village hall?" Rainwater asked.

"My guess is still Mayor Hodge. According to his journal, he visited with Whitman and didn't think much of him. He thought Whitman's poems were scandalous, but he had the foresight to know that the letter was important because it was in Lincoln's own hand. He preserved it under the hall and near the foundation, and it stayed there until Vaughn found it during construction."

Rainwater nodded. "That works with what we know from Vaughn. He said he found it in the failing foundation. He also thought it was a safe place to keep it hidden. He never knew his sister took it. Vaughn kept going back to the hall every day to work—I use that term loosely—on the foundation, when in fact he was looking to see if there was anything else hidden there."

"Was there?" I asked.

"He claims there wasn't," Rainwater said.

"I tend to believe him on that. He met Redding through his sister, and he, Redding, and Bryant Cloud crafted a way to sell the letter to a private collector and split the money. Bertie found out about it and thought this could be her way to get back at the village she felt had forgotten her. Am I right on that?"

Rainwater nodded. "And she could have had a nice retirement if she'd sold that letter too. She just didn't know where it was. She knew that Jo took it, though."

"Did Jo tell you why she stole the letter?"

"She stole it the day before Redding died with no idea of Bertie's plans. She knew it had to be given to a museum somehow. She didn't want to get her brother in trouble, but she knew it was wrong for him to sell it."

"What will happen to Bertie?" I asked.

"She killed two people. She'll spend the rest of her life in prison at best."

I grimaced. "I can't help feeling sorry for her. She felt like she was being pushed out of the only life she knew, so when that happened, taking that letter, which would have made my grandmother's museum world-famous, was a way to exact revenge on a village that had forgotten her. I know Grandma Daisy feels terrible about it."

Rainwater squeezed my hand. "She killed two people, yet you still have sympathy for her. You have a kind heart, Violet Waverly."

I stood up and walked over to the tree. "The strange thing is, I'm looking at the tree differently now. Because now I know Whitman looked at the same tree. It's hard to explain, but I feel a deeper connection with the shop now that I know about this literary connection and the connection of my family to Whitman too."

Rainwater smiled. "Literature has been your life for a very long time."

I looked up at him. "It might have been my whole life before, but it's not now. I have other things to concentrate on."

He wrapped his arms around me. "Things that are more important than long-dead poets? I don't believe you."

"You had better believe it, because you're one of them. I can't have you doubting my devotion to you."

Emerson sat on the step with that little feline smile on his face, and Faulkner flapped his winds above out head. "Have you dreaded these earth-beetles?"

"That's cheerful," Rainwater said.

I laughed. "He's quoting Whitman."

"I know." He looked down at me with those amber eyes, and I felt like I was melting from the inside out. "I don't care who your father is. I don't care that you have a magical book-shop. None of those things are important to me."

I looked up at him. "They're not? I would think a book-shop with flying books would be something to talk and worry about."

"I care about you and making you happy."

"I'm sorry that I kept the shop's secret from you for so long and made you doubt how I felt about you."

"I would never doubt you, Violet. That is something you can rest assured of. I have something for you."

Rainwater reached into his pocket, and I thought my heart might stop. I felt dizzy. Breath whooshed out of my body when I saw it was a piece of paper. "Open it," he said.

With shaking hands, I opened the note. There was a verse I knew very well from my time studying Whitman, both in grad school and over the last week while trying to find out who killed Joel Redding. It was from "Song of the Open Road."

Tears gathered in my eyes as I read it.

I give you my hand!
I give you my love more precious than money,
I give you myself before preaching or law;
Will you give me yourself? will you come travel with
      me?
Shall we stick by each other as long as we live?

When I looked up, he was on his knee.

Author's Note

Walt Whitman visited Niagara Falls twice in his lifetime, once before the Civil War in 1848 and once after the war in June of 1880 as an old man. He never visited Cascade Springs, as that is a fictitious village I created for this series.

While studying the self-proclaimed first American poet, I was struck by his complicated character and his poetry. The more I learned about Whitman while researching this novel, the more I wanted to know about him. He did not have an easy upbringing, and in his lifetime, he rarely received—with few exceptions—the acclaim he so desired. He was a conflicted young man who lived on the fringes and moved through the counterculture of New York City. Because of his willingness to embrace a different way of life and because of those he loved, he was judged harshly by both the general and the literary society of the time. As a result—and I doubt this makes it up to the great poet much—I felt the need to give him a more integral role in this novel than I had previously planned. The shop wouldn't just use his works to reveal clues to Violet, but

Whitman would be a character in the story. I had him visit my fictional village while he was on his 1880 visit to Niagara Falls.

There is no evidence that Lincoln ever read *Leaves of Grass*, let alone wrote Whitman a letter telling the poet what he thought about it. Had Whitman received a letter from the president, it is likely he would have published it with a future copy of his poems to increase sales, just as he had the factual letter he received from Ralph Waldo Emerson. However, I like to think there could have been such a letter, because I know it would have made Whitman immeasurably happy to have President Lincoln's approval. Whitman respected and idolized the president, whom he viewed as a savior of the country. When he was working in the hospital in Washington, DC, tending to the wounded during the Civil War, he would often see Lincoln there when he was out walking and the two men would tip their hats to each other.

The works of Walt Whitman can be read many different ways and are open to many interpretations. Everything about the poet was questioned in his lifetime, from his manners to his writing to his sexual orientation. He was a man of paradox, which is why I believe his poetry has withstood the test of time, and I, for one, am grateful that it has.

I took literary license with Whitman's life for this work of fiction. Any historical mistakes made in the novel are my own.